Six Days in Dirtwater

randall 'Jay' andrews

JaCol Publishing Inc.

Copyright 2018 by JaCol Publishing Inc.

FIRST PRINTING

August 2018

All rights reserved

JaCol Publishing Inc.

2008 Hoquiam Ave NE

Renton, WA 98059

818-510-2898

ISBN: 978-1-946675-21-7

JaCol Publishing

Cover Art by Wincat Alcala

Table of Contents

Acknowledgement

I can't begin to thank the wonderful writers who have graced my world. From Writers World, where thousands have come to learn the craft of writing and kick around critiques of their current projects, to the boot camps where writers take a vested interest in finishing manuscripts, they have been inspirational in pushing all of us to publish.

I thank Colleen Ries, who has been my partner in JaCol Publishing and did the groundwork for getting us up and flying. She put her footprint on the company and helped give it the quality we continue to maintain.

I thank those who have come aboard JaCol since then: Jessica Collins, who does editing, proofing, and covers legal issues. Kathy Johnson, who plays the best girl Friday, and has been there to see that we don't sink under the demand of jobs beyond my editing, and to be an ear to me. RL Andrew, one of the authors who has helped me with many small projects needed to run a successful publishing company.

To the cover artist, Wincat Alcala, from Family Guy for his wonderful rendition for this book.

Finally, I thank my family. They have to put up with a writer for a husband and dad.

To those I have regrettably not mentioned, know you aren't forgotten.

Chapter 1

At some point you'll be held accountable; not for your actions, but for which side of right and wrong you are on.

Lyle's heart raced; a bleeding in his soul as he stumbled fast over cold wet ground farther into a wilderness unfamiliar to his childhood Ozarks. He stumbled away from terror, through spindly alders and drenched bows of cedars, the smell of tilled earth and fern covered soil with debris of decaying leaves from the previous year's canopy. The echo of hard breaths and crunching footsteps pushed panic into the abyss. He turned, needed a breather, knelt down and held a hand up for a time out. He'd gone as far as he planned and smiled as Danny Gates closed in with an ax in one hand and a knife in the other. "You know you can't win?"

Danny swung the ax like a majorette's baton. "Really, and what makes you think so? I chased you out here in the middle of my nowhere."

"You didn't chase me out here."

Danny tilted his head. "No?" He looked amused.

"You followed me out here."

1

"Well then!" Danny shoved the knife in a sheath and clutched the ax with both hands, holding it as though he stood at the plate, the next batter up. "You look pretty scared for someone who led me out here."

"Scared? Not really." Lyle caught his breath and relaxed. "Worried you would stop and go back, but not scared."

"Geez, You and your sister are crazy. I give you credit, you might be the boldest nitwit I have ever killed."

"Maybe, but you won't be killing me."

Danny peered into the night sky; the clouds had parted and the moon glow beamed down. Danny asked, "And what makes you think so?"

"I just know, but I'm sorry I didn't meet you sooner."

Danny hovered over Lyle. "You have a trick up your sleeve, huh?"

"No, that's not it." He rolled over and sat on a log, studied Danny's face. "The trick already played out," Lyle held his wrist up, "Nothing up my sleeve."

Danny thumped his chest with the flat side of the ax. "Little ole' me? Caught and don't even know it."

"Yeah Danny, I think you do."

"Well, you remember my name!" Danny sat on a stump opposite him. "At least you paid attention."

"I told you, you didn't chase me out here, you followed me."

"Look, you nitwit, this is my field, sits right out back of my house. You have no idea where you are."

"You think I don't know where I am? You think the logging roads behind your property are out of the way? You think I wasn't ready for something odd to happen? I decide to run instead of have an ax fight? Wow!" He pointed at Danny. "How unlucky were you?"

Danny squinted and showed interest. "You drove down the logging roads? So, you came in this way?"

"Of course I did."

"And you meant to get caught?"

"Yeah, I meant to get caught. I meant for you to follow me all the way out here."

"Why would you do something so stupid?" Danny bent over and stared.

"The answers written all over my face, can't you see it?" He closed the gap between them, the light of a full moon shining upon them.

"What should I see?"

"My sister was everything to me, she was my twin, her name was Lauren, and we were connected in ways you would never understand, and yes, my face is her face."

Danny pulled a lighter from his pocket, struck it with his thumb, and illuminated the space between them. "You two do look a lot alike."

"You didn't know Lauren, how could you kill her?" a tear slid down his face.

"She had it coming to her." Danny nodded. "Just like you."

"Calm down, Danny, you'll get your chance if you were a careful man."

"Careful?" Danny laughed. "So why would you come out here? I'm twice your size; you can't possibly believe you can overpower me?"

"I found my sister out here. I'm guessing you buried her because you didn't want to get caught. I saw what you did. She fought you, and she was tough." Lyle focused his rage, "Then you separated her head with an ax."

"Pretty much, pretty much how this one's going down too."

"Are you sure, Danny?"

Danny stared back, studying Lyle. "If you are anything like your sister, it is. You're dressed the part, but you don't have a weapon on you, you pea brain." Danny looked around. "Oh, let me guess, your sister's gonna' rise from the dead and exact revenge. Damn, sorry, Little Lyle, that ain't happenin' and you know it."

"You're right, that's not going to happen. As much as I want my sister back, she's dead and she's not coming back."

"So what's your surprise, Lyle, you gonna' talk me to death?"

Danny amused Lyle. He relaxed, he'd won and Danny didn't realize it. "You look a little sweaty, Danny. You feel okay?"

Danny rubbed the back of his neck and tried to speak, "shhhh," He shook his head and started to stand but fell back.

"Ah, this must be part of that talking to death, huh?" Lyle nodded, "Right?"

Danny dropped the ax and cleared his throat. "Whaaaat's happpp…"

"What's happening? Is that what's you're trying to ask?"

Danny swayed, his torso heaved and fell off the log; he quivered, trying to roll to his back.

"Here let me help you, Danny." Lyle used his foot to roll Danny over so they could see each other. Lyle snapped his fingers. "Look at me, Danny."

Danny's eyes followed Lyle.

Lyle sneered. "You can hear me, Danny, so let's have a conversation, okay?"

Danny was stiff but paid attention.

"I laced the trail with a drug called Tetrodotoxin. You probably were stuck by needles a half dozen times. I missed it. Good thing I'm so much smaller than you." Lyle grabbed Danny's chin, picked up the lighter and flicked it on. He twisted Danny's face. "Oh yeah, look at those marks, you took a few good ones."

Danny was stiff but paid attention.

"You're probably wondering what Tetrodotoxin is?" Lyle nodded Danny's head for him. "Yeah?"

Danny was stiff but paid attention.

"It's famous for coming from Puffer Fish. It's a neurotoxin and it puts you in a death state. Eventually it either kills you or you slowly recover, really depends on how much you get. I hope you didn't get too much. But don't worry, I have something to counteract it. I'll fix you up."

Danny was stiff but paid attention.

Lyle stood and walked to a corner of the clearing. "So, now you want to know what we are doing out here?" Lyle turned back to Danny. "I will take your silence as a yes."

Danny was stiff but paid attention.

Lyle cleared a patch of brush and located his shovel and flashlight. "I located my sister and asked her what she wanted me to do with you. She said she would like to spend some time with you, Danny. She really wants to get to know you, and I hope you'll get to know her."

Danny was stiff but paid attention.

Lyle came back and shined the flashlight on Danny's pupils. "You are a large human, Danny. I hope you don't mind getting a little wet? I have to roll your fat ass about twenty yards." Lyle pointed the beam of light to an area not far away. "I have a resting spot for you. You can handle that, can't you?"

Danny was stiff but paid attention.

Arm by arm, Lyle rolled Danny from back to stomach, from stomach to back, and over again. The flashlight illuminated a hole in the ground, a large wooden box down below, his sister littered inside. "Danny, I wanted you to see where you will be spending the rest of your life." He sat Danny up and held his head so he could see down in the hole. "That's my sister." A torso, a hand, and a head. "Don't worry, I will leave you with some light so you two can get to know each other a little better, for when you come back around. The ground isn't packed too tight and with the gravel content, and as long as it doesn't rain, you should be able to breathe." With that, he slid Danny down and into the box. Lyle jumped down and stuck a needle into Danny's hip, "An antidote, I want you to be awake." He placed the lid over the box; he hammered dozens of nails so it was snug, climbed out and whistled 'Kumbaya' as he shoveled dirt and buried his sister, Danny, and the box.

He was sure Danny was stiff but paying attention.

Chapter 2

Lauren and Lyle, such beautiful creatures, born to doting parents proud of twins with such angelic features, had looks mirrored by those of their parents. Lauren was wily, keen of thought, and quick to suggest. She was blonde like virgin clouds, silk white brows, pale skin, innocent looks she did not merit.

It was fall in the Ozarks, Smoke trees turning their brilliance of color, orange and red of hickory and maple. It was Halloween night of 79 when Lauren's mother brought forth her and her brother, a festive night for everyone on Potter's Mountain, everyone but the Thibodeauxes. Larry and Loretta Thibodeaux gave birth to their first children, the fruit of their union, exhaustion and work for the former doctor and his wife. Potter's Mountain was small, all the easier for Larry and Loretta to keep to themselves. Larry and Loretta had their reasons; they weren't Baptist or Methodist like the residents. They kept to themselves; they came from the bayou of Louisiana, arrived with the pulse of lowlanders, with charm, urban mystique, and an intense desire to escape.

Larry and Loretta didn't need to work. They'd sold their inheritance; he stopped practicing, packed up and moved to remote parts of the Arkansas-Missouri state line. Together, they raised their ten children alone, home schooled in the stone masonry three story home, built upon a lake the Thibodeuxes would rename after themselves. They taught their children to play piano, violin, and the cello, as well as astronomy, biology, and chemistry. They taught them civility, nobility, and the bible. Those ten kids would do well and attend schools of medicine, law, literature, and business. They would make the Thibodeaux family name proud, and they were all led by the twins, Lauren and Lyle.

Lyle was attentive, kept time, notation of events. He was quiet, calculating and at times dismissive. He was a wonderful big brother with one weakness of giving in to his sister on any disagreement. He loved his twin; he shared his soul; he shared his secrets. Lauren and Lyle would leave the mountain together; they were never to be separated.

They found their way to California, and studied together at Stanford; he in chemistry, she in law, but as was their lot in life, he excelled, where she learned to use her guile to succeed.

"Lyle what do want to be when you grow up?" A teasing thirty-three-year-old Lauren asked her brother.

He laughed, "Consistent, sister, consistent."

"You are no fun." She watched as her brother finished drying the last dish.

"Maybe, but well-made plans lead to fruitful endeavors." He crossed the floor and sat beside her at the kitchen table, his dish towel draped over his shoulder.

"We're thirty-three years old, Lyle, we both have great jobs, we don't own homes, and we don't have aspirations?"

They both finished school years earlier; he finished grad school; she finished law school. They remained in the San Francisco area and roomed together ever since leaving home. Driven by education, neither dated, seldom did either go out. They had become much like their parents, reclusive. But they had each other, they understood each other. They laughed at the same jokes; they fought over the same section of the newspaper; they were twins.

Lauren was fair height for a woman; Lyle was the same height, not fair height for a man, always a rub with him. Lauren was athletic, Lyle was not. If they stood together, it was obvious they were twins, the same Thibodeaux cheekbones, the same crystal blue eyes, bleach white eyebrows, and downy white hair, but she had elegance to her gait, powerful, sure; where he did not. Lauren caught many an eye of young men over the years, but she never took interest. There was the Romanelli kid when she was fifteen, but he was killed falling off Lookout Point Bridge over Arbuckle Gorge, and there was a young man her freshman year, but he drowned in Half Moon Bay. Her luck was predestined to be poor. Likewise, Lyle's luck wasn't much better. He was sweet on the McGarvey girl when he was fourteen, but the girl disappeared on a vacation with her parents to Mardi Gras.

"Let's move." Lauren insisted.

"Where do you want to move to?"

"Portland."

"Maine or Oregon?"

She smiled. "Oregon."

"Can I get a job in Oregon?"

"Brother, you can get a job anywhere." She would never admit it, but she loved his organizational skills. She knew he could walk into any business that needed a genius chemist and get hired.

"What do you have in savings?"

She waved her hand. "Not enough, but I know you do. Besides, it doesn't take that much to move us. We don't have that much."

"I'd need to give two weeks' notice and we need to scout out the area. I don't want to live in a bad part of town."

Like that, she was quick to suggest, he was calculating, and he gave in to her wishes. They were twins.

Chapter 3

Swaheenie Road ran north out of Dirtwater, a lonely road with farmers' fields of seasonal crops and split log posts, barbed wired fence barriers keeping the cattle in. County planners built the road to serve as a dike and then forgot about it when the state decided to build the highway twenty miles to the east. They wanted Swaheenie to be a shortcut through the two mill towns of Dirtwater and Bradenton, but Dirtwater dried up when the timber industry evaporated, and Bradenton already had a road to the outside world; there was no reason to go south into a town with nothing to offer. They brought in excavators and dug out two large gravel pits back in 1947 and used the earth to run a swath of road through the Gates' property. Paid the Gates well, turned out to be better than well when one considered Swaheenie was nothing more than a driveway to the Gates' farm.

No one came to fix Swaheenie road when the floods washed away a quarter mile of it in 1974, so old man Gates did the best he could to repair the road. He left a long stretch of gravel, a stop gap for the passersby who thought to take the road to the timber ridge as a short cut to Bradenton. It also served as a deterrent for the local kids who raced the half mile before the dip, or if someone entertained the notion of dropping an old car off in Harper's pond;

one of the two gravel pits used to make the road. The pits were deep; cars that went over, the deep black waters swallowed.

A forgotten road and that didn't bother the Gates. Old man Gates died of a heart attack in 1998, left behind one son, Danny, and a wife, Louise. Louise followed him eight years later of cancer, leaving Danny heir to eight hundred acres, and a fat sum of cash for letting the county build Swaheenie.

Danny wouldn't have to work, but Danny did; he was a farmer. He was more than a farmer. He kept up the farmhouse like a gardener, loved colorful flowers, evergreens, rhododendrons, azaleas, hanging baskets of petunias and dusty miller. All that while attending to crops and raising cattle. The area folks knew on occasions he'd double as a logger and hauled timber down off the northern slope of his property. He mowed on Fridays, painted the place every three years, washed windows twice a month, dusted the furniture, vacuumed, did the things his mother and father always did. Although he wasn't the most social person, he did give to the booster club of Huggins high, even though he'd been a star lineman years before for Dirtwater, but since Dirtwater shuttered the doors of the Mighty Mustangs, he turned his allegiance to their rivals, the Hawks of Huggins.

Danny wasn't much of a dog person. They irritated him. He didn't mind the feral cats who worked as mousers around the place, but when his mother passed on, he took the two terrier dogs she had and sent them to the pound. He didn't much care for shooting animals, thought any animal deserves a fighting chance; giving them up settled the situation.

Danny liked justice. Justice didn't mean you couldn't extract a pound of flesh, but it had to be warranted. Every decision he made was his own, no one had a stake in it. Danny wasn't thirty yet when he had to make it on his own, but he was okay with that. Had he been younger he would have been what the military wants as a serviceman. He'd thought about it, had thought it would have been dutiful to serve his country, but he was a farmer and leaving wasn't a realistic possibility. He already secured his life's path, besides, at 6'10" he didn't know if they could fit him with good threads.

A mountain of a man, a brown bear nearly killed him one spring when it crossed the backyard and Danny ran out with a gun and an ax. He put the handgun in his waist and wondered who was tougher. He started swinging the ax, exhilarated, alive, the challenge of a fight with an equal, but a bear has a thick hide and just because you connect, doesn't mean you're going to do anything other than piss that kind of creature off, which Danny did. When he landed the blade against the shoulder of the bear, it turned and swatted the ax to the ground. Danny held his position and growled. The bear charged and in a weak moment, Danny pulled the handgun out, and a lucky thing he did because it took the fourth shot to penetrate the bear's skull. By then, he'd already taken Danny down and ripped into his arm. Danny needed forty stitches to close the wound.

He remembered the night the salesman stopped by his house after dark.

Who the hell comes by to sell something at that hour?

One late fall, the doorbell rang; he looked out the side window and saw a man, a kid really, holding a clipboard. He answered the door. "Can I help you?"

"Hi, my names Jason, I'm working my way through college, and I'd like to know if you subscribe to any of these magazines?" He handed Danny a paper with a list of fifty magazines.

"Is Playboy on the list?"

"No, sir."

"Then I don't." He didn't want one, but he thought watching the kid squirm would serve him right for coming over so late.

"Do any of those magazines interest you?"

Danny shook his head. "Not really." He handed the kid back his paper. "Sorry, you wasted your trip out here."

"Where the hell am I?"

Danny laughed. "That's what everyone says. Just go back the way you came, and you will be okay."

"Your road is pretty wicked. It's gravel for about a half mile."

"Yeah, no one came to fix it when it washed out so my dad did the best he could."

"I nearly drove into that lake of yours."

"Good thing you didn't. That's no lake and if the fifty-foot drop doesn't kill you, the depth will. Not to mention, it has no shore, just a wall. It's a gravel pit."

The kid shook his head and started to walk away. As Danny stood at the door, the kid caught him off guard when he turned and brandished a gun. "Maybe you don't want to give up your money for magazines, how about for your life?"

Danny smiled. "Really, you plan on shootin' me if I don't cough up a buck?"

"Wouldn't be the first time, so if you don't want to join my list of victims, maybe being smart would be a good plan."

"Maybe you're right, son."

"I ain't your son."

They stood there in a stare-fest before Danny said, "Well, I don't carry it on me, so if you want it, you're going to have to come in with me."

The kid stepped a little closer and assured Danny, "Try anything and I'll kill you where you stand."

"Fair enough."

Danny walked in first and without the suspense of a cat and mouse affair, the kid barely made it to the welcome mat before Danny turned and had the gun in his big paw, squeezing both the kid's hand and the iron with so much force that the boy yelped, "Okay!" He went to his knees and Danny elbowed him in the face, hard enough to knock him unconscious.

Danny shook his head and picked the kid up with one arm and hauled him to the couch.

"What am I going to do with this nitwit?" Danny went to the kitchen to call the Sheriff and noticed the ax sitting beside the back door. He grabbed the tool and slung it over his shoulder. He grabbed his hunting knife and put it in a sheath on his belt. He damped a cloth and stepped back into the living room. Danny wrung water out over the kid's face and the boy coughed to attention.

"Damn, what hit me?"

Danny handed him the cloth to clean up the blood oozing from one of his eyes. "Hey kid, I'll make you a deal."

"What kind of deal?"

"I will buy every magazine on your list if you can get out of here alive." Danny grinned.

The kid looked amused and laughed. "Just call the cops!"

Danny quit smiling. "I'm not kidding."

"Fuck you, mister."

With one hand, Danny extended the ax and pointed it; his arms were massive, years of working the farm, the trees, and the earth. They extended from his shear height like pieces of lumber. "Careful what you say in my house."

They glanced at the front door, then back at each other.

"You think you can make it?"

"What do you want?" The kid oozed desperation in his voice. "I was just screwing with ya, I wasn't going to shoot you? I'm sorry."

"So, you were just going to rob me?"

"It was a joke."

"That was funny. I'm laughing pretty hard, don't you think?"

"Fine, just call the cops."

"Nope. I'm gonna give you a head start. You can go out the back door and through the forest. If you can out foot me, you'll make it to another farm, or maybe a road."

"It's pitch dark, I don't know where I am."

"Don't go left or right and you'll hit a road about a mile up, it's a logging road." Danny cleared a path for the kid to run past him and to the back door.

The kid stood still. "This is a joke, right? You're screwing with me, right?"

Danny stepped a foot closer. "You don't start running; I'll kill you at my front room." He stared cold steel, serious and unforgiving.

Tears welled in the kid's eyes. "Oh shit, oh shit. Please, dear God please don't do this."

"Oh, I'm not God, and God has nothing to do with this." Danny teased him, "Know your audience, Boy."

The kid bolted, and Danny watched as he emptied out the back door. Danny turned and walked out the front door, standing on the lighted porch. "Hey Boy! I'm sure you're hiding out back, probably wondering if you can make it to your little car." Danny stepped off the porch and approached a sedan. "Just to let you know you better start running, let me help you." Danny swung the ax at the front tire and it hissed as it bled air. "How many spares you have?" He circled around to the other front tire and pounded until it whistled air. He could hear the kid scream and run toward the forest. Danny turned and followed the sound of scared huffing, of feet kicking clods of dirt, of his prey.

About a half mile in, the landscape rustled, the kid had found the thickest part of undergrowth, and total darkness settled in as the clouds hid any moonlight. Danny knew this spot; the brush was heavy; a person could be entwined for hours in that stuff. "Hey kid, you need some help?"

Nothing moved.

"You know I hear you, and it's only a matter of time before I find you. We can wait all night and then daylight might either help you or hurt you!" Danny laughed, "Come on, be a man." Danny sat and listened.

Two minutes passed—a crackle of branches, followed by the sounds of running footsteps. Danny stood and walked down his worn path, following sounds to his right. "Kid, you aren't even on the path! You nitwit, you can't get very far very fast if you aren't on the path." Danny heard crying. "Geez, stop it. I'll kill ya just for pissing me off if you start crying."

The kid exited the brush. "Mister, I'm a bad guy, I know that. I shot a couple over in Bradenton a few nights ago. You'll be a hero if you turn me in. I think there's a reward for me."

Danny sighed. "I'm sorry, I took this way too far. He slung the ax over his shoulder, let's get you back to the house and call the sheriff."

"You're not going to hurt me, are ya?"

Danny threw his free arm out and pointed to the house. "Let's go!"

Danny wasn't sure if the kid had tried to figure a way out or if he had a moment of quick decision, quick bad decision, but as he passed Danny in the pitch dark, he lunged for the ax. What the kid didn't know was Danny had released the knife from his waist and had it in his other hand. As the kid gripped the handle, Danny grabbed him and plunged the knife into the kid's side by accident. It must have hurt because the kid let out a visceral scream. Blood ran down Danny's wrist, warm and sticky fluid clung to him like oil from a dirty car. The kid dropped to his knees and let the ax go. Danny knew that couple in Bradenton, a nice elderly couple.

The kid jumped up and rushed Danny, a sparkle of metal reflected a glint of moonlight as the ax sailed through the air; Danny wondered if the kid's last thought had anything to do with the ax coming in contact with his neck. Danny had swung the ax and caught the kid about the shoulder; it sliced through his neck like butter.

Danny had a mess, but what a judicial mess it was. He looked back in the direction of home and hoisted the body up. He grabbed the head by the hair and walked back to the house. He needed to deal with the car, so he tossed the kid's parts in and drove the flat tired Honda to Harper's Pit. He pushed it over the cliff and watched it sink into the dark murky water. He used a broom to brush the gravel, hide the evidence a car had gone over. As the sun came up, he surveyed the land. That had been too easy, and justice had been served. He wondered if he'd ever get the chance to do it again.

Chapter 4

Lyle and Lauren packed up and loaded the last of their boxes when a pair of detectives from metro stopped by to ask about one of their neighbors downstairs.

"Knock knock." Someone shouted; echoes in the empty apartment bounced into the front room where Lyle and Lauren enjoyed a final wine together in their humble third floor setting, overlooking steep hills and a view of the Golden Gate Bridge in the distance.

"Come in." Lyle shouted.

Two official looking sorts worked their way to the front room, and Lyle stood with alarmed interest. "Can I help you?"

"I'm Detective Heath and this is Detective Kappler. Wondered if we could ask you some questions about a neighbor of yours?"

Lauren snapped to attention, rising behind her brother. "Which neighbor?"

"Jeff Lambert."

Detective Heath's partner scanned the empty room. "You two moving?"

Lauren interrupted, "What's happened to Jeff?"

Kappler frowned. "That's what we'd like to know. Apparently, no one has heard from him in a week."

Lauren corrected the detective. "Six days to be correct."

"Six days?"

She stepped around her brother and put her hand out. "I'm Lauren Thibodeaux and this is my brother Lyle." She shook each detective's hand with polite grace. "I went to a movie with Jeff last Saturday night."

"And?"

She smiled. "And that was it. I mean, Jeff and I went out on occasions. I think he was sweet on me, but it was strictly platonic."

Both detectives stepped closer; a surge of electricity in their demeanor changed their focus. Heath stared at Lauren. "What time did you come home?"

"Oh gosh, tenish."

"Did he come here, or did you go there?"

"Neither. He saw me to the elevator, and I came home alone."

"And you didn't think it was unusual that you haven't heard from him since?"

Lauren laughed. "Why would I? We were Saturday night buddies."

"So, he never contacts you during the week?"

Lauren tilted her head. "You mean ever?"

The detective shrugged. "Yeah, ever."

"Sometimes, but he doesn't make a habit of it. I sort of let him know that we can hang out on the weekends." She crossed her arms. "Detective Heath, I'm an attorney and my weekdays are pretty busy. Jeff is a night clerk at a hotel, sort of different hours for us to be much more than weekend friends."

Detective Kappler asked again, "You two moving?"

Lyle responded, "Yes, we are moving to Portland." Lyle wanted to ask if Detective Kappler's skills came with a magnifying glass. The place was empty save two boxes and a lamp. He smiled. "Is there something suspicious about Jeff's disappearance?"

Kappler stared at Lyle. "I didn't say he disappeared. I said he hasn't been seen for a week, or as your sister has offered, six days."

"And that's not disappeared?" Lyle held his ground.

"Just seems an odd word to use."

Lyle raised his eyebrows. "How about vanished then?"

"Another odd word."

If you say so. People who haven't been heard from usually don't have the authorities knocking on the neighbors' doors unless something nefarious is suspected."

Detective Heath stepped in. "What do you do for a living, Mr. Thibodeaux?"

"I'm a chemist."

"For who?"

"SteadyWell."

Heath smiled. "Big company. Why are you leaving a job like that?"

"My sister is going to work for a law firm in Portland and I'm going with her."

"You're not married?"

"No sir, I am not."

"Are you going to be working when you get there?"

"Probably. Getting work in rejuvinetics isn't hard." The conversation, albeit engaging, didn't get Lyle closer to where he needed to be. He picked up one of the boxes. "I don't know how we can help you, but we are on a schedule."

"Cell phone?"

Lyle looked surprised. "Excuse me?"

"Do the two of you have cell phones?"

Irritated, Lyle answered. "Of course we do. Why?"

"May we see them?"

"I don't see any reason why I should let you see my cell phone." Lyle nodded at the door.

"Brother, let them see it." Lauren turned to the detectives. As you probably have guessed, I'm pretty versed on the law, and the truth is, I should say no; however, in the interest of finding Jeff, I freely give you my phone to look at, and my brother will too."

Lyle shook his head in disgust but let his sister snatch it out of his pocket. The detectives studied the numbers, of which there were only calls to each other. The twins seldom made calls unless it was to let the other one know where they were.

"Whose number is this one?" Detective Heath held the phone up to Lauren.

She nodded. "That's Lyle's."

Detective Kappler who had Lyle's phone, held up a screen with another row of identical numbers and showed it to Lauren. "I take it this is your number then?"

She smiled. "Yep."

"I'm going to jot these numbers down in case we need to get a hold of you. Is that okay?"

Lyle huffed. "I think your partner already wrote them down. Asking to do so is a bit disingenuous."

Lauren rubbed her brother's back. "Don't be a pill, Lyle; they are only doing their jobs."

Lyle smiled with disdain. "I guess." He held the box up and out from him. "We are in a hurry, may we leave now?"

Detective Heath scanned the empty apartment. "Can we look around your apartment?"

Lauren tossed him a key. "Have at it. When you're done can you return it to the manager in 101?"

Kappler nodded. "Will do."

Lauren put the lamp on top of Lyle's box and lifted the last remaining one. They exited and made their way to the elevator. Lauren whispered, "Wow, Jeff is missing. That is so weird."

Lyle agreed. "Bad luck follows us everywhere."

Chapter 5

Danny stood over the gravel pit, a cliff over water, and wondered what to do if the sheriff came by and asked if he saw a kid selling magazines? Should he tell the truth and confess he accidentally killed a killer after teasing him, running after him with a knife and axe like a lunatic, and then stabbed and cut his head off. Could he prove that accidents happened? After all, he cut the kid's head off with one swing of the axe. Should he say yeah, the kid came by but left? Should he say he didn't see anyone? Danny needed a story, and it had to be convincing. Last thing he wanted anyone to think is he killed someone on purpose. That would be terrible. "I didn't see him!" That's what he decided on. The kid went down with the car. Danny read a quick prayer for him and disposed of the materials associated with the kid, wiped away not only the presence of the kid but any thought of him as well.

A day went by and no one showed up. A week and then a month went by and no one showed up. No one ever showed up. "Hmmm," Danny sat on his porch one evening, winter biting with teeth of ice.

No one looked for the kid. How sad is that. Poor kid.

A noise broke his thoughts, spooked him to hear something while he wondered about the kid. "Bad omen, erase thoughts of the kid." Gravel spit up from a spinning tire. He stood from the porch and stepped onto the lawn. Someone, probably some kid, tried to work a car into the pit. Danny would have to put an end to people doing that. After all, he now had evidence in that pit to a bad event. He jumped in his truck and drove by moonlight down Swaheenie Road. He coasted up to the pit and flicked on his lights when he closed in on the activity and whoever was up to mischief. A single kid, maybe eighteen tried to solve how to drive the car into the pit without being in it. The slight incline prevented pushing it so that was out of the question. The kid didn't look like he wanted to try and drive it and jump out at the last second. When Danny arrived, he watched the kid trying to rig the gas pedal.

Danny stepped out of his truck. "Hey, knock it off and go home." He recognized the boy, Huggins' town hoodlum, Jamie Schmutz.

Jamie had a cigarette dangling from his mouth, a bright red cherry glowing in the brisk night air. "Why don't you go home and just forget you saw me, Mr. Gates."

The kid had a wiry frame, acted like the toughest kid in town. He might be tough, but Danny had a hundred and twenty-five pounds on the boy and knew the kid didn't want to test that. "Or what?"

Jamie pulled the cigarette from his mouth. "I ain't afraid of you, Gates."

"Then you're stupid."

He sighed. "Look, it ain't like there aren't a bunch of cars in this pit, just let me drop this one, and I will be out of your hair."

Danny offered, "Okay, but not this pit, the other one. This one is starting to get full!" Danny laughed, and Jamie returned with a chuckle.

"Okay, so how we get to that pit, it's a hundred yards off the road?"

"I have an access road we can take."

"You mean that dirt road with the deep ruts?"

Danny shook his head. "I see you've been on it."

"No offense but we might get this car stuck."

"It's freezing out, those ruts are solid as rock. We'll drive out there with ease."

Jamie shrugged. "Why not, I'm game. You want me to follow you?"

Danny thought about it. "No, let's hop in that thing in case I'm wrong. No need to get both rigs stuck."

Danny stepped out of his truck and came up to Jamie. "I'll drive."

Jamie climbed in the passenger side, and Danny turned the car around and found the access to McCleary Pond. The second pit rested out of the way, lonely, it didn't have the road butting up next to it and as Danny promised, the ground felt like rock under tire. "Damn, this car might break before we get it there."

"Hell, this is a Bronco, it'll make it. Sort of a shame to ditch it. Who does it belong to?"

"Jamie lit up another cigarette. "Fuckin' ex-girlfriend's dad's car. Dick is responsible for us breaking up."

"He's probably gonna know you took it, don't you think?"

"Knowin' and provin' are two different things."

Danny smiled. "I guess you're right about that."

Jamie puffed his chest as if trying to match Danny's girth. "Say, you ain't gonna say anything are ya?"

"If I was going to say anything I would have let you drop it off in Harper's pond."

"Why's it called Harper's?"

"My mother's maiden name."

"Why this one's called McCleary?"

"My dad's mom's maiden name."

"I should have figured. No offense but we live in a backwoods hillbilly valley. We not only name shit after family, half the time we marry them."

Danny's lips started to move but thought the kid sounded half right. Besides, he didn't need to entertain Jamie. "How were you gonna get home?"

"I got my bike in the back."

Danny twisted. A small trail bike lay in the back. "That's going to be a cold long ride home."

"It's worth it." Jamie winked.

They came around a corner and stopped at a tuft of grass.

"Why'd we stop?" Jamie stuck his head out the window at blackness.

"We're here. The other side of that grass is fifty feet of cliff."

"Really?" Jamie whistled. "Damn, I would have driven right over that."

They exited the car and went to the edge, the lights of the Bronco shining out over the cliff, an empty darkness below them.

"How far down is that?" Jamie picked up a rock and dropped it over, cupping his ear, he listened for a plunk.

"Fifty, maybe sixty feet."

They stepped away and walked back toward the Bronco. A round-house punch from Jamie caught Danny off guard. Blood drained from Danny's lip. He felt like he'd been hit by a rock. He went to a knee and a boot caught him in the ribs.

"I told you I wasn't afraid of you, Gates, and I sure as hell don't trust you to not tell anyone. I guess you are going over with the Bronco."

Danny hunched in front of the car, the lights illuminating another punch coming his way. He could see Jamie had a pair of brass knuckles; he turned so the blow cracked him in the side of the head instead of the face. He rolled to his right and as Jamie ran toward him for another kick, Danny caught the boy's foot and yanked him to the ground. Danny stood and towered over the Schmutz boy. He bent and grabbed him by the nape of the neck. "I said I wasn't going to say anything, boy, what the hell are you thinking?"

Jamie wasn't done. He tried to kick Danny but missed. Danny, with hands the size of frying pans, palmed the boy's head, lifted him up and bounced his face off the hood of the car with enough force to dent the metal. Jamie panted but managed to swing a roundhouse, missing Danny in a windmill of activity. Danny tripped the kid and pushed him down into the rocks. Jamie's head hit with a thump, and he stilled like a mannequin.

"Get up." The kid didn't move.

Danny pulled the kid off the rocks and brought him around to the headlights, blood ran out his head, and his eyes were wide open.

"You okay, kid?" No answer.

Danny put his head to the kid's chest—lifeless. "You nitwit." Danny had planned to let the kid dump the car in McCleary. It beat having the sheriff sniffing around Harper's Pond, but he didn't give a crap about McCleary. Now he had to make a quick decision. He picked the boy up and tossed him in the Bronco. Danny sat in the driver's side, depressed the clutch, revved the engine, put it in gear and stepped out as it lurched forward. In one motion, he caught the door and pushed it closed as the car rolled over the cliff and plunged to the water below.

He walked back up to the road and hopped in his truck, turned around and went back to the house. When he made it home, he called the Sheriff. "John, this is Dan. I was sittin' on my porch when I heard someone drivin' off road. I think somebody went in my back pit. I heard a loud splash."

The sheriff said. "It was probably a dump."

"They dump in Harper's, not in McCleary.

It was too dark; the sheriff didn't seem too worried. He said if anyone turned up missing, he'd be out in the morning.

The sheriff arrived around noon the next day. He rapped on Danny's door.

Danny answered. "So, somebody turn up missing?"

Sheriff looked put out. "Yeah, the Schmutz kid. "Mind if you take me out there?"

"No, let's go." Danny had finished up dishes and a drying cloth draped over his shoulder. He laid it on the porch bench and walked alongside Sheriff Scott as they made it out to his cruiser.

They drove to the access and the sheriff noted, "Looks like a car was out here alright." They bounced over ruts with recent tire marks.

"What kind of car does he have?"

"He doesn't but his girlfriend's dad's car is missing. Something tells me we're going to find it out here."

"Right here, sheriff."

"Damn, I always forget how quick that comes up on ya!"

"It's not real safe out here, not in the daytime, definitely not in the nighttime."

Sheriff Scott gazed off into the distance. "You remember when we we're kids jumping in that thing and your dad having to get us out with a winch?"

"Damn near killed us."

They stepped out and walked up to the edge. Visible tire tracks ran off the edge, but they couldn't see a car. However, a thin sheet of ice was missing where something big had gone in. "Son of a bitch. That looks like something big went in. I'll call the divers."

"Sorry, Sheriff."

"Damn kids!"

Danny and John went back a long way. John picked up a rock and threw it, Danny did the same, seeing who could toss a rock farthest across the pit, their breaths billowing vapors of steam from a brisk winter day. Alder trees stripped of beauty, just skeletal branches. The landscape dotted with evergreen firs taking their place as sentinels around the pit. They waited for a team of local volunteers to show up, deputies with diving gear. When the local team of deputies, no more than the Huggins' fire department showed up, Sheriff Scott lowered a winch cable for the divers to get in the pit. It wasn't easy getting them in, but when they did, they discovered Jamie Schmutz and the Bronco at the bottom. Bubbles and a head bobbed up; a diver pulled his mask off. "He's down here, and yeah, it's the Bronco."

The sheriff waved them up. "We'll winch you up; get the body and leave the rig."

Danny apologized, but the sheriff thanked him for calling. He said they would never have found him had Danny not notified them. Truth is, Danny didn't need them snooping around Harper's pit.

That night when Danny sat alone, he twisted the top on a bottle of beer as though champagne. He toasted, how easy dispensing justice had been, but that's justice. He wondered if the old adage of things coming in threes would bring him more trouble.

Chapter 6

Lyle and Lauren put San Francisco behind them, as they did every place they left. They drove up the 101, through wine country fit for tourist magazine covers, spending all of Saturday crisscrossing from vineyard to vineyard, purchasing fine wine for their new life in Portland. Lauren had an offer she would accept on Monday. Her striking platinum features had much to do with her landing a position with a notable firm. She was engaging and crafty, but her looks Lyle knew carried her far in her career. Lyle didn't worry for himself, his job security rested with the knowledge he possessed; people wanted it. Landing a job would be easy.

"So, Brother, tell me about our new digs?"

"We've saved a lot, and I found a condo in the west hills."

"Is that a nice part of town?"

He smiled. "It is." They sipped on red wine outside of Napa.

Lauren hesitated.

"What's wrong?"

She stared off into the distance, a resignation on her face. "Thinking about Jeff."

Lyle passed the conversation off with disregard. "I never much cared for him."

Lauren frowned and shook her head. "You never care for any of the guys I like."

Lyle admitted, "He wasn't good enough for my sister."

She chided him. "Whenever you say that, bad things happen."

"Don't go there; I already have suspicions about my thoughts. I don't need to believe I can will bad things."

She eyed him. "Will them?"

He put his hand to his chest and winked. "Surely you aren't suggesting something more sinister?"

She sniffed the bouquet of wine circling in her glass, and whispered, "Of course not."

"So tell me more about this office where you will be working?" He leaned into the conversation and propped his chin up with his hand.

"Well, it's an estate firm working with the farmers around the area. They cover from central Oregon up to central Washington. I'm going to be a field rep for new client acquisitions."

Lyle scoffed. "Sounds like a glorified ambulance chaser."

"Maybe, but it's good money."

"Money isn't everything, dear Sister."

"Easy for you to say. One look at your portfolio and companies drool over acquiring you."

He smiled. "You are in a service-oriented profession, one which I might say, is rather despicable at times, where I am in the field of extending lives. Is there a comparison?"

Lauren raised her glass. "And yet we coexist so well together."

As they sat on a veranda overlooking a grape valley, the sun smoothly caressed the afternoon sky. The wine loosened their spirits and they wondered aloud about their siblings, wondering if their brother's and sister's lives invited such opportunities as theirs. In the midst of their reminiscing, a young attractive sommelier approached them with samplings of wine.

"Would you like to try our Pinot Noir?" She stood the bottle onto the table and wrenched the screw over the cork, lifting it out of place before craning it free. She handed the cork to Lyle.

He sniffed the fragrance and stated, "You're very young to be a wine expert."

She thanked him. "My father is the proprietor, so I came by it naturally."

Lyle marveled at her beauty. "Naturally."

"This Pinot has a baked cherry aroma with a smooth but crisp finish." She deftly twisted the bottle as she poured, first Lyle's, then Lauren's."

She waited for Lyle to swirl the glass and take some in. She lifted a spit can and Lyle gently expelled the wine. "Very nice. We'll take a bottle, and we'd like to keep this one for the table."

"Very well." She excused herself.

"She likes you." Lauren still nursed her other glass.

"Why do you say that?"

"She poured your glass first."

"She's supposed to. I'm supposed to taste it."

"That doesn't change the fact that she likes you."

"Sister, look at me. I'm rather peculiar looking."

Lauren protested, "I should say not. We look like twins."

"You're right, but snow-white hair, snow white eyebrows, pale skin works for a girl. It's unusual for a man."

She reached across the table and touched his cheek with the back of her hand. "Not to me, Brother, not to me."

Lyle took her hand and squeezed it. "No, I suppose to you, I look lovely." He grinned and clinked his glass to hers.

"My goodness, I need to go to the lady's room. I don't think my bladder can wait much longer."

She stood and Lyle stood with her. "I'm glad you suggested it, I too need to do the same."

When they returned, they continued where they left off, enjoying the afternoon and finishing their wonderful bottle of Pinot. Lyle looked around for the sommelier and when he caught the attention of an employee, he raised his hand for service. A gentleman approached and Lyle caught his attention. "We had a young lady helping us and she doesn't seem to be around anymore."

"Ah yes, Linda. She felt ill, something came over her rather suddenly and she said she needed to head over to the house." He pulled a ticket from his pocket. "I believe you had the Pinot plus a bottle to go?"

"Thank you." Lyle and Lauren followed him to the counter. They paid for the wine and made their way out to the parking lot.

A large mansion at the north end of the estate had an ambulance parked outside. Lauren stared with interest. "I wonder what's going on?"

Lyle moved his sister along. "I don't know." He held the door open and hurried her in. "Let's go."

Chapter 7

Winter gave way to spring. In the Pacific Northwest that meant the beginning of spring rains. Every year, the valley worried about floods. Slow meandering rivers rose quickly, crests were met and exceeded; water seeped up through the ground like filled sponges. Danny sat on his porch and worried the cattle might get stuck on island knolls of undulated ground. They weren't the brightest creatures. "Better get em' in." He lifted off the chair and grabbed his bright yellow parka, bundled up and made it through the downpour to his truck.

He wondered why he kept tending to cattle. He should just butcher the lot and be done with them. They were more trouble than they were worth. He only kept them because it was easier slaughtering for meat than to drive into town for groceries. He pulled into the barnyard and gave his horn three honks. They might be stupid, but they knew three honks meant feeding time. He sped up the wipers, a deluge warped the view ahead of him. He waited, turned on the heat, and flipped the radio to AM music. Ten minutes passed before the first set of cattle wandered in, he counted four, twenty-two more to go. As the number grew, he flipped the hood on his parka over his head and stepped out of his truck, trudged through the mud to the barn and greeted the girls with grain and bales of hay. "You girls want Timothy or Alfalfa?" They lined up in their troughs, necks pushing through with greedy snouts plunging into feed containers. He waited until twenty four of the twenty-six made it in. He knew who the slow pokes were, and they were already in. He kept a rifle locked in the barn. He retrieved it and exited through the back, locking in the herd. He hoped he didn't have a stuck cow he'd have to put down. He followed the trail of hooves; he could see they had come from high ground, away from the river. The back forty had timber and pushed all the way to the lumber roads. The girls didn't normally go that far. Bear and coyotes had an advantage, so they stayed in the open.

A crack echoed from the trees; someone fired a rifle. Danny hurried his steps and bent low in the field to conceal himself. When he made it to the tree line, he reached in his pocket and drew out two more .308s, opened the chamber and dropped them in. He worked his way toward the logging road when he heard one of his girls writhing in pain followed by another shot.

Son of a bitch.

He followed the sounds of happy voices, laughing and cheering a kill. He reached the last of the trees, those standing between his property and the logging road and noticed two men winching up one of his cows. He scanned the area and noticed only two rustlers. Hidden behind a bush, he called out, "Those your cows?"

One of the men looked in Danny's direction, trying to find him. "Who's there?"

"Since you're on my land, that's my question to you."

Danny watched in amusement as the two men gave hand signals to each other, as though Danny couldn't see them. They intended to flank Danny. One of them ducked down beneath the Angus and started firing in Danny's direction.

Danny calmly took cover behind a tree and followed the second man as he ran toward the same tree line to his left. Danny knew his advantage would disappear if he let the armed cattle rustler make it to the forest. He raised his rifle and one shot later it was one on one.

"Son of a bitch! You killed him." A voice hollered over the belly of Danny's cow.

The gunfire stopped. Danny guessed the man reloaded. "What'd you expect? You're on my land and you killed my cattle." He steadied his rifle and took aim an inch above the mound of belly of the cow. Danny held it steady, waited, droplets of water cascading around him, the cedars acting as an umbrella. He waited for a splinter of color to show over the belling before he fired. He saw it and pulled the trigger. "You want to give up?"

Nothing.

"I'll ask again, do you want to give up?"

Nothing.

Danny had another bullet left, cocked and ready. He walked out from behind the cedar and into the clearing, his gun raised and pointed directly above the belly of the Angus. As he neared the cow, he could see someone sprawled face down behind her girth. "Hmm, good shot." Danny stepped around his cow and used his foot to roll over the cattle rustler; a bullet hole tattooed the man in the forehead. He bent down and snatched a wallet from the back pocket. He flipped it open. "You and that other Nitwit come all the way from California to rustle my cows?" He walked up to the logging road and looked in the back of their truck, his other cow lay inside. "Well girls, sorry to say I didn't make it here in time, but your murders have been avenged.

Danny left the one Angus in her spot, gathered the two rustlers up and tossed them into the cab. He drove their pickup to the barn and dropped off the girl, then headed to McCleary and rolled out as the truck danced over the edge and plunged into the pit.

He had started a graveyard service with all the undesirables, all who took Danny as an easy mark. He walked in the rain back to the barn and rolled out his cherry picker. He chained up the Angus and lifted her up by her hind legs, slit her throat and let her bleed out. "Guess I'll be having steak tonight."

Chapter 8

"So how was your first day of work?"

Lauren dropped her briefcase in the center of the front room. "Marvelous! I'm going to like the freedom to move about the countryside."

Lyle went back to scanning the stock section of his newspaper. "I see."

Lauren circled behind his chair and bent over and down along his shoulder. She put her arms around his chest. "Did you hear me?"

"Yes Sister, I heard you. I do hope being so free isn't dangerous."

"I'm dealing with farmers; do you really think that's dangerous?" She let him loose and walked toward the kitchen. "Besides, I always have you looking after me."

He craned his neck and looked over his shoulder as she passed the counter to the fridge. "Officer Heath called. His number is on the counter."

"I know, he called me too." She picked up the Sticky Note with his number and crumpled it in her hand. "What did he ask you?"

"If he could speak to you. He didn't want me. What did he ask you?"

"The usual stuff, did he have enemies, other girls, did we have a fight." Lauren reached back and slipped off her heels before stepping onto the brick flooring. "You didn't see him that night did you?"

Lyle sighed, exacerbated with the question. "Lauren, do you seriously think I went to see Jeff?"

She smiled. "Just asking, Brother."

"No, you're not asking, you're hinting." He shook his head at her bad memory, or how much she chose to not remember.

Lauren returned with yogurt and a spoon.

"You know you shouldn't eat in the front room."

"Yeah, yeah, yeah." She plopped on the couch and tucked her feet beneath her. She stared at Lyle. "Don't you think it's odd that so many of my boyfriends, and your girlfriends for that matter, have disappeared over the years?"

Lyle studied his sister. Did her eyes know something? "I do, do you?"

"You know," She hesitated, a sister's understanding. "I care more about you than life itself. Nothing will ever stand between us."

He turned toward the window, the Willamette River in the background, picturesque green trees dotted with incoming fall yellow, serene, a pleasant and unaware community around them. He whispered, "No, nothing ever will." He asked again, "Do you think it's strange?"

"What?"

"About all our bad luck?" He wondered what she knew, what she remembered.

Lauren shrugged, her kinetic energy bouncing. She changed the subject. "Let's go to a movie!"

Lyle spun back around and smiled. "No, I have too much to do. I haven't unpacked the bedroom. I have resumes to finish, too much work."

"Can I go?"

"Lauren, we don't know the neighborhood yet. This is a dangerous world."

"You act like I'm a little girl, besides, it's not like we live in the bad part of town."

"I just think you should wait until we're set up. Play after you finish your duties."

She laughed. "Play before you do your duties, now let's go. She stood and yanked on her brother's arm. "Come on."

He guessed it was better he be with her than let her go alone. "Very well."

Just down the road from their condo, a multiplex theater rested on the landing. Inside, a tempting array of movies led them to a sparsely attended comedy. Mondays were quiet, entire rows were empty and they sat centered in the room, Lyle ushering her into the middle.

"Can we sit further up?"

"The sound is best presented right here." He patted the seat and directed her to sit.

She shook her head. "You are so anal."

"It's not about being anal; it's about the best possible experience in any given situation."

"Popcorn."

"Excuse me?"

"I'm going to go get some popcorn." She stood and started to cross over her brother.

"I'll get it. You stay here." He blocked her and stood in her place.

She insisted, "A coke too."

"Yes, Sister."

As he exited, he turned to make sure she wasn't following him.

When he returned, he grumbled because she wasn't there. Their seats had been taken by someone else.

"Pssst! Up here." Lauren caught Lyle's attention.

There in the back row. She sat under the projector.

When he made it up to her, he huffed. "Seriously, right here?"

"Yeah, I want privacy."

"I thought you'd left."

"Honestly, Brother, I went to the bathroom, and when I came back, I discovered there are more anal people than just you. The entire room and they take the very seats we had, so I didn't think I should tell them that was our seats, or that we should sit right behind them."

"Yeah, I guess that's a good move, but right here?"

"Privacy, Brother, privacy."

"For what?"

"So, we can make fun of the movie and not bother people."

He raised the popcorn. "Popcorn?"

"Mmm." She snatched the bucket and patted the seat. "Sit down."

Together, they watched the movie. Lyle substituted for Jeff, her weekly movie date. The twins thought so much alike, the scenes one thought funny so did the other, and the scenes which weren't too good they both agreed. When the movie ended, Lauren wanted to leave, but Lyle had to watch the credits roll; it was who he was. He watched with interest as the credits scrolled upward.

"Can we go? Do we have to see who was the janitor on set?"

"Patience, Sister." When the final words disappeared like a crawling insect, up and through the top of the screen, Lyle stood. "Okay, let's go."

Lauren pushed her brother down the aisle. "Come on, hurry up. I want to go home."

"Don't be in too much of a hurry; we still have to set up the bedroom when we get home."

"I'll sleep on the couch while you work."

"That's just like you." He held his arm out for her to pass him as they made their way out of the row.

From darkness to light, they entered the hallway of theaters, ruby red walls, and sconce lighting. Toward the front of the building, in the concession area, paramedics attended to someone. "Look."

Lauren followed her brother as he walked closer to the activity. On a gurney, a blanketed woman writhed in pain. Lyle caught the attention of a theater worker. "What happened?"

The kid acted disinterested. "Food poisoning." He pointed out, "But not our food. Probably brought something in and it didn't agree with her."

Lyle and Lauren waited for the activity to die down, making their way after the onlookers dispersed. "I told you it's a dangerous world."

Lauren clutched Lyle's arm as they exited to a cool Portland evening. "That's why I have you."

Lyle whispered, "Yeah, I suppose you do."

Chapter 9

The meeting of the Dirtwater Restoration Committee requested the presence of the esteemed Daniel Gates. Danny read the embossed letter and laughed. Mrs. Kelman pulled out all the stops to entice some of the wealthier gentry of Dirtwater to help fix up the twelve two story buildings that made up the historical downtown of Dirtwater proper, in the great state of Washington.

On the day of the meeting, a parade of pickup trucks utilized the diagonal parking on both sides of Main Street. With a single street intersecting Main, that being First Street, the downtown was symmetrical, three buildings on the southwest corner, three on the southeast corner, and three on both the east and west on the North side. Chipped gray paint covered the eight empty buildings; the post office was lime green, the corner grocery store a putrid orange color, and the Ronners painted their two second-hand stores black. A flashing red stop light hung high over the intersection to keep traffic from roaring through without regard to human frailties, and the state came a few years earlier and rebuilt the sidewalks and tended to the potholes. Outside of that, nothing had changed for nearly a hundred years. Danny supposed the people naming the town Dirtwater early on doomed it. Someone had the bright idea to name a town after the flood plain's pretty clay dirt color that rolled in after every inundation. Still, Dirtwater was the town he grew up in, and when he went to school, they had the meanest eight man football team in the state, anchored by one six foot ten, two hundred and forty pound Danny Gates. That was sixty pounds earlier and a whole lot of years.

Danny stepped into the post office, removed his ball cap, and sat in one of the empty barber chairs. The post office doubled as a hair cuttin' place on a count of Mrs. Kelman's husband acted as both a postmaster and a barber. Mr. and Mrs. Kelman both cut hair, and both delivered mail. "Danny Gates! Great seeing you make it."

Danny knew they were happier to see his money make it. "Well, I couldn't miss the meeting with such a nice letter inviting me."

Mrs. Kelman's round cheeks dimpled with pride as she smiled. "Why thank you, Danny." She walked up beside him and touched his ear. "Why say, you look like you could lower those ears a little."

Danny put his cap back on and grinned. "I've seen your cuttin' Louise. I'll come back on Leroy's day."

She slapped his shoulder. "I cut your hair for the first eighteen years of your life."

"And look at me now, no wife and not a prospect in sight!" They laughed about old times before the rest of the farmers made their way into the building.

Dirtwater might have been sparsely populated by farmers who tended to stay to themselves, but everyone showed up. They understood the importance of having a town, a meeting place, a place important enough to warrant a sheriff living close by. If Dirtwater dried up completely, they might lose the one source of protection needed for the backwoods. When Louise, who'd spent several years conducting Toastmaster meetings called the meeting to order, she insisted everyone say the pledge of allegiance. She stood in the middle of the room and put her hand to her chest, looking up above the door where she had a flag pinned in place. In the middle of the recital, Sheriff Scott came in and interrupted with, "Jesus, Louise, it's a group of farmers for an impromptu meeting, not a high school football game. Get on with it."

Everyone stopped, thankfully so, and before Louise could move on to the business at hand, Sheriff Scott said, "John, Harold, Ken, I found your cattle."

Danny didn't know anyone had missing cattle.

Harold griped. "What kind of shape are they in?"

"Eatin' shape. I found a refrigerated trailer up on Bahalis logging road with all your cattle inside, shot dead. My guess is whoever did it must have seen me comin' because they never came back for their prize." He turned to the other farmers; Danny included. "Any of the rest of you lose any head?"

They all shook their heads. Danny said, "Any idea who it was?"

"Trailer appears to be from California, but the plates are stolen so who knows." He snapped, "You think I should get a fancy fingerprint expert up here?"

Ken interrupted, "The meat still good?"

Scott replied, "Damn near frozen. Trailer's running cold."

Farmer John said, "Forget it then, I'll just cut mine up." The other two nodded, and Harold added, "I hope they come back, I'll have a grave waiting for them."

Sheriff Scott cautioned him, "Be careful, they might be armed and dangerous."

Danny knew. They were neither armed nor dangerous anymore.

Louise stepped in. "So, if that's settled can we get on with new business?"

The sheriff laughed. "New business? Geez, just ask the boys to pretty up the town."

Louise sneered. "Well, as Sheriff Scott has so wonderfully spilled the beans on, we would like some participation in attracting new business to Dirtwater."

Danny observed. "We have twenty family farms that take up most the valley, maybe another twenty families related to those farms. What new business are you thinking about attracting?"

The Ronners, Marl and Helen, who'd stayed out of the fray, outsiders to the farmers, offered, "Maybe one of you farmers could open a meat store in one of the buildings."

The farmers chuckled and the Ronners looked confused.

Danny laughed. "Who would we sell meat to? We all cut our own, and what we do sell we sell to Tom."

Tom stood by the door, looking out for any customers who might wander into his grocery store. His interest piqued by the offer. "That would cut into my sales."

Danny calmed him. "Don't worry, no one is opening a meat store."

Louise bellowed. "We have these buildings that are going to waste. Our town is disappearing, and wouldn't it be nice if we could have a little bit of vibrancy around here?"

Jack Henricksen, sitting in the other barber chair, oldest of the farmers, childless, and nearing the end of his life, suggested, "I think I can solve your problem." His voice had old written all over it but strong for a man his age. He still tended to the farm, along with his wife, both into their late eighties. "Pat and I are considering retiring to a sunny place. We've given this a lot of thought. All of you men have been like our sons. We didn't have kids, instead we cheered you on when the Mustangs were high and mighty, and the truth is we miss that. The town needs some juice. We've been thinkin' about dividin' up the homestead and having a contractor come in and put a couple hundred houses in." He raised his hand to the clamor. "Don't worry, most of the division would be on the Huggins side of our property, so they would see the real growth, but some of it would spill over, enough to make people attracted to those empty buildings."

Danny turned in his seat and scolded Jack, "When were you plannin' on telling us about you moving? My folks been dead a lot of years now, and I sort of count on you two as my second parents and this is the first time I've heard of this."

"Well, it was sudden. We've been talking to a firm out of Portland about settling our estate. We haven't set anything definite yet, but when we do, they're going to send someone out to see us. We just need to be ready and doing something for Dirtwater is high on our list."

Louise had tears in her eyes, as though Christmas had come early. She mouthed, 'thank you,' to Jack.

Danny wasn't done. "That's a lot of change for our area. Two hundred homes?" It was an empty argument. The sheriff looked more than happy along with the Ronners, Tom Benck, and the Kelmans. This was town versus farmers. The concern for the farmers was unclear. Danny turned to Ken and Ken shrugged as if he didn't know what to think. "Well, I guess we'll cross that bridge when we get there." Danny wondered if it would affect him. He lived at the other end of the Valley, would his solitude be broken by more trouble, and would that trouble fill up his pit?

Chapter 10

Lyle had sat around the condo long enough. Two weeks of taking it easy, walking the neighborhood, seeing the bustle of a city that felt more like a town, and he knew the time had come to re-employ himself into the working world. As a chemist in the field of biogerontology, a wide range of companies existed in Portland that would jump to have him. He'd done the supplemental nutrition and the bio engineering, but what intrigued him was a job vacancy listed online for a disease decelerator chemist, experimentation with slowing the onset of disease. He wasn't surprised when his phone rang that the company wasted less than twenty-four hours to respond to his application; after all, he'd just come from the largest gerontology chemistry company in the world. His references were stellar.

"Hello?"

"Is this Lyle Thibodeaux?"

"It is."

"Hi, I'm Gladys Newberry of Decelerex."

Lyle moved to the counter and picked up a pen. He jotted down her name. "How may I help you, Gladys?"

"We just got off the phone with your former employers and we'd be very interested in seeing you."

"That would be fine. When would you like to set up an appointment?"

As though they feared they may lose him, Ms. Newberry insisted, "Could we see you this afternoon?"

"Ms. Newberry, if you're worried, I have other interviews, and you think I will make a decision before seeing you, don't be. I don't mean to come off as sure of myself, but I chose you."

The conversation went silent, a calm static. "So, we are the only company you have applied with?"

Lyle's voice came to life. "As my former bosses must have told you, I'm one of the leading chemists on the west coast. I don't apply to companies; I offer my services."

Lyle had an arrogance allowed to men who tell the truth about themselves. As uncomfortable as Lyle made Mrs. Newberry, she could only accept his words.

Lyle knew what his references thought of him. He was the bar by which the industry set their standards.

"So, I'm confused, do you want to have an interview today?"

Lyle offered, "I would, and I'd like to start tomorrow."

"But we haven't discussed the work or the compensation."

"Ms. Newberry, do you have my resume in front of you?"

"Yes, I do."

"Do you see salary expectations, insurance requirements, and vacation accrual?"

"Yes."

"Then we know what I'll be paid."

Ms Newberry dispensed with the pleasantries. "Can we meet with you at one o'clock?"

"I look forward to it." Lyle thanked her and turned off his phone. He'd already showered, anticipating the call from Decelerex, his slacks were on and he'd pressed his shirt.

He composed a text to his sister who called before the text had time to settle. "You got the job?"

"Well, I have to go in and make sure I like the work environment, and if everything is copacetic, I'll agree to work for them."

"That's great, but I sort of hoped you would have waited a little longer, I could use company on these road trips out here to the middle of nowhere."

"Are you lonely, Sister?"

"It's just that some of these farmers see an attorney and they think the worst."

Lyle laughed. "There is a certain parasitic quality to a lawyer."

"You're talking about your sister here." Her voice hollowed out from being in a car.

"Are you driving?"

"Yes."

"You need an earpiece."

"Trust me, out here, no one gives a rat's behind if you have a phone to your head, hell, I only see a car every twenty minutes."

"Still, a surprise pullover could be very costly, Sister."

"You are so suspicious of people."

"And you should be too."

"Are you worried a country sheriff might take advantage of me?"

Lyle detested her talking about being defiled. Nothing set him off more. "Don't talk that way, it's disgusting."

"Brother, you need to relax. As long as I have you, nothing bad is ever going to happen to me."

"I hope so."

Lauren changed the topic. "So who are you going to see?"

"I don't know. A Ms. Newberry called me and only referred to 'we' in her conversation."

"Did she sound pretty?"

Lyle dismissed the question. "I don't know what that means."

"Did she sound young?"

"Young as in she didn't sound like a senior citizen." Lyle thought about Ms. Newberry's voice. It was Midwestern, a slight accent like she'd been on the west coast many years but didn't grow up there. "A brunette."

"You could tell that from her voice?"

"I'm guessing. I'm guessing she wears pant suits, has hair done up and not long enough to reach her shoulders. Tall, as well."

"Is that what you think or what you wish?"

"Oh please, if I was wishing I would want her to have platinum blonde hair and pale skin like my sister."

Lauren laughed. "Now you're funny."

"Timing is everything."

"Oops."

Lyle heard her phone drop and the sound of tires locking up. "What's wrong?"

There was no answer.

Lyle panicked. "Lauren?"

With a jostling of sounds, Lauren returned. "Damn it."

"What's going on?"

"I missed my turn. These roads are horrible out here. Half of them don't have signs, the other half are gravel. I am in the middle of fricken' nowhere."

"Please be careful. I don't want to lose you, Sister."

"Fear not, I am back on track, and I have farmers to see. Hey, I will catch up with you later. Let me know what Ms. Newberry looks like."

Lyle cautioned her about going into anyone's home and told her to make sure the places she went looked reasonably well kept. He worried about his sister. He disconnected and jotted, 'Buy Lauren a Bluetooth.'

If she planned to be working with farmers and their estates, an earpiece she could have on would give him the peace of mind if she ever had doubts. Some of those places were pretty secluded. He worried.

With time to kill, he returned to the paper, to the obituaries, to see how the area farmers were getting along.

Chapter 11

The Dirtwater Restoration Committee meeting adjourned, and the dozen men gathered on the sidewalk across the street from Tom Benck's corner market. A rumble from the east echoed up Main Street as a string of bikers paraded into view.

"Geez, just what I need." Sheriff Scott spit a stream of tobacco.

Danny spoke over the muffler sound, "Just weary travelers, John."

"Yeah, well, hopefully they're just passing through."

One by one the bikes came to a stop and backed into diagonal slots in front of Tom's store. The farmers held their ground and watched as two dozen, leather clad, tattooed bearing men dismounted from Harleys and approached the store.

"Danny, can you walk with me to Tom's."

Danny shrugged. "Sure."

They crossed over and entered; the bell above the door barely audible over the din of a full store. Sheriff Scott and Danny caught the tail end of a biker's question, asking if there were any bars in town. Sheriff Scott interrupted. "Closest bar is in Huggins."

The man leading the group turned. "Yeah, well, we sort of didn't feel comfortable there."

"Well then I can't much help ya." Sheriff Scott rested his hand on his holster.

"You mind if we clean you out of your beer and Alcohol?" He looked at the Sheriff but spoke to Tom.

Tom, ever the businessman, said, "Be my guest."

Sheriff Scott wanted to keep his town safe. "And where would you be taking that alcohol?"

The biker, barely as tall as Danny's shoulder, stepped toward the sheriff. "Do you have a park here?"

"Nope."

"Anywhere we can go?" He sighed. "Look, I know we look bad, but truth is, we're tired and cold. Riding around in March in Washington isn't the smartest move we've made lately. We just want to hole up for a day, build a fire, keep warm, and move on tomorrow. How bout it, Sheriff?"

"We have no hotels, no parks, nothing but wilderness, and the last thing I need is to scrape dead bodies from the elements."

He smiled. "It's Washington and overcast, how cold can it get?"

The sheriff kept his composure. "If it starts raining, it won't matter how cold it gets, it's unbearable."

"Trust me, we've figured that out already."

"Where'd you boys come from?"

A woman stepped from the crowd of bikers. "Not all of us are boys."

Sheriff tipped his hat. "Sorry Ma'am. So where are you from?"

"Came up from Bakersfield. We were making a run because Jerry over there," he pointed to a tall skinny fellow who raised his hand. "Said there was a warm front that was supposed to be here for a week."

Danny laughed. "A warm front in Washington, in March, usually means fifty and raining."

"Yeah, so we are learning."

The Sheriff apologized. "Well, I can't help ya all. The best thing to do is to go back the way you came and get to the 5, get back to civilization."

Their leader had a noticeable worry. "Well, that's the other problem. Half of us are on fumes. We need a gas station."

The sheriff uttered, "Unbelievable."

Danny offered, "I'll help em."

The sheriff tilted his head and pulled Danny away from the crowd. He whispered, "You are inviting trouble, Danny. You might be the biggest bear I've ever seen, but there's over twenty of them. You get them out there to the farm and you're liable to disappear in one of those ponds of yours."

Danny couldn't help but find irony in the sheriff's words. "Don't worry about me. I got a feeling about these boys."

Sheriff Scott broke away. "Suit yourself." He pointed to the leader and signaled for him to step into the conversation. "This here's Daniel Gates, he's a friend of mine and a pretty stand-up guy.

He has gas and diesel pumps at his farm, of which you will pay for, up front before you leave this store. Are we good with that?"

"Fair enough, Sheriff."

Danny leaned down to the biker. "What's your name?"

"Don, but they all call me Duke."

"How many bikes need fillin'?"

Duke turned to his gang. "Show of hands, how many need gas?"

Everyone raised their hands.

Danny counted twenty-two. "Can you get by on two gallons each?"

Duke nodded. "That'd be great."

"Forty-four gallons, how about a hundred and twenty bucks."

Duke pulled out his wallet and handed Danny three fifties. "Keep the tip."

The sheriff took the money. "I'll keep this in the patrol car. I'll follow you out to the farm."

After Duke and his boys bought all of Tom's cases of beer and his couple dozen bottles of hard liquor, they, along with Danny and the Sheriff, made their way to the street. Danny turned to Duke. "I've got the Silverado over there, follow me north."

As Danny and the Sheriff crossed, the sheriff's radio squawked. He had a call and was needed elsewhere. "Damn it."

"It's fine, John. I'll be okay."

"I don't know."

"Just go do your job."

"I'll be there when I'm done."

Danny patted him on the shoulder. "Later." Danny turned as the group of men tried to secure liquor in saddle bags and bungee cords. He laughed. "Hey Duke, tell your crew to put it in my truck."

He waited until they had the cases and bottles in the back. He put the truck in gear when someone tapped on his door. Startled, he spun his head around and the one woman from the group motioned for Danny to unlock the passenger door. He tapped the lock, and she opened the door. "Can I ride with you?" She was wet leather and shaking, a damp smell of nature. The bikes came to life and one by one they pulled up behind Danny. Danny craned his neck and Duke nodded it was okay if she took the ride.

"Hop in."

"Thanks, Mister."

"Name's Danny."

"I'm Trixie."

They waited for Danny to pull out and followed him to the farm. He pulled into the barnyard, his pump was there, and he figured if they wanted to rest, they could use the barn for cover.

Danny offered them access to park inside, he shooed the cattle out of the stalls and back to the field. The rains weren't as hard as they predicted, and the rivers receded. The girls would be safe again in their own pasture.

Duke thanked Danny and noticed the large metal room in the corner of the barn. "What's that?"

"Meat locker." Danny had cut the two cows the rustlers had shot. He had more meat than he could eat in a year. "Your gang want to hole up the night, you can spend the night in the barn, you can have a fire in the fire pit out front, and I have a side of beef you're welcome to."

"No shit?"

"Yep."

"What do we owe you?"

"On me."

"Why so nice to us when no one else is?"

Danny looked him in the eyes. He whispered, "Sometimes you can tell by lookin' at someone who is good and who is bad." Danny towered over Duke and said matter of fact. "You know what I mean?"

Duke hesitated; a warm smile crossed his face. "Yeah."

Danny walked to the meat locker. "Hope you have proper bedding. I can't offer ya more than hay for cushion."

Duke followed him. "We got bags."

"Good. And if you need any clothes dried, let me know and I'll dry em for ya."

"Well, since you mention it, I think we all have a set of wet clothes."

Danny eyed Duke's chaps. "Those don't keep you dry?"

He smiled. "To a degree, to a degree."

Danny started the pit fire and put a screen over it for the meat. He gave Duke a sheet of flat steel to place the cooked meat on, apologized he had no plates, and took the clothes that needed drying. The gang started into drinking and celebrating a place to stay. As Danny pulled out of the barnyard, he saw the headlights of the sheriff coming up Swaheenie road.

They met at the house and Sheriff Scott stepped out with a question, "Let me guess, you are letting them stay the night?"

"Yep."

He shook his head in disgust. "You have your mama in you, that's for sure."

"They're fine."

"Now they are. Wait until they have enough booze in em and they want to see how tough a bear is." He looked in the back of Danny's truck. "What the hell? Are you their maid too?"

"Hospitality, John." Danny stopped and turned to the sheriff. "You know, they gave me an idea for the restoration."

"Do tell."

"A bar, a hotel, and a gas station." He picked up a stack of clothes as big a haystack.

The sheriff nodded. "I like the gas station. The other two, not so much." His phone rang. "Oh boy, that's Nancy wantin' to know where I am." He turned anxious. "You be okay without me?"

"I'll be fine." He shooed the Sheriff off, who drove out and made a pass in front of the barnyard first. The car slowed to a stop, the headlights illuminating the road. A minute passed, the spotlight shining at the barn and bikers. Danny whistled for John to move on, and the cruiser roared toward Dirtwater.

Danny figured he'd leave the gang alone, let them do their thing in peace. After he ate, he took to the porch and sat out in the cool dark evening. With no city near, a blanket of overcast, it was as dark as it gets in his little world. The pit-fire the lone rescue from total black. The coyotes competed with drunken bikers for breaking the silence.

Danny had no issues until he heard a shot ring out. "Son of a bitch." Danny retrieved his rifle and jumped in his pick-up. When he pulled into the barnyard, more chaos than calm danced about the place. He stepped out and fired a shot into the air, the party of bikers silenced. "What was the gun shot?"

Duke stepped out from the crowd. "Nothing, just an errant mistake."

Danny reached in his pickup truck and pulled out a flashlight. Shining it around, he saw a pool of blood next to the tractor. He turned the light to the group who looked like students waiting for a teacher's request. "Duke, I'd like to speak to you." The group moved in unison toward Danny, but Duke held his hand up and stopped them.

When Duke moved out of earshot of the group, he stepped closer to Danny and whispered, "What do you aim to do with that gun?"

Danny knew if he spooked the group, he'd have no chance. No telling how many of them had guns. "Nothing." He put it in the truck and held his hands up so everyone could see him unarmed. The two men faced off, the cab of the truck, his flashlight, and the fire behind them casting shadows of dim perspectives. "Is the person missing that blood alive?"

Duke was frank, "Nope."

"Did he have it coming to him?"

Duke pulled his jacket away and blood seeped from the side of his stomach. "Yep."

Danny rolled the flashlight to Dukes side. "Good Lord, is that a stab wound." Danny could see sweat beading up on Duke's forehead.

"Yep."

Danny watched Duke wobble. "You got enough energy to quiet your mob?"

He labored. "What do you have in mind?"

"You tell them I'm going to take you up to the house to patch you up and not to worry. You also tell them to leave the body to me."

"Can we take Trixie with us? She's sort of the catalyst for the problems."

"That's fine."

Duke called over one of his men and gave an order. After calling for Trixie, the three of them hurried to the house. By the time they arrived, Duke started losing consciousness. "Duke, if you're in this bad of shape, I don't know what I'll be able to do."

Duke said, "I'm not in that bad of shape."

"You're about to pass out."

He laughed. "That because you have the damn dome light on and I'm squeamish about blood. Hell, I was fine until you shined that damn light on it."

Danny laughed. "What kind of biker are you?"

"Honestly?" He whispered, "One who never did any dirty work."

So who shot the stabber?"

Trixie tilted her head and raised her hand. "That would be me."

Danny put the truck in park, exited, and walked around to the passenger side. He gave Trixie a handout and lifted Duke up with one arm. He cradled him like a baby.

Duke marveled. "Damn Dan, you are one big son of a bitch."

"So how did you get stabbed and why did Trixie do the shootin'?"

Trixie offered, "We have a couple of undesirables, namely Bobby Huntsman, with us, and after a few drinks, he wanted to see what was under my clothes. Duke stepped in between us and Bobby stabbed him. Bobby pulled it out to stab again, and I shot him. Got him in the Adam's apple, a quick gurgle and damn if he didn't die fast." Trixie frowned. "You gonna call that sheriff friend of yours?"

They made their way into the house, and Danny carried Duke to the kitchen table. He placed Duke flat, pointed to a cupboard. "I'm a big believer in justice, justice settled between parties, so no, we'll leave the sheriff out of this, but right now I need you to get that sewing kit up there in that cupboard." Danny pulled a chair up and tore Duke's shirt open. "Looks pretty clean. Trixie," he pointed to another cupboard, "Grab some alcohol out of there."

As she did, Danny pulled a hook shaped needle out of the kit. Duke panicked. "What the hell, is that a fishhook?"

Danny laughed. "No, it's a suture hook."

Duke looked petrified. "What do you have one of those for?"

"When you live on a farm, far away from help, you have to have many talents, and one of mine is stitches."

"God Damn, I can't watch this." Duke couldn't look away fast enough before fainting.

Trixie worried. "He's okay, isn't he?"

Danny pushed on the wound, nothing gushed. "Yeah, he's not bleeding badly." He whispered. "Your boyfriend's a pussy."

She whispered back, "Shhh! don't tell anyone."

Danny cleaned up the wound and put on his glasses so he could see up close to stitch him up. "Damn eyesight!"

Trixie frowned. "I shouldn't worry about that should I?"

Danny smiled. "Not as long as I have my glasses." When he finished, he sat Duke up and called his name until Duke came to.

"Is it over?" Duke was groggy.

"You are right as rain."

"I didn't throw up, did I?"

Danny took his glasses off and stood over Duke. "Nope."

Duke's eyes widened. "Damn, did you grow while I was out? You seem to be bigger than before."

Danny shook his head. "No, you probably just have a higher opinion of me now."

Duke said, "That I do, that I do." He stood and wobbled a little. "I suppose I should get back to the barn and make sure no one else is dead." He sighed, "What am I going to do?"

Danny told him, "You leave that to me. You stick him in the meat locker tonight and leave his bike in the barn. After I gas you all up and you leave, I'll deal with it."

"What are you going to do, make it look like we ran after we killed him?"

"Trixie, can you go check the dryer in the laundry room over there and see if the second load is dry?"

After Trixie moved out of range, Danny said, "No one will ever know anything." Danny's gaze penetrated Duke. "And that will mean you as well, do we understand each other?"

Duke nodded.

"And if there's a commotion with your boys, there might be more than one body that disappears. We get each other?"

Duke nodded again.

"Good. Now, let's get you back to your gang."

Trixie came back. "Everything is dry."

"Perfect. Let's pack it up and get you both back."

Danny took Duke and Trixie back to the barn and dropped them off. He didn't know what was said, but early in the morning they filled up and headed out without mentioning the night before. Danny knew Sheriff Scott would be by to make sure he was okay, so he hurried and cleaned up the scene of the shooting. He hauled the bike and biker to McCleary, tied the body to the bike with a chain and tossed it over. Danny sighed. "Guess that's three. What a night." As the bike and biker sank, Danny offered, "Justice is all about."

Chapter 12

"Decelerex is a pioneer in slowing the onset of illness. We have made great strides to suspending progression of cancer and aging cycles within the body by chemically slowing specific pathogens."

Lyle listened to the lead researcher as he glowed over his work, but Lyle focused on the documents handed him on the processes used. "It would appear you have retarded actual processes and diseases, slowing them chemically."

"Very good, Mr. Thibodeaux, you are a quick study."

Lyle looked up from the papers. "Quick study? This is not cutting edge."

"Excuse me. Where else in the world would you find this sort of research?"

"I abandoned these procedures four years ago with SteadyWell. We discovered ancillary issues with prolonged nerve deadening chemicals." He dismissed the documents and gave them up with a look of disgust. "You are better off strengthening the surrounding tissue." He spoke to his new colleague with suspicion. "Unless of course, making them buy, and buy for failed results but large profits is your goal."

"I assure you, our results have extended the lives of every test subject we have tested."

Lyle read his name tag one more time. "Niraj, I have no doubt that you are wonderful at your job, and that you have gone far, but extending lives and eliminating life threatening illnesses are two different things." Lyle took a breath and relaxed his disposition. "I hope we can learn much from each other and that I can bring something new to the table." He smiled. "May you show me the experimentation logs for what didn't work?"

Niraj looked puzzled. "You mean our failures? Why would you want to see failures?"

Lyle corrected him. "They are not failures; they are all the ways which we don't want to go." They walked through the hall and to the lab. "I am going to have an open mind. I may be able to work in my research with the work you have done, we might be able to salvage your work."

Winning friends was never Lyle's forte. He left that to Lauren. In the short two days he had been with Decelerex, he had managed to alienate himself from every chemist in the department, but that wasn't of concern because the CEO had quickly come to realize, Lyle held the keys to a new future. After the interview where Lyle interviewed his prospective employers instead of vice versa, Mr. Deeds, the president, declared the thirty-one-year-old newest member of the team would be leading a new team of researchers, but there were advantages on both sides. Decelerex received an employee at a much-reduced salary than expected, and Lyle had access to all the cutting edge drugs in the world. He would be free to experiment with chemicals that could change the way humans live and die.

His phone buzzed. "Hello, Sister."

"How's work?"

Lyle smiled at Niraj and stepped out of the lab. "Like my last job."

"That bad huh?"

"I'll have them whipped in to shape in no time."

"I called because I wanted you to be the first to hear me on my earpiece you got me."

"Good." He leaned against the wall and relaxed. Hearing his sister's voice relieved him. "Are you wearing your seatbelt?"

"Brother, why do you do that? I think I am old enough to decide if I should wear my seatbelt. It's my life."

"Do you want a ticket?"

"I don't care. I'll fight in it court."

"You aren't a litigator; you are an estate attorney. What a ticket does is raise one's stress level. It ties up a day of work, it leads to long lines in courthouse counter windows, and it takes hard earned money and throws it out. Not to mention, it puts you face to face with the law when they pull you over."

Lauren whispered, "I like that last part. Those are the confrontations I win."

"I would like you to put on your seatbelt and quit testing fate. Please." He could hear her clicking the lock of the belt. "Thank you."

"You are no fun."

"Well, I will be fun in time. I will be able to take days off so I can go with you on drives to some of your country clients."

Lauren's voice spiked, "Really?"

"Yes, I need to watch out for you, make sure you are safe."

"I'm so excited. That will be fun. Maybe we can make a few weekends of it and drive out to the coast some time."

"Maybe. Be safe and I will talk to you when you get home."

"Love you, Brother."

"Love you too." Lyle pulled the phone away and lost himself in thought.

"Was that your girlfriend?" Niraj interrupted.

Lyle straightened. "Excuse me?"

"Was that your girlfriend?"

Lyle frowned. "Why would you say that?"

"I apologize, but you look so happy. I thought perhaps it was a love interest."

"Hardly, that was my sister." Lyle placed the phone in his breast pocket and passed Niraj back to the lab.

Niraj followed. "Oh, oh! I didn't know." Niraj pulled up alongside Lyle. "You seem very close to your sister."

Lyle admitted, "We're twins so there is a bond which is unmistakable."

Niraj laughed. "I too am a twin."

Lyle grinned. "Brother or sister?"

"Twin brother."

"Do you live with him?"

Niraj stared back. "Live with him?"

"I mean, aren't you two close?"

"But of course, but we are both married and have families. I only see him on holidays."

Lyle tried to comprehend. "Holidays? You mean you don't see each other every day?"

"He lives in New York."

Lyle stammered, "New York?" How could he live so far apart from his twin? That made no sense.

"Do you live with your sister?"

Lyle hesitated and said with reservations, reservations that perhaps the oddity was his own. "Why yes." He looked around and said quietly, "Yes I do."

Chapter 13

Danny needed to leave the house. Too much happened over the last few weeks. Death had become too comfortable and concentrating on other things might ease the stress. He'd thought about Jack's decision to leave the valley, to pick up, carve his land for new homes, and do it all without saying a word. That hurt. Jack and Pat were best friends with his mom and dad and when they both passed, Jack and Pat stepped in as surrogate parents. They may not have seen each other every day, but they spent holidays together, celebrated birthdays together, and they agreed to discuss any major news together. He made a quick breakfast, put on better clothes than overalls, nearly Sunday's best, and jumped in the truck for the drive across the valley.

He could make that drive in his sleep. From the dip before the tracks, to the poorly banked turn at Mill's Creek, Danny knew when to slow down and when to push it.

He made it over before nine, exited his truck, and Jack's dogs greeted him with excitement. "Get off me, you mutts."

"Why don't you like dogs?" Jack carefully stepped off the porch, his stiff leg a little stiffer in the cool weather.

"I don't know, but can you lock them up or something." They continued, three Brittany spaniels, to jump as though longing for an owner.

Jack insisted. "Trudy, Tess, Wilbur, get over here!" Jack shooed them into the house. He turned to Danny. "Son, good to see ya."

Danny grumbled in a foul mood. "Let's go in the house and talk." He followed behind as Jack worked his way back up the porch.

"Danny, good to see you." Pat came out and pulled Danny down for a peck on the cheek.

"Don't think I'm not mad at you too, Pat."

"I heard Jack spilled the beans at the meeting. Believe me, I let him have it. This was supposed to be something we were going to talk to you about before we told anyone. You know Papa Jack; he doesn't like to wait."

They walked to the door, and Danny whistled for the dogs. They scurried out onto the porch and Danny closed the door as he entered. "Dumb nitwits."

Jack smiled. "You better get used to them. Iffin' and when we move, you're taking them."

"I am not taking your damn dogs."

Pat reminded him. "They aren't like those yapping terriers your mother had. These are good dogs, they are protectors."

Danny chided her. "They aren't protectors. They're Brittany spaniels. They'd show you the family jewels if you were a burglar."

She led the men into the kitchen. "Doesn't matter, you're still taking them."

Danny toggled his head, he wasn't winning the argument, and he didn't want a change of attitude toward dogs.

Jack patted a stool. "Come sit here at the counter and tell me what you think of this proposal."

Danny had to spread his legs and sit outward, his size wouldn't let his lower body rest comfortably, his knees would hit the wall under the counter. He jockeyed getting comfortable. When he finally came to rest, he picked up the papers and followed the wording down the page, stopping when he made it to the section regarding the ridge. "What's this?"

Jack patted Danny's knee. "You know I have a thousand acres here in the valley, and I have the eight hundred that horseshoes around the valley on the ridge. Well, I want you to have the ridge land."

"Why? I thought you were giving that to Dirtwater."

Jack admitted, "What is Dirtwater? It's a defunct town that we are going to have to set up a committee to decide what to do with the five hundred they are already getting. Chances are, votes will be cast by most land, and if you have an additional eight hundred, you will have a big say in what is done with this land. As for the ridge, it touches your land, and you have all that privacy out there, you need to keep it."

Danny winked; Jack had no idea the truth of his words. "You know you don't have to do this."

"I'm embarrassed that I'm not giving it all to you."

Danny acknowledged. "I like Dirtwater just as much as you do, and I want to see it come back. I think the five hundred will go a long way, and I think with a development far enough away, we will grow just enough to open the school back up."

"So, you aren't too mad?"

"Jack, I'm only disappointed you don't want to spend your days here. How am I going to see you? I can't get up and hop on a plane. I have cows to tend to, fields to grow. It's like you're dyin'."

"I know, Son, but this isn't about you. It's about some sunshine, spending some easy time, lounging in a desert somewhere."

Danny knew the conversation would have been unfair had he bellowed about his own selfish needs, it was after all, their lives. He accepted the truth and their graciousness for the willing of land and the endowment to the town humbled him. "So when are they going to start building houses?"

Jack said, "First tract starts in the summer, a total of thirty-five homes by Christmas."

Huggins sat only a mile from the outer edge of Jack's property. Two hundred homes would technically be in Seefer Valley, divided by a ridge and ravine that the Huggins Prairie Road traveled through. That meant they would be Dirtwater residents, but Dirtwater proper sat on the southeast corner of the triangle shaped

Seefer Valley. Danny's Land occupied the upper North section of the triangle, and Jacks property the southwest. All the rest of the farmers had the area in between. The residents of the new housing would find Huggins their town, not the dried up Dirtwater.

"Make sure my land never gets annexed by Huggins."

"I don't think that'll be up to me. Chances are, quadruple the population of Dirtwater and anyone who is anyone will push for annexation."

"That's why you need to put businesses in Dirtwater."

Danny raised a brow. "So, I take it that's what the five hundred acres is for?"

Jack stood and hobbled over to a desk, grabbed a rolled up blueprint. "I have the solution."

He laid it out on the table; Danny unrolled it and whistled. "You want to put a small plane airport on the land?"

"Why not? Huggins will be forced to put a hospital in place of the clinic, real grocery stores, chains, you name it. They can build congestion and we can put an airport, a golf course, maybe a few nice restaurants."

Danny grinned. "For an old fart, you have quite the dream."

Jack fired back. "Dirtwater cannot become the slum of Huggins, but we can make the opposite true if we make it a luxury to live out here. The homes being built out here aren't going to be small dwellings. I'm building beautiful well-constructed homes, two hundred of them with a golf course running through the heart of it all. That'll keep anyone here from wanting to be annexed."

Pat interrupted the men. "I see someone coming down the road. Must be the estate attorney."

Danny stood. "Well, I better leave. I should let you two do business."

Pat sounded disappointed. "I thought you would stay and listen."

Danny had no expertise. "Jack has this way more under control than me. I'm a simple farmer. I had no idea Jack was a city planner!" Danny and Pat shared a laugh.

Jack, Pat, and Danny made it to the porch and watched as a dust plume rolled in with a little red car that parked behind Danny's truck. When a slender attractive snow-white blonde exited the vehicle, Jack hollered, "Ms. Thibodeaux, I presume?"

The wind whipped her hair, and she used her briefcase to poorly shield her locks from being plastered across her face. She scurried up the gravel and onto the cement, her hand extended and reaching for Jack's. "Hello, Mr. Henricksen."

Jack put his hands on Ms. Thibodeaux shoulders. "Well, look at you, Darling. You are pretty as a snowflake, and your hair is just as white."

She smiled, and as a gentleman followed up behind her, Danny couldn't help but notice the platinum white hair on his head as well.

Jack looked back and forth, "I'm going to guess that either this is your brother, or you pick your men by looking in the mirror."

Ms. Thibodeaux laughed. "Both!"

The remark caught Danny by surprise. What did that mean?

Her brother broke the tension. "My sisters a little crazy, but a great attorney. I'm Lyle, and she wanted some company coming all the way out to the country."

Danny's heart lifted to hear him say sister. He found something about Ms. Thibodeaux intriguing. She had a power to her, wrapped in innocence. She had striking looks like nothing he'd seen before. Danny nudged Pat and whispered, "Well, since they parked behind me, I suppose I could stay and listen."

Pat winked and responded, "I'm sure that's the reason."

Jack shook Lyle's hand and replied. "I don't blame her and you're a good brother to tag along." He made a path and introduced the two people behind him. "This is my lovely wife Pat, and this is the son we never had, Dan."

Ms. Thibodeaux commented. "I keep looking up and you keep going, Dan."

Danny gazed down at her, her beauty intoxicating. "Well, the bad part is, I feel a storm coming before anyone else."

"Oh, and witty too."

Danny stepped forward, shook her hand and then her brother's. "Nice to meet you."

Ms. Thibodeaux's brother had a cold steel to him. Danny wondered if being there might be a distraction, and as much as he wanted to stay, he could see her brother's agitation by Danny's presence. Leaving would be better for the business at hand. "Would it be possible to have you move the car? I need to be leaving."

Pat and Ms. Thibodeaux rang out in unison, "No, why don't you stay." Her brother took his sister's keys. "I'll get it out of your way."

Danny could see his anxiety to remove a dumb farmer away from his sister. A rivalry of sorts, but Danny supposed he didn't blame him; he just wanted to protect his sister. Danny turned to Pat. "Call me after the meeting to let me know how it goes."

Ms. Thibodeaux offered, "They are being sent off in style, I promise."

Danny took in Ms. Thibodeaux one more time, the wind pushing the scent of jasmine up and around him. Its fragrance lovely. "Pleased to meet you, Ms. Thibodeaux."

She stepped close enough to whisper, "Call me Lauren."

"Fair enough, Lauren."

He hoped he would see her again.

Chapter 14

Lyle liked control.

He'd risen in the company and as six months had passed Decelerex performed as Lyle wanted it to. His bosses had fallen into line. The other chemists accepted Lyle as the genius, and his direction worked best for the company.

Christmas had come and gone, winter had passed, and spring promised great things. Things were good, but a tension lie beneath the surface, a lid rumbled to be lifted. He decided to take a day off and travel with his sister.

"Amazing you are letting me drive, Brother."

Out the window, plowed rows of pattern, miles and miles of it stretched from farm to farm. His thoughts rested uneasy and heavy. His concern deepened. "I hope all this monotony doesn't eat at you, Sister."

"It's been nearly seven months, and I have enjoyed my job. Both of us have. It's been quiet, we've been good."

"Have we?" Lonely farmhouses passed—silent testimonies to privacy.

"We have." Lauren tapped her brother's shoulder. He turned and she said, "What's eating at you?"

"I'm feeling as though you want to explore a little too much, Sister."

"And I want you to come with me."

He sighed, "I don't mean that. I mean you seem restless. You haven't become smitten with a man, have you?"

She giggled. "Maybe a little with one of the office attorneys."

Lyle covered his face and rubbed tension from his temples. "What's his name?"

"Hamilton."

Lyle smirked. "Is that a first name or last?"

"A first name." They looked at each other. "I know it! How pretentious is that?" She laughed, and Lyle shook his head.

"Office relationships are a bad thing; you know that right?"

"What about you and that missy working in HR?"

"Who?"

She huffed, "Ms. Newbody."

"Newberry, and nothing could be further from the truth."

"Good, because I have never thought a brunette would look good with my brother."

"Quit changing the subject. I mean it when I say to back off office romances, Sister."

"Is this what you're sulking is about, about me being interested in someone?"

"Of course it is. It always is." He didn't want to bring up the white elephant in the car. They knew the issues; they knew the risks; they knew what they really wanted. "I don't want to lose you, Sister. Just promise me you will step back."

Lauren's shoulders slumped. "You always get in the middle of my life." She wiped a tear. "I'll try, but it's so hard. I want to feel that emotion again."

"I know you do but remember me. Remember what you mean to me." He hesitated. "And what I mean to you."

Her tears flowed. "You throw that in my face every time. I'm a big girl and you act like I am a complete wreck."

Lyle cautioned, "You would be lost without me, remember that."

"Maybe not."

Lyle spoke with force, "What's that supposed to mean? Have you been acting on your emotions?"

Lauren gripped the wheel with both hands and narrowed her gaze, staring forward. "Maybe."

"Has Hamilton gone on vacation yet?"

She smiled. "Not yet."

"Then I don't believe you. I know you too well. You would have told me if there was someone else you were interested in, someone you'd danced with."

"You don't know that. I work in the field every day; I could have met someone out here in these lonely little farm towns."

"Like I said, had you, you would have come home crying as you always do. I would pick up the pieces because I always do. Just be happy with me, come home and wind down, and life will be wonderful."

Lauren slowed down and dried her emotions. "Dirtwater. We're here."

Lyle adjusted his eyes. "Dirtwater? Who names a town Dirtwater?"

Lauren scanned the first road sign. "Chamalea. Should be the next road."

"What are we looking for?"

"Henricksen Road."

"There it is." Lyle pointed and Lauren turned onto a long gravel driveway, a large ranch home a half mile beyond rows of cherry trees and planked fencing. "Nice grounds."

"It's over eighteen hundred acres."

"And they're selling? Unusual for farmers."

"No, they are retiring, developing two hundred homes on five hundred acres and willing the five hundred to Dirtwater."

"Where's the other eight hundred going?"

"To a family friend."

"Ah, that's where you come in."

"White Shadow Development and Dirtwater would like to make sure it's done properly." They pulled up to the home, and Lauren parked behind a dusty gray Silverado. Outside, an elderly couple engaged in a conversation with a large man, as tall as he was big. Lauren and Lyle stepped out, and the elderly man spoke up. "Ms. Thibodeaux, I presume?"

She hurried ahead of her brother, dancing across the gravel and up onto the cement portion of the driveway, her hand extended and her briefcase shielding a slight breeze pushing strands of blonde hair into her face. "Hello, Mr. Henricksen."

Mr. Henricksen put both hands on her shoulders. "Well, look at you, Darling. You are pretty as a snowflake, and your hair is as white."

She smiled, and as Lyle came up behind, Mr. Henricksen took a double take. "I'm going to guess that either this is your brother, or you pick your men by looking in the mirror."

She laughed, "Both!"

Lyle broke the tension of his sister's awkward remark, "My sisters a little crazy, but a great attorney. I'm Lyle, and she wanted some company coming all the way out to the country."

Mr. Henricksen shook Lyle's hand. "I don't blame her, and you're a good brother to tag along." He made a path and introduced the two people behind him. "This is my lovely wife Pat, and this is the son we never had, Dan."

Lauren commented. "I keep looking up and you keep going, Dan."

Dan smiled. "Well, the bad part is, I feel the storm coming before anyone else."

"Oh, and witty too."

It disgusted Lyle. Lauren flirted with that monster of a man, more human than she could handle, and certainly someone he wouldn't want to tangle with.

Dan stepped forward and shook his sister's hand and then his. "Nice to meet you."

Lyle stiffened. He hoped the gentleman didn't plan on sticking around. If only a family friend, perhaps he would leave and not bother his sister while she conducted business. Tension developed between Lyle and Dan; Lyle could feel it. Lyle needed the farmer to back off.

When their guest started to move toward his car, Lyle let out a sigh of relief. "Would it be possible to have you move the car? I need to be leaving."

Mrs. Henricksen and Lauren spoke in unison, "No, why don't you stay." Lyle took his sister's keys. "I'll get it out of your way." His curtness rang loud as he made quick with the remark.

Best to remove his sister from that poor dupe. He could see how awe struck his sister made him; he could see it in the farmer's stare; how preposterous a notion that the farmer would ever have the opportunity to engage his sister in anything other than idle chit chat, but he supposed he didn't blame him.

Their guest turned to Mrs. Henricksen. "Call me after the meeting to let me know how it goes."

Lauren said, "They are being sent off in style, I promise."

Their guest took one more look at Lyle's sister, His chest heaved as though he breathed her in. "Pleased to meet you, Ms. Thibodeaux."

Lauren stepped close enough to whisper. Lyle guessed she gave him her name.

As if on cue, the guest said, "Fair enough, Lauren."

Lyle hoped that ended it and they would never see him again.

Chapter 15

The phone rang, Danny lifted the receiver. "Hello, Pat."

"How did you know it was me?"

"Because no one but you uses a land line anymore, besides, I knew you'd call to tell me how the meeting went."

"It went very well. That young lady had everything already drawn up for the land divisions. Jack signed the papers, and we worked out a deal for the remainder of the year at the farm."

Danny felt relief. "Glad to know you aren't leaving tomorrow."

She chuckled. "Who wants to go to the desert with summer approaching. We will wait until it's winter."

"How's Jack? Any regrets?"

"I think he regrets leaving all he knows, but I think he's excited to turn Dirtwater around."

Turning Dirtwater around had an appeal to it, but it meant intrusion, and intrusion hadn't served Danny well over the last year. "I suppose."

"Don't you feel the same way?"

"I do, I just have to adjust to more people, more people who will bring more problems."

Pat changed the subject. "That young lady asked about you."

"Really?" That intrigued Danny. "What did she ask?"

"About whom you were, what you did for a living."

Danny laughed. "Everyone in Seefer Valley is a farmer."

"Yes, I told her you were the most eligible farmer in all of Dirtwater."

"How'd that brother of hers take that?"

"He's protective, like a brother should be."

Danny thought something else. It felt creepy protective. "He struck me as weird."

"He's a very bright man."

"I didn't say he wasn't bright, I said he was weird."

Pat dismissed it. "Would you like to come to dinner tonight?"

Danny had promised to help Harold plow the north end of his field. "I can't, but I could make it tomorrow."

"Oh, that would be fine. We will be having your favorite."

Danny loved her meatloaf. "I can't wait. Haven't had much besides steak lately."

He finished up his conversation, happy the Henricksen's were happy, not too worried about anything else. Worry wasn't something Danny dwelt much about. He fired up the tractor from a winter rest and traveled through the field until he met up with Harold's property line on the south side of his. Danny helped his neighbor over the previous ten years, ever since Harold started slowing down. They were neighborly enough to have a gate on the fence line.

A man does a lot of thinking runnin' rows, back and forth, paying just enough attention to keep them straight, but wondering thoughts about life. He wondered about his existence, living there in Dirtwater, never marrying and never having any kids. He supposed someday he'd be like Jack, ready to retire and looking for some young farmer to take over his land. Of course, with three bodies in McCleary, he might have some explaining to do in the afterlife.

Two hours passed, and he'd barely plowed a quarter of what he'd promised. He'd have to run all the way to eight, dark in the month of March, to finish it all. Wouldn't be the first time, wouldn't be the last. He plugged along, running rows. Harold dropped in a new crop. Instead of peas he decided to grow corn. Danny wasn't a fan of the corn, by late summer he wouldn't be able see Blanchard Road as it came up to Swaheenie. That meant travelers were on his road before he noticed them. However, with a mile of distance before they made it to the house, he had plenty of time to see them coming.

He didn't see the sheriff when he caught him off guard as he did a sweep and turned. There Sheriff Scott stood, about twenty feet in front of him. He stopped the tractor, let her diesel down and gurgle to quiet. "John! What brings ya out here?"

Sheriff Scott walked down a row and stood looking up at Danny, still perched on his seat. "You remember seeing this guy?"

He handed Danny a picture of the man dumped in McCleary with the bike."

"Should I?" Danny handed the picture back.

"He was reported missing by his sister. She says he took off with his motorcycle gang, the same gang that passed through here and stayed at your place."

"Honestly, I didn't hang out with em', and they all sort of looked the same to me. Leather jackets with a hornet and Bakersfield written on the back."

"Bakersfield police might be callin'. I gave them your name and said if anyone could help it was you."

Danny jumped off the tractor and reached for the photo. He looked at it again, thinking about the guy's last moments when he stuck a knife in Duke's side and received a bullet in the throat by a woman. "Not sure how much help I can give em', but I certainly can let them know they seemed like a nice bunch."

Sheriff Scott changed the subject. "So did Jack decide on his property?"

"Yep, he's already signed it over."

"No shit. When?" John crossed his arms and looked up.

"Today." Danny could see the wheels turning in the sheriff's head. Land meant money and money to Dirtwater meant a possible raise for him. The county paid him, but he earned a stipend from Dirtwater to run his jurisdiction out of Seefer Valley.

"How long you think it'll take for his housing development to get going?"

Danny pulled his gloves off, set them on the rear tires and pulled a sandwich out of the toolbox. He offered half to the sheriff, who waved it off. Danny took a bite. "They're starting this summer."

"What about zoning?"

Danny shook his head. "Seriously, John?" This is Dirtwater. Who's coming out here to stop two hundred homes? If the farmers don't bitch, this is going through."

Sheriff commented, "I think this would be good for Dirtwater."

"I think it would be good for the Sheriff of Dirtwater."

Sheriff Scott offered, "Maybe we could change it to a police department, get an actual town going, maybe turn those pits of yours into a fishin' park."

"Slow down, Nottingham. They haven't even broken ground yet; and leave all the growin' to that side of the Valley. This here's my own paradise and I'd like to keep it as private as possible."

"Just thinkin' about making a Mayberry community."

Danny grinned. "Would that make you Andy Taylor or Barney Fife?"

Sheriff Scott pointed at Danny. "I do a good job here."

"Yes, you do, but you also don't have to do much. You prepared to work a twenty-four seven? Worse, you might get some new resident who wants your job. You have about a 100 people in

Dirtwater who you grew up with. Two hundred new homes potentially is four times as many adults, adults who aren't hillbillies like us. They might want someone more like them. You thought about that?"

He shrugged. "If that's the case, maybe I'll open that bar you were talking about."

Danny finished off the sandwich. "I'll wait for Bakersfield to call. Thanks for the warning."

Sheriff nodded and turned.

"If you see a snow-white woman with a ghostly looking brother, she's doin' the estate for Jack."

Sheriff spun back around. "Saw her! They came into town about an hour ago and went into Tom's place. Kind of an unusual looking pair, like something out of Children of the Corn."

"I thought she was pretty."

Sheriff stared back. "Unique."

Danny stepped up and turned the key over on the tractor. It came to life, and he continued plowing a new row. His mind raced over what the sheriff said about the changes. He realized this sort of change would only bring situations into his life, and as much as he found the events of the last year memorable, he didn't want to make a habit out of cleaning up the trash.

Chapter 16

"Your dogs are beautiful." Lauren patted her lap and all three nestled their heads against her. She alternated between each dog, briskly petting them. "Such affection."

Pat admitted, "When we leave, we have to leave them with Dan, although he's not much of a dog lover."

Lauren sighed, "If we had the room, I would take them all."

"We? Are you married Ms. Thibodeaux?"

"No, I live with my brother."

Lyle sat nearby and nodded. "One day, somebody will take her away and she will be happy. Until then, she has me." He calculated his remarks. Lauren too freely gave hers. He glanced her way and she weakly smiled. "We've only been in the Pacific Northwest for about a half year, and we share a condo. No dogs."

"That's too bad. They sure do like your sister."

Lyle smiled. "Everyone seems to find my sister alluring."

"I think Dan found her alluring."

Lauren grinned and Lyle cautioned, "That would be a very odd pair. My sister is an attorney, and well, Dan seems like a nice enough guy, but what possibly could they have in common."

Jack, who'd been reading the paperwork, stepped into the conversation. "Dan's an interesting fellow. Self-made in many ways, well read, and very intriguing."

Lyle wanted the conversation to end. He couldn't think of anything worse, but he didn't want to step out on a ledge and upset his sister's new clients. High maintenance on the order of extreme best described Lauren. "Yes, I suppose to be such good farmers, one must be a jack of many trades." He wanted to keep his sister intact and get out of there. He made eye contact with impatience, and she held her hand out and closed her eyes to calm him. Would she be okay? Would she twenty-question her clients about Dan?

Lauren smiled. "Where is Dan's farm?"

Pat responded, "He has the last farm in the north end of the valley."

Jack said, "And soon, the entire western ridge. I'm willing that to him."

Lauren's eyes widened. "My goodness, that will be a large chunk of land."

Jack continued, "With the addition of my eight hundred acres, he'll have the most land in Dirtwater."

"Who's the lucky woman sharing that with him?"

Pat scoffed. "Who? Danny?"

"Danny?" Lauren smiled. "He goes by Danny?"

"Yes, and Danny doesn't have a girlfriend. He's a good-looking man but he's as big as a house. I think women are intimidated a little. Plus, he's a little awkward at times."

Lyle could see where this was going. "Lauren, let the man be."

Pat turned to Lyle, "Oh, I think he would be tickled to find out such a beautiful woman was asking about him."

This is how it always started. She'd been so good since they made it to Portland. The San Francisco incident blew over and no one was the wiser. The last thing Lyle needed to deal with was another of his sister's romances. He always found it distasteful cleaning it up so she could keep focused. It wore on him. Why couldn't she just be happy with her brother?

He waited his turn as Lauren conducted business in between questions about the big burly farmer. When the business wound down, Lyle asked his sister if she'd like to see the town of Dirtwater. He knew she would want to continue through and find Dan's farm, but he felt sure he could distract her enough to stall her. However, trouble percolated.

When the time came to go, Lauren said all the right things. "I will come back and see you. You have been my favorite clients, and I truly hope you get what you deserve out of this sale."

Lyle prodded her to hurry. As they made it to the car, he said, "I'll drive."

"Why are you so upset?"

"Because you're getting restless."

"I'm bored, Brother."

On the porch, the Henricksens carried on a tense conversation. He smiled and waved, put the car in reverse and pulled away. Driving out the gravel driveway and to the main road, he continued, "Don't be bored. What am I? Are you forgetting me? I'm here, I'm not going anywhere."

They drove east, toward Dirtwater proper. When they made it to the dingy little downtown, Lauren asked to stop at the corner grocer. When they stepped out of the car, Laurel caught sight of a man in uniform and said to her brother, "I like a man in uniform."

She teased Lyle, and it irritated him. "Leave him alone."

They entered the grocery store and the grocer stood on a stool restocking the beer aisle. She whispered, "I like a man in an apron."

Lyle resigned himself that she had no plans of letting it go, that he would have to take matters into his own hands. This had the ear markings of ending badly, he could tell. "What do you want me to do, Sister?"

"I want you to let me be me. I want to explore."

"I can't let you do that; do you understand me?" Lyle asked for green tea and the grocer acted like he spoke a foreign language.

"We have Lipton, sweetened and unsweetened."

"How about soy milk?"

He stared at Lyle. "What kind of milk?"

Lyle threw his arms up. "Never mind, do you have bottled water?"

"Right over there." He pointed to the last cooler.

Lyle paid for two waters and escorted his sister out and to the car.

"Lyle, can we drive up north out of town?"

"You want to see the farmer?"

"Please."

Lyle smiled. "I suppose." He handed his sister her water and watched as she tipped the bottle and drank it down. He started counting, sitting in the car, still parked out front of the grocery store.

"What are you doing?" Lauren watched Lyle counting.

"Waiting."

Lauren frowned; her face saddened. "You didn't."

"It's for your own good, Sister."

"You're horrible sometimes." She leaned back and closed her eyes.

Lyle watched as her head tilted and she fell unconscious. "Sorry, Sister. I can't go through this again, it's unfair to me. I love you dearly." Lyle turned the car around and drove back to Portland.

Chapter 17

Eight o'clock rolled around and Danny tired from sitting in a tractor seat for nine hours. He'd finished his portion of plowing and ran the tractor back through his field and to the barnyard. Even though the sun had gone down, he washed down the tractor and cleaned it up; he didn't like to wait on chores. He gave his truck horn three blows, and the ladies worked their way back to the barn. He grained them, washed the shit off them. He couldn't believe they'd sit in their own crap. God his cows irritated him. They were dumb. He finished around ten and headed back to the truck when he saw the headlights of a vehicle coming up Swaheenie. Danny couldn't make out the color or model of the car, too dark, but it pulled in and sat idling in front of him. Whoever drove it shifted to high beams and Danny had to shield his eyes to keep from turning away. "Who's there?"

Danny backed up and worked his way to the barn, and with each step the car crept closer. "I said, who's there?"

The car shut off, and a gentleman step out brandishing a handgun. "Sorry, Sport, but I'm sort of lost, and I'm sort of in trouble."

"And that is my problem because?"

"Because I have a fucking gun, and I want your truck."

He was tall. Not many men passed Danny shoulders, Danny guessed his assailant stood a good six-four. "What kind of trouble are you in?" Danny figured if the man offered it up, he would probably shoot Danny, so it disappointed him when the man did. "I robbed some Podunk bank out here in Dumbfuck, Nowhere, and I'm lost, and I think they know what kind of car I'm driving."

"And if I give you my truck, what are you going to do with me?"

Danny's question brought a gaze of irritation. "Oh, I'm not asking you for your truck, I'm taking your truck, as for you, I am putting a hole in your head."

He raised the gun and Danny said, "You might want to wait."

The bank robber lowered the gun. "And why?"

"The keys to the truck are at my house and I can guarantee you if you fire a round, my wife and sons will be locked and loaded. Just sort of how it is in these parts." Danny stared back with a look of amusement.

"Yeah, so I've noticed. I've already had a rifle pointed at me when I knocked on a door." Danny figured he met up with old man Ronner. He'd point a gun at his own wife if she didn't identify herself.

"So what are your plans?"

"I'm taking the truck, so let's go get those keys. I'm sure if they see me holding a gun on dear old dad, they'll do as I ask."

"Still might not work."

"Why's that?"

"I'm not going to let you kill my family. We get to the house, I just tell the boys to get their guns."

"How many God damned kids you got?"

"Four, all boys."

"You ain't that old, they can't be too big."

"We marry young in these parts, and I'm a bit older than I look."

He aimed the gun at Danny's head. "I'll take my chances. Let's walk up to the house."

"It's a quarter mile."

"I don't give a shit. I sure as hell don't want a boy your size sitting next to me for too long. I can't drive and hold a gun on you at the same time."

"Okay, let's walk then." Danny didn't know what to do, but at least he'd bought some time. "What bank you rob?" Danny led the way, his captor a few paces behind him.

"Some bank in Bradenton."

"Boy you must be lost. How long have you been driving around?"

He whistled in disgust. "Since noon."

"What makes you think they know what you were driving?"

"Gut feeling. Besides, I don't want to find out if I'm wrong or right."

Danny reasoned. "Yeah, I suppose that's a smart move."

They made it up to the house, the lights were off. "Looks pretty quiet."

Danny suggested, "They might have seen us coming."

"Doubtful, it's as dark as shit out here."

"You don't hear my hounds baying, do you?"

"So."

"Someone's got em' shut up. Let me say something to them."

"Like what?"

"I'll calm them down." Danny shouted, "Boys! No need to worry, this here's a friend of mine." Danny whispered over his shoulder, "Stand a little closer so they see ya." The man stepped close, a little too close, Danny half turned and had his paw on the pistol before the bank robber realized what happened. Danny took his second hand and placed it over his first and with both hands yanked it away. His assailant, unfazed, punched Danny's face with three quick jabs. Kicking his arm and jarring the gun into the ditch. In the darkness, the gun disappeared, and it turned into man on man. They stood toe to toe, and Danny realized his foe had a fighter's touch, was big, and every bit the worthy adversary. He caught the man's fist as he threw another punch, yanked his arm down and followed with a punch downward onto the man's collar bone. The guy let out a yelp, and backed away, pulling his arm free.

"Son of a bitch. I am going to beat you to death."

Danny backed up, closer to the porch, a lone pole light casting a dull glow over the driveway. He needed him out of the darkness.

He caught a streaking body approaching just in time to wrap his arms around a lunging figure. As they hit the ground, Danny rolled and settled on top, throwing a heavy punch to his foe's face. He felt something explode.

"Mother fucker." The man rolled to his stomach and was up as quickly. Danny guessed the man had wrestled in his day.

In the modest light, Danny could see the man's nose gushing blood. Danny offered, "I'll tell you what. If you beat me, I'll let you kill me and take my truck, and if I beat you, I'll let you drive out of here with your car."

"Yeah, right. I'm sure that family of yours has already called the cops."

Danny motioned with his finger to step closer. "There is no family, I live alone."

"Well hell, I should have just killed you when I had a chance."

"Shoulda, coulda, woulda. Now you're going to have to earn it."

His foe danced like he was in a ring, but every time he neared close enough for a punch, Danny leveled him with a hard straight jab. When he fell to his knees, Danny gave him an upper cut with his knee, flattening him onto the gravel. "Okay, okay," he bounced his words off the ground, his arm raised in submission, "I give, you win." His breathing labored and his body lay exhausted.

Danny grabbed him by the neck and brought him to his feet. He dragged him to the porch and bounced his head hard enough to disorient him one more time. Danny opened his door, reached in and up for a rifle he kept above the molding. He flipped on the porch light and pointed the rifle at his assailant's head. "Now I'm going to follow you back to your car."

"Dude, you might as well call the cops. I can't get out of this place. I don't know where I am."

Danny pitied the man. "You nitwit. I'll give you a route out of here, up a dirt road and over the hill. Just stay on the path and you will get out of here."

"Excuse me? Why the hell are you helping me?"

"Let's just say, I like having my blood pumping. I owe you this one."

"Do I get to keep the money?"

"I don't need your money." Danny laughed. "I probably have more in the house than you got from Bradenton."

They walked a marcher's pace back to the barn, Danny keeping the man in file with the shove of the rifle when he'd slow down. "Dude, I'm gushing blood from my nose, relax, I'm good with getting out of here. I don't want to do the whole fighting thing again."

When they made to the barn, Danny did a quick look in the man's car to make sure he didn't have another weapon. "I'll follow you as far as the hill, just in case you get stuck."

"Yeah, okay. Just get me out of here and I promise I'm never coming back."

"No, I don't think you will."

Danny followed him up Swaheenie and planned on giving him a dirt road to the logging trails, but something spooked the bank robber and he turned onto an ill-advised path. He followed the bank robber as far as he could, as the man worked his way over the rutted road. They were a few hundred yards in when Danny stopped, waited, and watched the sedan disappear into the darkness. He rolled down the window and heard a loud splash. He took his flashlight out and walked to the edge of McCleary and shined the light over, catching the last of the car sinking into the murky abyss. He studied the water, an occasional bubble surfaced. "If you're lucky you died on the sixty-foot impact." Either way, his trip to Dirtwater officially ended. Danny held his jaw and opened his mouth. "You got some good punches in." He had a split lip and felt sure he had a mouse under his right eye. "Nitwit, he could have been gone if he'd listened."

He hoped he didn't have to start a new 'things come in threes' moments.

All in a day's work.

Chapter 18

Lyle carried his sister, cradled in his arms, to the elevator. "Excuse me, but can you push up?" Lyle had his hands full and counted on a fellow condo owner. Lyle looked odd, his carrying a sleeping sister early in the evening. "She's fine, just sleeping off an afternoon drink." The door opened and he stepped inside.

When he made it to their door, he leaned his sister against a wall and unlocked it. Inside, he made his way to their room and lay her down in a fetal position. He pulled the blankets over her and kissed her on the forehead. "Sleep tight, Sister."

She mumbled, "Come here."

She came out of the drug. "I'll be in later. You rest." Lyle turned the lights off and closed the door. Making his way to the living room, he pulled a blanket from the closet and carried it with him. All his life he'd taken care of his sister. She didn't understand his devotion. She thought he interfered but how could she know all he did for her?

He turned on the TV and skipped the channels, found a mindless showing of reruns, programs of a time less stressful. He sat in the room, the only light the flickering rays of television static. He felt defeated. How could he continue to go on with this excuse for a life? All he had was his sister, the twin he shared his life with, from the cradle on, the first face he saw every day for the totality of his life, the one soul who knew him better than God, and the one soul he knew as well as his own.

He hated these moments, the moments when his sister felt restricted, feeling as though life cheated her. She couldn't be satisfied with a life he planned for her. This is what was best for her, she needed to understand that. She would flaunt it in front of him, tease him with desires of the flesh, of desires he couldn't compete with. She treated him unfairly, why did he have to care?

His eyes grew tired; his thoughts turned the clock from early evening to late night. His hand held the remote like candy, random changes to keep his mind occupied. Sooner or later, she'd wake and ask, 'why?' His answer would be the same as usual, 'Because you don't realize what you're doing to me.' She in turn would push it back on him as some selfish motivation, as though he was to blame. She always did this, always the same, from the first moment he felt something between them, something united in their souls.

Would she sleep through the night? Perhaps he could step out and relax, relax with a drink. He checked in on her; she slept soundly, at peace, an angelic peace on her face, such innocence, such beauty. Lyle slipped on his shoes, grabbed a wool coat and quietly slipped out the door. He walked in the hall as though she might hear him, light steps, hurried, he worked his way like a thief to the elevator. "Please give me a moment." He uttered as he punched the ground floor. Outside, he walked over a lighted sidewalk, concentric circles casting shadows from front to back, and front again. He turned up his collar, and warmed his hands in his coat pockets, head down, moving briskly to find a drink.

He made it to the Fisherman's Reef, a quiet lounge a half mile from the condo, jutted out on a pier over the Willamette. He stepped inside to orange lighting casting dim shadows in a darkened room. He walked to the bar. "Do you make Manhattans?" A pretty barmaid smiled, pretty in a hard-working sort of way.

"Absolutely."

Lyle opened his wallet and handed her a fifty. "Whatever this will get me, keep them coming."

She winked. "You got it."

In a nearly deserted place, he found a seat overlooking the river, lights across the bank casting long streaming beams in reflections on the water, scenic wooden poles of dead piers dotted the landscape, tugs moored, river bells clanging. He drank to escape. Lyle wasn't a heavy drinker, so fifty would go a long way, and his bartender kept them coming. An hour went by, and he stopped her on one of her rounds. "What's my total up to?"

"Honey, you still have a few more to go."

He thanked her, and she lingered. "I've never seen you in here. Are you a traveler?"

Lyle smiled, so few women paid enough attention to him to notice if they'd ever seen him. "No, I've been here about a half year, but I work a lot."

She suggested, "You're the last customer, if you want to keep me company, why don't you sit at the bar."

He hesitated, the peace of the view kept him from wanting to leave, but Lauren wasn't around, what harm could it be to flirt a little. He picked up his drink and followed her to the bar.

"So, you don't worry about working alone at night?"

"Honey, this is the West Hills. It isn't the projects."

Lyle smiled. "I suppose, but you can never be too careful."

"True, but I live upstairs, so it isn't like I have far to go."

Lyle remembered his manners. He stuck his hand out. "I'm sorry, my name's Lyle."

She reached across the counter and took the ends of his fingers and squeezed, "I'm Cindy." She leaned into the bar and rested across from Lyle. "So what do you do?"

"I'm a chemist for a longevity company."

"You mean you help people live longer?"

Lyle smiled that she wasn't a dish of soap, that she could grasp his job. "Yes."

"Do you help healthy people live longer or sick people live longer?"

He smiled. "Both, but my job is with those who are sick."

"Do you believe in fate, Lyle?" She grabbed a bottle of whiskey and vermouth and started making another Manhattan.

"I don't much follow fate, but if you knew my life, I guess I can't discard it."

She finished making the drink and slid it to him. "If I took you home with me tonight, could you help my mother?"

Lyle didn't need her to take him home. "What's wrong with your mother?"

"She's dying of cancer." Cindy shook her head. "She's still functioning, but they gave her six months. You think you have a cure?"

"I can cure anyone, but you don't have to take me home to get my help."

She grinned. "Can I take you home anyway?"

Lyle wondered how long his sister would sleep, chances are it would be through the night, and she would wake up and go to work. Maybe she would be okay; he worried she might wonder where he wandered off to. Either way, he wanted to risk it. "Only if you have a drink with me."

She reached under the counter and pulled up a bottle of gin, added the vermouth and said, "You're on."

When they finished, and they had closed the place down, Lyle had enough drink in him to loosen up. Cindy put her arm around him to keep him steady and he kissed her. They kissed passionately. He knew it was wrong, he barely knew her; he knew his sister would object, but what she didn't know would be his secret. Cindy locked the door, turned the open sign off, and together they found the stairs to her apartment upstairs.

Cindy surprised him, meticulous, tidy in her tiny one room apartment, an efficient housekeeper. He liked order, he liked her. He worked her blouse off and pushed her toward the couch, but she stopped him, "Uh uh."

"No?"

She laughed as she took his coat off, pulled his top over his shoulders. "Let's shower."

Lyle had never showered with a strange woman before. It aroused him. They worked their way to the bathroom, undressing as they went. Cindy had full breasts, her bra strained to hold them in, her waist slender, tapered to a flat stomach. When she kicked off her pants, Lyle noticed her legs. "Are you a runner?"

She smiled, "I am."

Lyle felt embarrassed when she slipped his underwear off. He had an erection and he wanted to turn away. "I'm sorry."

She reached down and gently put her hand around his penis. "Don't be." She kissed him more passionately than before, and he kissed her back with the same intensity. They circled until they made it into the shower. She turned it on, and as the water cascaded around them, shards pelted them with respites of warmth. She lifted a leg and slipped him inside her.

They made love under the shower; they carried it to the bed and made love through the night, on and on.

Lyle never thought of Lauren, and perhaps that was a blessing. Perhaps she would be better in the morning. Lyle certainly believed he would be.

Chapter 19

Danny woke up the next morning with a splitting headache. Having someone punch him didn't happen often. In his entire life, he avoided punches, mostly because half the guys didn't want to try, and the other half had a hard time reaching that far up. Those quick punches the bank robber gave him rung his bell.

He staggered to the bathroom and noticed his lip—a cut split wide. The mouse under his eye was incidental and would go away pretty quickly. "Damn Danny, how do you attract so much trouble?" He bent down and splashed water into his face to bring the full force of morning into the day. Five comes early and with his own fields to plow, he didn't have much time to waste.

He took his pajamas off, hung them over the towel rack and worked his way to the shower where he ran the water cold to bring him to life. Not many men could use the shower head as a mike, but Danny stood even with the top of the shower and had to bend down to get water to cascade over his scalp. He held the neck of the shower with his hand and soaped up with the other. Taking a cold shower kept him from hanging out too long, something his father recommended all those years ago, something he continued doing throughout his life.

He dressed in overalls, made it to the kitchen, grabbed a full package of bacon, fried it up, used the grease for eight eggs and sat a half gallon of milk on the table. This wasn't a big meal; it was a normal one. When he finished, he used a sixth slice of bread to wipe away the rest of the egg yolk and finish up the rest of the milk.

He caught the time. "Damn, late start." He needed to be on the tractor and in the field by six, and at a quarter to, he needed to hurry. Danny felt calm for a man who had been in a fight the night before and watched that guy plummet to his death. He barely thought about how it ended. Life was like that. If you plan on playing on the dark side of life, expect dark things to happen. He didn't have much sympathy for those who had bad intentions.

He made it to the tractor, fueled up and headed out to his acres of farming. He had a field of peas to prep, and with the rains at bay, he knew it was time to finish his work. He waited until noon before he shut down the tractor, pulled his phone out and gave Jack a call.

"That you, Danny?"

"You need me to come over there and plow the fields?"

Jack laughed. "Be no need this year. I'm done."

Danny thought if Jack wasn't leaving until Christmas, he would at least get another yield in. "What about your cows?"

"I got plenty for them. Besides, by summer, I won't have any cows, and the land will be in the hands of Dirtwater and White Shadow."

It sounded so final. Danny sighed. "What the hell. What are you going to do all summer?"

"Oversee my Dirtwater project, what else?"

Danny sighed. "So, is everything finished with the attorney?"

"Just finished. That pretty little ghost of an attorney came out here with another attorney and handed me the signed documents."

Danny quizzed Jack. "Another attorney?"

"Sorry pal, she seemed to have her eye on him." He laughed, "Had the damnedest name. Hamilton! Who names their kid Hamilton?"

Danny figured she had too much city in her for him. "Oh well, I sure thought she was a pretty thing, but I guess it'd be too much to ask for something like that to come walking into my life."

Jack cast it aside. "She's a girl with needs. Too much needs if you know what I mean. Get yourself a girl who can drive a tractor and clean a house. Something tells me that girl has never done neither."

Danny said, "I'll be there for dinner tonight, so tell Pat I want meatloaf with mash potatoes and gravy, dark gravy."

Jack promised, "Dark gravy is what you make with meatloaf, don't be a goof."

"Good! Talk to you tonight." Danny disconnected and continued running rows, back and forth, through the acres and acres he owned in the north end of Seefer Valley.

Two days straight, Sheriff Scott startled him. This time Danny nearly hit him when he made a quick turn and the Sheriff walked up a few feet away. Danny shut the tractor off and yelled, "You want to get killed?"

"Son of a bitch, watch where you're going. I whistled and shouted. I swear you're getting deaf in your early years."

Danny laughed. "Is that what we are, in our early years?"

"Damn straight." The sheriff leaned on the rear tire.

"You don't come out here unless it's important. What is it?"

"Guy robbed a bank over in Bradenton and he came out this way last night."

"How do you know that?" Danny stepped down from the tractor.

"Ronner scared him off his property, and if he continued on his way, it would have led him out to here."

"I didn't see anyone."

Sheriff Scott looked to the south. "You think he could have driven off into Harper Pit?"

"No, I would have heard it. I was working until ten and at the barn until midnight."

The sheriff took a step closer. "What happened to your face?"

Danny paused, paused uncomfortably long. "One of my girls kicked me."

"How the hell one of your cows kick you?"

"One of the Angus' had a limp, and I was checkin' her hoof and she kicked me, hit me in the face."

Sheriff frowned. "Did a number on ya'. That's the worst I've ever seen you hit."

Danny smiled. "Ain't that the truth."

"So, this guy gets away with twenty grand. That's not bad pocket change." He looked up at Danny, "And you don't think he could have skidded off into the Harper?"

"I would have heard him."

What if he took a wrong turn and wound up in McCleary?"

Danny laughed, "Hardly."

"Just sayin, if he did, there's twenty grand in that pit."

Danny needed to stop his friend. "John, he wasn't up here. I can promise you that. Ronner probably didn't see shit. He points a gun at anyone."

"No, he described the car. It was him. How about I send Hal up here to swim around?"

Danny said. "I don't want Hal up here swimming around in my pit. Tell you what, I'll check it out."

"You? Have you ever scuba dived in your life?"

"You're kidding right? I had to fish my cows out fifteen years ago if you forgot. I have gear, and I will check it out." Danny dismissed Hal coming in by suggesting, "If I go in and find the money, it'll be our secret."

Sheriff winked. "You give me half?"

Danny shook his head. "He won't be there, but yeah, you can have half."

The sheriff grinned and turned toward the road. He whistled with joy. Trouble pissed Danny off. The ponds had become a problem. Sooner or later, he would have to fish out the bodies.

He stepped back on the tractor and started the engine. Sooner or later, but for right now he needed to finish the plowing.

Chapter 20

Lyle woke up with Cindy curled in his arms, the sun not visible through the windows yet. He slid his arm from under her head and moved quietly across the room to the bathroom to gather up his clothes. He dressed in silence, but his heart felt light. He'd enjoyed himself but knew he'd betrayed his sister. She would never understand any of this.

Before he left, he bent down over Cindy and whispered, "Thank you."

As he made his way to the door, she said, "You're welcome."

He turned around. "You're awake."

She opened her eyes. "Yeah, I wanted to see if you'd slink out of here."

"I assure you…"

"Shh, you were a gentleman. I enjoyed last night, and I hope we can see each other again."

Lyle felt wanted. "Really?" He hadn't prepared himself for women wanting to spend time with him. "I'd love that. I mean, I hope we could do something eventful; I mean, this was eventful." He stumbled over his words, "But I mean, we could go out or something."

She sat up, her breasts staring back at Lyle.

He found himself aroused.

"I think that would be great."

Lyle wanted to take his clothes off and jump back into bed. He couldn't. "I have to go."

"Work?"

He frowned. "Among other things."

"Woman?"

"Not exactly. My sister. She's going to freak."

"You live with your sister?"

Lyle sighed, "It's a long story, but yes I do."

Unabashed, she stepped out from under the sheets and walked to Lyle naked. She put her arms around him. "There's something about you, something oddly attractive."

Lyle could see his reflection in the mirror, Cindy's back side and his face staring at him, her tan figure and his snow-white features. "Yeah, I have an odd look."

She pushed away. "I didn't mean that. I meant you are beautiful in a striking way."

Other than Lauren, no one ever told him that, and since Lauren was his twin, she had a reason to believe he was beautiful. "Thank you."

"Don't forget me." She touched his cheek and stepped forward, kissing him on the lips.

Lyle shook his head and chuckled. "Hardly." He grabbed his coat and made his way downstairs and to the street. His gait picked up, he felt alive, smiling at the morning crowd, saying hello to passersby. It was a great day.

When he made it to the condo, he erased the evening, forgot as much as he could. If Lauren had awoken, she would wonder where he had taken off to. He had to make a lie sound real. He unlocked the door to the condo and as he stepped in, his worse fear materialized.

"Where were you?"

"Huh?"

Lauren smiled. "When I woke up you were gone."

"Oh, I went for a walk." He put the keys on the counter and made it to the couch, picked up the blanket and folded it.

"But you didn't sleep here last night."

"Yes, I did." He looked offended.

"Oh, okay." She came around the counter from the kitchen and put her arms around her brother. She took a deep slow inhale and whispered, "Why are you lying to me?"

Lyle peeled her arms off him. "What are you talking about?"

"Lyle," Lauren smiled. Her demeanor light, she turned away and stepped a few feet back, looked to the ceiling and screamed, "Why are you fucking lying!" She turned and faced him, spit pushed out the sides of her mouth. "Do you think I'm a fucking idiot?" her position had turned dark. She stepped quickly at Lyle, hands raised and slapping. "Who is she?"

Lyle caught her hands. "Lauren, calm down." It had started.

She pulled her arms from his grasp and sat on the floor, her knees bent to her face, she buried herself. "You don't love me."

"Lauren, I love you with all my heart and soul."

She looked up, tears streamed down her face. "Then show me." She reached for his pant leg and tried to draw him down to her.

He crouched and faced her. "Stop, Sister."

She pushed herself to all fours so they were face to face. She narrowed their distance and tried to kiss him on the lips; she pulled her blouse away to show her breasts. Lyle turned and she caught his cheek. She sobbed. "You can't do this to me. I need you."

He knew if he didn't give in, it would start all over. He would have to cover up her indiscretions. He always covered them up. She acted wild. "We need to get you help."

She spit on him. "I don't need help."

Lyle wiped his face and stood. "You need to stay home today. I'll give you a sedative." He turned and felt something sharp in his thigh.

"You mean one of these?" Lauren pricked him with a needle.

"What are you doing, Sister." Lyle felt dizzy.

"Giving you a taste of you own medicine." She stood and helped her brother to the couch. She pushed him down and Lyle offered no resistance. His head spun, but he tried to keep conscious. He stayed awake as long as he could, hearing Lauren tell someone he wouldn't be able to make it to work and how, whoever she spoke to on the other line, it would be nice to meet with them.

The last words he heard were, "I'll take care of the people who are bothering you, Brother."

Lyle opened his eyes to a silent room. Alone, he wondered what time it was. He fumbled to get upright and found his phone on his lap. He tapped it and found a number on it with the name Cindy. He didn't put Cindy's number on his phone; he certainly wouldn't put her name on the phone.

Oh my God, Cindy.

He hit send on the number. It rang and went to voice mail. "This is Cindy, leave a message or I won't know who you are. If I'm not home, you can find me at the Fisherman's Reef."

He shouted, "Pick up!" He dialed his sister but heard her voice mail as well. "Call me, Sister."

He shook the numbness, went to the sink and splashed water on his face. His phone read noon. Lyle hurried out the door and ran down the street to the lounge.

Inside, a man working behind the counter looked up as Lyle rushed in. "Hey, Buddy, you okay?"

"Is Cindy here?"

"No Dude, she's not."

"Is she upstairs?"

He looked surprised. "Who are you?"

"I'm a friend." Danny pointed toward the upstairs. "Is she up there?"

The bartender came out from around the bar, concerned. "She's visiting her mother." He stared at Lyle. "You're the second person today who was looking for her and be damned if the first person wasn't a woman who looked like your twin."

Lyle sighed. "It was my twin."

"What the hell do you two want with Cindy?" He crossed his arms as though prepared to force it out of Lyle.

"My sister, did she bring anything?"

He stared at Lyle. "Like what?"

"I don't know, anything?"

He nodded, yeah; she brought a bottle of wine. Said it was for Cindy."

"Can I see it?"

The bartender stepped around Lyle and up a few flights of stairs, the stairs to Cindy's apartment. He returned with the bottle. "Here."

Lyle inspected it; he could see a tiny mark in the cork. "I need this."

The bartender squinted. "And why?"

"This one's been tampered with. Trust me." Lyle eyed the bartender square. "Trust me."

Lyle tucked it under his arm, and before he left, he turned one last time to the bartender. "Did you tell my sister where Cindy was?"

"Outside of at her mom's, I don't know where that is."

"Thanks." Lyle left and headed to work. With his sister foiled, he knew she had another person to deal with. He needed to get to work. From there he could centralize what needed to be done. He'd promised to help Cindy's mom, and there was a chance Ms. Newberry might be on his sister's list. Cindy had told him her mother had pancreatic cancer and that she was terminal, but his research had reversed almost every case of pancreatic cancer he'd come across.

He was late, extremely late and it didn't go unnoticed. Niraj said, "That must have been a great day off, you made it a day and a half off!" He grinned at Lyle.

Lyle said, "I need to push the Cyclene D1 experiment out the door. I have a need for it."

Niraj laughed. "You have been the master of this department, but those decisions come from above."

Lyle huffed and stormed out of the lab. He made it to Mr. Deeds' office and knocked.

"Come in."

Lyle entered and without pleasantries, sat opposite his boss. In a hurried voice he demanded. "I need a favor."

"And that would be?"

"I have a friend who needs the product from my research." Lyle wasn't sure why he asked, this was his product.

"Lyle, even if I could just release it, which FDA has a lot to say about that—"

"We are there. The FDA approves it tomorrow if you put it on the market."

"Let me finish. This product is going to make us millions. We aren't going to just give it to our friends."

"Excuse me?"

"We're grown-ups, Lyle. This is for the rich. We are going to make this drug the most costly cure on the planet."

"But I have someone who needs it."

Mr. Deeds stared across the desk as though Lyle wasn't there. "Well, I hope your friend is a millionaire."

"Mr. Deeds, with all due respect, I didn't make this drug for the sake of a profit."

"No, you made it for me. Let's remember that."

Mr. Deeds had no intentions of budging and Lyle didn't need to get locked out of his lab for fear of stealing, so he accepted. "I understand. Thanks for listening." Lyle was many things, arrogant, misguided about his sister, rude, but he didn't do his work for the rich, he did it for everyone. His heart sank.

Lyle stood to leave, and Mr. Deeds offered, "Great job by the way. Everything they said about you is true."

Lyle smiled through a dead gaze. "Thanks."

As he opened the door, Mr. Deeds added, "And that sister of yours, awfully nice to take Ms. Newberry out to breakfast."

Lyle spun around. "What?"

"Yeah, she took her to breakfast this morning."

"Has Ms. Newberry returned?"

"She did, but she went home. Said she wasn't feeling well."

Lyle nodded and left, closing the door behind him. He pulled his phone out and called his sister again, and again heard her voice mail. "Please Sister, call me. We need to coordinate. You are going to need me."

Chapter 21

Danny cut out early; he wanted to arrive at Jack and Pat's house before six. He cleaned the tractor at the barn when he noticed the sheriff's car racing up Swaheenie Rd. "What the hell?" John could only head to one location, and by the looks of it, he needed to see Danny in a hurry.

Sheriff Scott spun left and roostered a cloud of dust as he screeched to a halt. He jumped out. "Let's go! Old lady Collins found a body in Willow creek."

Danny shook his head. Dead bodies weren't a big surprise anymore. "I got dinner with Jack and Pat, you go."

"Damn it, Danny, come on. This is big. We don't get dead bodies here very often."

As much as Danny wanted to correct the sheriff on that one, he opted for, "You're the sheriff; you can take care of it."

Sheriff Scott stepped closer. "Olympia is sending someone down here. Would you please come with me before they do?"

"Why me?"

"Because we've been friends a long time, and moments like this are special."

Danny couldn't believe the Sheriff just offered that reason. "You're kidding right?"

"Look, I need another set of eyes to bounce thoughts off of and my only other option is a high school kid from Huggins who does ride-a-longs. I choose you."

Danny relented. "I'll follow you down to Willow, let me call Jack and tell him I'll be late." Danny pulled out his phone and called the Henricksens. Pat answered and Danny said, "Pat, I'm going to be a little late. I hope that's okay?"

Pat had a joyful tone. "That's fine. Don't be too late, we have a surprise waiting."

Danny didn't ask what kind of surprise; he guessed it wouldn't be a surprise if he did. "I can't wait. I'll call you when I'm on my way. Shouldn't be more than an hour."

"We'll keep the meatloaf warm."

"Let me talk to Jack."

Pat responded, "Jack is lying down. He said he wasn't feeling good and needed a nap."

"Anything serious?"

"No, he was fine earlier, probably just being old. Needs his rest." She laughed and they said their goodbyes.

Danny followed his friend, Sheriff John Scott, down south to where the Willow meets the Seefer, turned up Collins Road and not too much further. The sheriff stopped and Danny parked in behind him. When Danny exited, the sheriff had an anxious glow. "Come on, down here. Put these on." He handed Danny his own pair of latex gloves. They walked down a slight embankment, easy access, a clear view to a spot in the creek, careful to avoid tracks that the killer might have left. Plain as day, a body laid half in and half out the creek, as though gravity rolled it into place.

Sheriff noted, "Body's face down."

Danny took a step closer and noticed the body missed a head. "Huh, I don't know if you can technically call it face down. There is no head." Danny noticed the hands missing as well. "This body isn't local." Blood still trickled from the neck. "Body hasn't been here very long. Did Mrs. Collins mention if she saw anyone?"

The sheriff viewed the body like a science project, using a pen to probe a pocket. "Nope, didn't mention anybody." He added, "Nice clothes." He turned and scanned the bank. "Tire tracks lead almost down to the water. Body must have been in a trunk. Person who dumped it must have been small."

Danny laughed. "Or a woman."

Sheriff raised his eyebrows. "Or a woman."

Danny wondered if all of Dirtwater cleaned up the riff raff, and if maybe whoever this poor victim was had it coming. "Now what?"

"Olympia comes down here and hauls the body off."

"John, you have a mystery. No head, no hands, clearly whoever did this would like the body to take a while to be identified." Danny and the sheriff walked up to the road. "This is so wide open, so close to the main road, the person who killed that person," Danny pointed over at the corpse, "wasn't local either."

The sheriff grinned. "Good work, Dan. If they'd been local they would have taken the body out to your pits. Those things are bottomless."

Danny half smiled. They weren't bottomless but they were deep. "I suppose."

The sheriff intimated. "This is the worst thing we can have happen right now."

Danny said, "Uh, this is the worst thing that can happen any time."

"I mean, with all the plans for Dirtwater, the last thing we need is a murder. Jack and Pat are donating five hundred acres of land for Dirtwater proper to grow and another five hundred for two hundred homes."

Danny shrugged. "A body being dumped out in the country isn't going to shine poorly on Dirtwater. This will be old news in a month. They will catch some pissed off spouse from the city who was looking for a place to dump their cheatin' mate, or the poor soul they were cheatin' with."

The sheriff disagreed. "I'm not buying that one. Wives don't cut their husband's or their husband's lover's heads and hands off, and vice versa." He pushed at his temples with the tips of his fingers. "This could get messy."

The sheriff went to the trunk of his patrol car and pulled out crime scene tape. Danny developed respect for his friend. The sheriff had turned into a good crime scene investigator, taking precautions to preserve the scene. Sheriff Scott cordoned off the area leading to the body. He had a half dozen red flags on wire staffs he pressed into the ground around the tire tracks and what appeared to be shoeprints. "I thought you were a nine to five guy John. Get off work with as little noise as possible."

John winked. "I am, but it doesn't mean I don't take my job seriously, besides," he laughed, "It looks good on my resume if I actually solve something. We will have a bunch of new residents I'll have to impress." The sheriff took off the gloves and shoved them in his pocket. "I take offense that someone figures that the sheriff in our town is a bumpkin and dumping bodies in my jurisdiction is okay."

Danny stared back at the sheriff, wanting to applaud him for such a wonderful stance, but under the circumstances, anything he said would be ironically condescending.

Chapter 22

When Lyle was seven years old, Lyle's dad caught him and Lauren touching each other. They were seven, and kids do that, but Lyle's dad didn't seem to mind, he even smiled and said, "You two are meant for each other." Lyle never felt comfortable with the affection Lauren showed to him, but she was his sister, they were twins, and they had a bond undeniable between them. Lyle came to realize people are born into situations and they learn to function in that environment. What seemed odd to others seemed normal when that's all you'd ever known. His mother and father insisted upon allegiance to one another, and in that allegiance, Lyle and Lauren, being twins, had an especially close tie.

Home school left little interaction with the sparsely populated mountain town where they lived. Lauren was Lyle's first experimentation with everything from socializing to intimacy. At fourteen, Lyle met Jackie McGarvey, the cutest girl in the Ozarks. Not that Lyle had a chance with her, but she treated him well, and he had nothing but sweet thoughts for her. It would be the first time he discovered his sister's 'moments.' Lauren turned manic and became enraged over Jackie. She threatened the cute red head with her life if she ever spoke to Lyle again. Lyle accepted the fate that he should not become involved with Jackie, it was after all, something which upset Lauren, and it went against the Thibodeaux way. He promised his sister he would not make mention of Jackie ever again, and so it was, Lyle made true on his promise.

However, Lauren was not one to chance fate with good intentions, and one spring when Jackie McGarvey and her family made a trip to Mardi Gras, Lauren pleaded with her parents to take the family home to their roots, if for nothing else, then to dance the tempo of Mardi Gras. It was there, Lauren engaged Lyle to help clean up her first moment. She'd done her homework and knew how to find Jackie, and while the fourteen-year-old walked around by herself, Lauren used her father's drugs to incapacitate the object of Lyle's affection, lopped her head off with a saw, and took it back to Lyle to view. As horrified as it made Lyle, he went back to the scene of the murder, cleaned the area, and disposed of the body in a place no one would ever find her. Her parents were never the same.

Lyle had gone to his father, explained the atrocity, but his father forbade Lyle from saying another word about what his sister had done. Mr. Thibodeaux experimented with his daughter, using psychotropic drugs to treat her moments, teaching Lyle the chemistry he would one day become famous for, how to minimize her behavior. Lyle became her keeper, even though he ultimately became the object of her desire.

There would be more moments in their lives. There was Kenny Hall, the boy who liked her, who fell to his death, pushed by

Lauren on a friendly hike the two of them took, the two of them gazing out over Lookout Point Bridge. Lauren hated to be touched by anyone other than her brother, the thought repulsed her. She would take it out on boys when Lyle wouldn't play with her, play the way she wanted him to play. In college, a boy, Hal Lines who had a crush on her, drowned while swimming at Half Moon Bay. Lauren discovered the power the drugs her brother gave her had on other people. Her moments disappeared as long as Lyle gave in to her desires, but at times he found it difficult, and hard to function with the pressure she put on him, and when he refused, she rebelled; her moment in San Francisco came from rebellion. It forced their decision to move on. She escalated her use of more potent drugs, drugs that didn't incapacitate, but rather killed. She found ways to talk her brother into accessing the drugs from his work. She experimented with Arsenic and Belladonna. She used Arsenic on Jeff Lambert, but he convulsed, and she was so sickened by the sight she drove him out to the woods and cut him up. Lyle came and helped dispose of his parts. He, like Jackie, would never be found. She tried Belladonna on the sommelier, but her brother explained it was detectable and not a good drug to be giving to people. Finally, she settled on Aconite, slipping it to the woman at the theater. Lyle was to blame; he gave her the drugs; too afraid her moments would get her caught if he didn't help her conceal them. The alternative was to give in to her passion, which she really wanted; to make love to him. Lyle felt selfish when he denied her, but it was wrong to make love to a sibling, it never felt right. Now he wished he had continued pleasing her. Death had become too common.

Lyle called Cindy. She answered. "Hello, Lyle."

Lyle relaxed. I'm so glad you're okay."

She laughed. "What's wrong?"

"Has my sister tried to contact you?"

"I had a call that didn't say anything. From a 415, is that her?"

It was. "Yes," Lyle hesitated. "If she should call you, tell her nothing, and immediately call me."

Cindy sounded concerned. "What's this about?"

Lyle couldn't go into details, his culpability waist deep. "My sister takes medication for a mental disorder, and right now she's off of them. She hasn't come home, and I'm worried about her behavior."

Cindy suggested, "Have you thought about calling the police?"

Lyle dismissed it. "No, that's not an option." Lyle continued, "Be careful." Lyle disconnected and went about his job. He knew everything spiraled out of control and that life changed by the moment, his life especially.

Lyle made some calculations on an experiment. He called Niraj over. "Did you see these readings on the Cyclene D1?"

Niraj studied Lyle's calculations. "This can't be. I've run this test a dozen times. The cells have never broken down like this." Niraj was frantic. "This can't be."

Lyle calmed him. "I will work on stabilizing it."

Niraj insisted, "We need to let Mr. Deeds know. We are preparing to launch this."

"Just give me the rest of the day, this may be a glitch."

Niraj stood beside Lyle. "I am here to help."

"Good, I'll need you to access the prep data from the holding tanks."

"Anything you want, Boss."

Lyle worked quickly. By the next day, he realized he may not have a job, not because of his request for the D1, but because his sister might have changed their lives and Lyle wouldn't survive the damage. They video recorded the lab and scrutinized everything the scientists did. The only physical access the team had to experimental products was for disposal on faulty experiments. Lyle triggered the release button, the dump procedure. The canisters opened and he pulled out the vials of D1. With sleight of hand, he appeared to fill the dump containers with full vials of D1. Before Niraj could return, Lyle had deposited all twenty-six vials, or one subject dosage, into Test 29 canister: a canister not yet sectioned and free from inspection. He placed Test 29 on the shelf above his workstation and returned to seal the dump containers.

"What are you doing?" A confused Niraj asked, "Why did you dump, we don't know that the D1 is faulty."

Lyle nodded. "We can recreate it, better safe than sorry."

"But protocol says we are both supposed to observe the dump."

Lyle whispered, "I won't say anything if you don't." He handed Niraj the dump canister. "Do you want to open it?"

"No, I trust you." He frowned. "What a shame, all that work, all that promise."

"We will synthesize it, make it stronger."

"It will take a month, and another month of testing."

Lyle smiled. "All in due time."

Lyle's phone buzzed. It was Lauren. "Raj, I got to take this." Lyle stepped out of the lab and into the hall. "Lauren, where are you?"

The line was quiet.

"Lauren?"

A sure voice responded. "Worried?"

"Where are you?"

"I'm taking care of business."

"What kind of business are you taking care of?"

"Personal."

Lyle didn't like the sound of that. "Do you need my help?"

Lauren started to cry, the sobs of a lost little girl. "Yeah."

"What have you done?"

"I took Hamilton to his vacation."

"Is that all?"

Her voice trailed off. "No."

"Did you do something to Ms. Newberry?"

Lauren sounded tired. "She's a nice lady, but all wrong for you."

"Were you careful?"

Lauren said nothing.

"Do we need to clean you up?"

"I think we need to leave, Brother."

"That bad?"

"Uh huh."

"Tell me where you are, and I will come get you."

"I can't."

Irritated, Lyle asked, "Why?"

Lauren whined, "I have more work to do." She perked up, "But guess what?"

Lyle entertained her. "What?"

"Hamilton gave me a going away present."

"What did he give you?"

She started laughing, laughing as though telling a joke only she understood—one she thought was hilarious. "He has hands like an octopus, lips like a vacuum, a square head on his shoulders, and is a cut up!"

Lyle closed his eyes. He couldn't have imagined anything worse. "Lauren, wherever you are, don't come home. I will find you; call me when you need me."

"Okay, Brother, I have some nice people to visit; I will call you when I'm done."

Lyle checked his watch, it was four-thirty. He knew where she went. If he left right away, he might be able to stop her. He hurried back into the lab and took the Test 29 canister off the shelf and went to his desk. He placed his brief case between his legs and opened the flap. He opened the canister and dumped the contents in his bag. As calmly as he picked the canister up, he put it down and screwed the top, stood, and placed it back on the shelf.

"Raj, I need to go get my sister. Her car broke down." He put his bag over his shoulder and promised his lab partner, "I promise tomorrow we will get back on a new batch."

Chapter 23

The moment had an eerie hush as Danny drove up to Jack and Pat's house. The dogs neither barked outside nor inside. Even on their best behavior, they always barked when someone came to the door. He stopped and stared at his watch, it neared seven p.m., the clocks hadn't sprung forward yet, time still darkened at this hour, but he sensed a different kind of darkness. Maybe the image back at the creek spooked him, maybe not. He came to the porch, the sound of one dog scratching to get out, not barking—slightly whimpering, caught his attention. Danny opened the door and a blood-soaked spaniel darted out and ran past him, running beyond the fence and into the field, running at a sprint, running as though fleeing. Inside, two more soaked spaniels sat at attention, facing Danny as though they'd been told to 'stay.'

The lights were on; it hadn't been dark long. Whatever happened, happened within the last half hour. As Danny passed the two dogs, they turned and followed him with frightened gaits. When Danny came around the corner, into the kitchen, blood rested everywhere, as though water poured from the spigot a crimson red. "What the hell." Something, or someone had been dragged across the floor, smeared blood formed a trail onto the carpet in the dining room. The table had no tablecloth, and Danny guessed someone used it as a shroud. He stepped around the bloodied areas and came to the conclusion whoever tried to clean it up either quit halfway through, or someone interrupted them.

Danny grabbed a kitchen knife and called out, "Anyone here?"

The room contained his echo. The two dogs never left his side. Danny paused with worry and asked the two spaniels. "Where's your master?"

They shook with fear.

Danny walked down the hall toward Jack and Pat's room. He pushed open the doors to the bathroom and closet as he passed. Empty. The bathroom a sea of red, someone had showered, once white towels a ghoulish pink. When he entered his friends' room, he could tell the bed had a body under the covers, still, motionless. Danny held the knife out and reached for the end of the blanket at the foot of the bed. He pulled it hard, and it slid off a petrified looking Jack. His eyes wide open, his mouth in a gasping locked position, stiff from rigor mortis. Jack had been dead for a while. "Son of a bitch." When Danny stepped forward and reached down to close his eyes, he caught a scent he'd smelled before. It danced around him, sweet, full, Jasmine. He recognized that smell, and whom he remembered last wearing it—the attorney.

Danny pulled his phone out and called Sheriff Scott.

"Yeah?"

"Get to Jack's immediately."

"I'm here with the investigators at the creek, what is it?"

"Jack's dead, there's a ton of blood here, and none of it's his."

Sheriff Scott screamed, "Where's Pat?"

"I don't know, but the dogs are clinging to me like they witnessed something really bad."

"Shit, Gawd Damnit. I knew this was bad. This has got to be connected." Sheriff Scott whispered, "You think this guy in the creek is part of it?"

Danny's mind raced, more concerned about finding Pat. "I don't know."

"We'll be there in ten minutes. Don't touch shit!"

Neither said goodbye. He backed out and exited the way he came, careful not to tread on anything that might lead to a clue, but he had a hunch who had done this; he wondered if a sister and brother might have come here and executed his friends, but he couldn't understand why.

What the hell would be a motive?

As he passed the kitchen, he noticed a lid over a plate, fine silver, something Pat only used at Thanksgiving to cover the turkey.

Odd.

He grabbed a napkin and carefully lifted the lid on the dish. To his horror, he'd found Pat's head. He dropped the lid, and it skidded off the plate taking the head with it, both crashed to the ground at his feet. The dogs howled and backed up. They wouldn't shut up and Danny screamed, "Shut the fuck up, you two!" They looked at him with more fear than any animal he'd ever seen. He didn't know they could show that sort of emotion. He sighed, "Sorry guys, let's get out of here." He carefully stepped away from Pat and found clean flooring to walk over. The dogs followed and the three of them waited on the porch for the authorities to arrive.

In the distance, a car turned on its headlights, as though someone watched this house. The car did a U-turn and headed out toward the highway.

Danny pulled his phone out and called Sheriff Scott. It went to voice mail. "Pick up your phone. There's a car coming your way, stop it and see who is in it." He reconnected; again, it went to voice mail. "Pick up your phone!" He tried again and again, but when he saw two vehicles racing down the gravel entry, he disconnected in disgust.

The sheriff reached Danny first. The lawman trembled as he stared at Danny. "Did you find Pat?"

Danny sat on a porch step, the two dogs resting their heads on his lap. He pointed in the house. "She's in the kitchen."

"Don't tell me she's dead too."

Danny craned his neck. "Dead?" He raised his voice in anger. "Just her head is in the kitchen, John."

Two professional-type men, dark suits, detective like, walked up behind the sheriff, pads in their hands, ready to ask questions.

"What the fuck do you two want?" Danny stood and towered over them. "My friends are in there; go do your fucking job."

The older of the two said, "Look, I'm sorry that I have to ask, and according to the sheriff, you were just with him, so this isn't an interrogation, just a quick question before we go in."

Danny stood akimbo and tilted his head, staring at the questioner. "What?"

"Did you see anything suspicious, or have any idea who could have done this?"

Danny had a great idea who did this but kept that to himself. This was personal. "A car was parked out front that I tried to reach John about. I wanted you guys to stop it and find out who it was, but it's long gone now."

"Sedan or—"

"It was dark; hell, I couldn't tell you what it was."

The second gentleman pulled out his phone and called someone. "Put a roadblock on the I-5 entrance coming out of Huggins."

Danny shook his head. "There are a thousand country roads weaving through these hills."

The second man said, "Maybe so, but stranger things happen. Maybe they are feeling pretty safe."

Danny turned to Sheriff Scott. "Take care of Jack's dogs. I need to get home."

Sheriff Scott gazed at the two animals. "I don't think they're leaving your side, Dan; looks like they're yours."

The older investigator asked for Danny's number. "Ask John, he'll give it to you."

Danny walked away and the dogs walked beside him, flanking him on both sides. "Oh hell, these mutts aren't leaving me." He opened his door, and they jumped in. "John!"

Sheriff Scott turned around. "What?"

"I don't know which one's which, but the third one took off running north, dead sprint; never looked back. You might want to see if you can find it."

Sheriff Scott walked to Danny's truck and turned on his flashlight, the animals covered in blood. He stated with confidence, "That one's Trudy and that one's the boy, so that's Wilbur. Tess must have run off. We'll find her."

Danny turned the truck over and flipped on the lights. "Well kids, welcome to the Gates plantation." He put the truck in gear and headed for home, headed to avenge.

Chapter 24

If Lyle knew his sister, the couple she wrote the contract up for, had to be her target. Their love for each other would have irritated his sister. That the old man could love his wife, and how she wanted Lyle to treat her like that, followed by Lyle enjoying the company of another woman had sent Lauren over the edge. He knew she would hunt down every person she came into contact with over the last two days.

Lyle raced against time. He'd left several messages for his sister, all of them going unanswered. By the time he'd reached the cut off from I-5 to Dirtwater, the sun had nearly set. He wouldn't make it there before sundown.

He didn't know how many police patrolled those back roads and he didn't care, hitting a hundred on the straight stretches and the corners at seventy. When he reached Dirtwater's valley, he didn't fully remember where to go. He had last gone there during the day, and he didn't drive. "What was the name of that road?" He tested his memory. "Mills Creek!" Find Mills Creek Rd. He knew to travel past the road leading to the town, if you could call it a town, keep traveling some indeterminate number of miles and then veer off onto a road called Mills Creek. He hoped the signage would be visible in the dusk. It was. Now he had to spot a mailbox with Henricksen on it.

Lyle was sharp, not a man who had many peers when it came to pure knowledge. However, he lacked a compass to put his foot down on family. Regardless of the act, he held a blind eye to anything other than allegiance. He found Henricksen's box and turned down the tree lined entry. Lauren's car came up the driveway. Lyle slowed and as they crossed, Lauren stopped and lowered her window. She had her pale features camouflaged behind a mask of crimson red blood. It appeared she'd combed the blood into her hair, and applied blood for eyebrow shading. "What have you done?"

"Thank you for finding me." Her voice breathed exhaustion. I'm going to go into town and get a soda."

"Lauren, you need to find a place to dump your car, find a lake somewhere. Call me when you do. I'll clean this up. No one will know."

She gazed into the distance; her words separated. "Okay."

"Lauren, listen to me. Get rid of the car and hide away."

She drove off as though she didn't listen. Lyle worried she had an irreversible moment.

"Oh. Sister," he spoke to himself. "I don't want to lose you." He turned his car around and drove it back to the road, hiding it behind a pile of discarded farm brush along the road. He went to the trunk and pulled out industrial coveralls, a hood, gloves, and shoe protectors. He hurried up the entry way and to the house. Lauren had left it unlocked and inside the dogs howled over the loss of their masters. "Sit!" Lyle commanded the trio of spaniels. Two of them sat at attention by the front door while the other whimpered to be let out.

When he went into the kitchen, his sister's brutality horrified him. Much like her killing of Jackie and Jeff, this was personal and savage. The body of Mrs. Henricksen lay on the floor, the head he couldn't find. He put the hood of his sterilization suit on and began the process of cleaning up the kitchen. He pulled Mrs. Henricksen's body to the dining room table and rolled her up in the tablecloth. He smeared the tracks of Lauren, who'd walked through the scene in her bare feet. He could see she, at one point, stripped completely naked, imprinting her body on the kitchen floor; a snow angel pattern in blood. Lyle would have a hard time eliminating all her prints. He thought about what she did, how she traveled, he followed it, wiping as he went, "She would have touched this," he wiped. "She would have pushed that," he wiped. "She would have grabbed those," he wiped. Not sure if she had cut herself, he took all the towels to the bathroom. He laid them in the tub and ran water, rinsing the blood away, turning the linens pink. He repeated himself, each time turning the bathroom redder and redder, but eliminating his sister's presence.

Lyle heard someone coming down the gravel road. Outside, a truck traveled halfway there. He ran back out to the dining room, yelled to the dogs, "Stay!" He did a quick search for Mrs. Henricksen's head. He wondered if his sister took the head with her. "Where is it?" He checked in the oven, the refrigerator, he had no more time. He threw Mrs. Henricksen over his shoulder and slipped out the back door, dark, he could hear the truck pull to the front as he worked his way through the field. Making it to the road, he laid the body in the ditch and retrieved his car. With the lights off, he parked next to Mrs. Henricksen and placed her in his trunk, then waited, watching to see if the owner of the truck hurried out of the house. Ten minutes went by, and Lyle realized his position in the road looked bad. He flipped on his lights and turned the vehicle around. He needed to find a hiding spot as well; he needed to wait out the telephone call from his sister. He headed to the main road back into town. Halfway there, he passed two speeding vehicles, the first with lights flashing, a sheriff's vehicle, the second following close behind. Lyle realized he'd miscalculated his stay and sighed relief. Perhaps with the authorities, of whom there couldn't be many of them, tied up with that scene, he could stop Lauren before she created a new scene.

Chapter 25

Danny headed home, driving east out Mill Creek Road and over to
Main instead of north and across the foothill. He could go north
out of Dirtwater proper to get to Swaheenie, and he wanted to get
some food for the dogs at Tom Benck's before heading home. "Kids,
you wait for me." He parked out front and started to open the
doors. As he did the two spaniels sprang to their feet and pushed
forward into Danny. "It's okay, I'll be right back." He backed out of
his truck, pushing the two dogs in as he closed the door. They
started howling echoes against the glass that vibrated the panes; a
cry so loud he couldn't bear it. He sighed and opened the door.
"Come on." They looked in horrible shape. He hoped Tom
wouldn't freak when he saw the blood on the dogs and realized
who they belonged to. They stayed close to Danny, but when he
made it to the door of the market, they backed up and growled.
"What is it, you two?" He leaned over. "Come on." They didn't
budge. Through the glass door, Danny noticed Tom wasn't in his
usual spot behind the counter. He cupped his face and closed the
gap between him and the glass. The floor looked wet, wet like
blood.

He turned back to his truck. "Come on, you two." They ran
with him to the cab. Danny shoved them in and pulled his rifle off

the rack. "Stay here, you two." He left the door open in case they changed their minds. Danny approached the door and swung it open with his back against the outside wall. He shouted like a fireman clearing a building, "Is anyone in there?"

No one answered. He took a quick look in and pulled his head back. As the door slowly closed, he pushed it again. He shouted louder, "I said, is anyone in there?" No one answered. He checked the clip and the chamber of his gun. He went in with the gun raised eye level and pointed in the direction he walked. It was quiet, just the buzz of refrigerator coolers. He looked at the dark cement floor and ran his shoe over the slick fluid. When he turned the sole over, he could tell it was blood. "Tom, you okay?" He dropped the rifle to his side, still pointed forward. He walked down the rows, past the cereal, the cans of soup, the toiletries, and the auto products. He walked farther, past the candy and the chips; he grabbed a bag of beef jerky. He opened the bag and continued. When he made it to the dog food, he pulled a bag and slung it over his shoulder. He circled the row and came up the second aisle, past the cases of soft drinks, the spices, feminine hygiene, hair coloring products, and condoms. When he made it to the front, he put the bag on the counter and continued down the cooler aisle. When he came even with to the Boars Head ale, he noticed a crooked case; it appeared to have blood on it. He reached up and pulled the case out, and as he did, he found Tom, or Tom's head anyway. Tom's head rolled out and dropped on Danny's foot. "Damnit!" Twice in one day he'd found a friend's head without a body. Danny dropped the case, bottles flowing beer mixing with blood on the cement below. Danny put the gun back up and scanned the horizon. He walked to the back cooler and opened the freezer door. Inside, the rest of Tom's remains lay on the floor. Danny found a pair of scissors in Tom's back, along with several holes in his shirt, as though the scissors had plunged in many times. He also noticed a meat saw next to his body.

Danny stepped out and went back to the counter. He grabbed the dog food and went to his truck. He pulled his phone out and called the sheriff.

"Yeah."

"You better get over to the market."

John sounded irritated, "Why the hell for?"

"Why do you think?"

"You better be fucking with me."

Danny raised his voice, "Do I sound like I am?"

A frantic sheriff asked, "Is it Tom?"

"Yeah, just like Pat and the stiff at the creek."

"Headless?"

Danny wanted to correct him, technically Pat was bodiless. "Yeah, but all his parts are here."

"Jeez, I hate to tell you this again, but don't leave and don't touch shit."

Danny returned. "The place is secure, I know nothing. Body is in the refrigerator and head is in the beer aisle. If you want to see me, you know where I live."

John tried to say something, but Danny shut the phone off. "Alright, you two, let's get you guys home and see if you want anything to eat." Danny shook his head. "Sorry, Tom, all I can say is I hope they come to my door."

Danny drove north and made it to Swaheenie Road. As he drove in the dark, he noticed a gravel tire trail veering right, straight through into Harper Pit. "Good God, just what I need." He stopped and pulled his flashlight out to view the pit. When he stepped out of the truck, the dogs acted up. "What is it you two?" They growled. "Really? Something out there you don't like?"

Danny stepped back in, too dark to let the element of surprise beat him. He drove slowly, checking for more disturbed gravel. He drove up to the barn. He positioned the truck to shine on the area around the barn. Everything under the dim pole lights looked the same. He continued to the house. He gauged the dogs' reactions to test the safety of exiting his truck. They jumped out and sniffed the ground, they smelled the air and let out blood curdling howls, but they weren't afraid. Danny retrieved the food and motioned to the spaniels. "Let's get you two cleaned up and fed. Danny unlocked the front door and locked it when they were all safe inside.

Chapter 26

Lyle wondered if the police might block the main accesses in and out of the valley. He used his phone to locate a map of the area, to find a country road that might lead him to a back way to Portland. In the night, the country roads were dark, almost too dark to drive safely, but he needed to get back, he needed preparation for Cindy's mother.

His phone rang. He looked at the number and answered, "Lauren."

"Brother, I'm having an up and down day."

"Did you do as I said? Did you find a place to get rid of the car?"

"I did." Her voice childlike. "I drove it off into a big deep hole with water at the bottom."

Lyle slowed down, stopped, and prepared to turn around. "I'll come get you."

"No, please don't. I have some work to do."

"Sister, no more work, okay?" He tried appealing to her. "You've done enough. You've shown me the error of my ways. I will come to you; I will hold you, just us, forever."

She screeched, "You filthied yourself! You had an unnatural relationship with another woman! I will need to work through this, and I'm getting there, Brother. Tomorrow, you can come get me tomorrow."

"Where will you stay tonight? It's cold?"

"I have my coat, and I have Hamilton to keep me company. He's going to have his hands all over me tonight!" She laughed and laughed, hysterical fits.

Lyle waited for her to gain her composure. "Sister?"

"What?"

"You know I love you, right?"

She sounded as though she wanted to cry. "I know, I know you do. Brother, I am so glad you want me. We can move to a sunny place, maybe the desert this time." Lyle looked around; he stopped high on a ridge, a rural pass road with deep ravines. As he spoke to his sister, he opened the trunk and worked Mrs. Henricksen out. He frowned that the poor woman had suffered at the hands of his sister. He felt guilt that he went this far. He couldn't ask Lauren why she killed her; it wouldn't have made sense if she answered, or worse, she'd fly into a tirade of how he made her do it. He pushed the body hard and heard it tumble down the ravine, down and into heavy brush. He guessed the animals would find her before anyone discovered her body. Either way, there wasn't much more he could do.

"Brother, I met a really nice man tonight."

He didn't want to ask. "Where?"

"At the grocery store. I cut out some coupons, I was really careful and cut on the dotted lines."

"Did you buy something?"

"I wanted to but the meat saw broke."

Lyle started to weep. He held the phone, cupped in his hands as he held his face and cried. He did everything he could. He'd let his parents down. They made him promise he would be her keeper, but she had gone too far, he couldn't help her anymore. "Sister, you take care tonight, stay warm and safe."

"Oh, Brother, are you weeping?"

"I'm okay." He squeezed his eyes with his thumb and forefinger. "I'm okay."

"You miss me don't you?"

He was silent. What could he say? She had lost her sense of reality, so far out there; bringing her in wouldn't be easy. "Yeah, I do."

"Well, you go home and get some rest." She laughed, "And don't you worry about that horrible Cindy girl. I patched things up with a nice bottle of wine."

Lyle answered, "I'm sure you did. You've always looked out for me." He'd at least saved one of the people who'd come into his life, for once, he'd intervened in time. "Good night, Sister."

"Good night, Brother. I see my ride coming."

Lyle continued driving over the hill. When he pushed down into another valley, he found a major country road with road signs to the towns of Longview and Kelso, two towns which sat on the major highway. He could be back in the West Hills in two hours. He looked at his watch; he could get to the Fisherman's Reef before Cindy closed up.

Lyle rolled into Portland around one a.m. He stopped and tossed his sterilization suit in a trash bin and took the bloody car seat covers out and tossed them as well. He checked himself over, clean of blood. He went straight to the Fisherman's Reef, straight into the waiting arms of Cindy, so happy when he saw her smile. "Miss me?" He came in with a bouquet of roses and his briefcase.

"I was worried about you. After what you told me about your sister and what our day bartender said happened, I was afraid you might be in trouble."

She had no idea the accuracy of her statement. "Nothing I couldn't handle."

"How's your sister?"

"She's staying with a friend." He dismissed his problems with the help of a comforting soul, a normal soul who made him feel normal; one who drew him in.

"Good." Cindy came out from behind the bar, stepping into the center of the empty lounge. "You look like you need a kiss and a drink."

"I definitely need the first." He didn't feel guilty, for the second time, he didn't feel guilty kissing a woman. He felt relaxed. He pulled away and smiled. "I have something for you."

"They are beautiful."

"These?" He handed her the roses. "This is not what's beautiful." He pulled her to a table. "I've done something illegal, something that's probably going to get me fired, but it's the best thing I've ever done."

Cindy looked concerned. "What are you talking about?"

"You have no idea how special I am in the field of bio medical research. He pulled his briefcase up. "The drugs I make are more advanced than any other on the planet, and until today, I had no idea that I was working for the rich and famous, lost in my own belief that I was changing the world. I wasn't. I was proving that money is the only way to survive." He started pulling out vial after vial. "Twenty-six of these injections and your mother's cancer will be eradicated." He cringed, "They need to be localized in their injections, but a qualified physician will know what to do."

"Are these from your work?"

"Yes, but I made it, and I will determine who gets it."

"What will they do to you?"

He thought about that, probably not much. He might be branded a thief, but a genius thief, and they weren't going to kill their goose laying golden eggs; however, that trouble meant nothing compared to what lay on the horizon. His sister had numbered their days in Portland. He knew his actions covering up Lauren would come back to haunt him, or worse, kill him.

Chapter 27

Danny lived on the farm his entire life. In those years, he knew the uneasy feeling of a coyote prowling, of a bear foraging, of a mountain lion lost, and of a human nearby. He had a feeling that night. "Kids let's get you two bathed." The two spaniels had crusted blood from paws to withers. Danny corralled them into the bathroom and ran water in the tub. He lifted the girl; her nerves sputtering as he placed her in the water. "So, you're Trudy, huh?" He patted her head. "Lets you and me forget I ever said mean things to ya', okay?" The water turned a dirty red as he lifted a bucket and doused water over her body. He took his own hairbrush and stroked her fine silky fur. He closed the gap between them. "You're gonna be okay."

She lifted her head and licked him on the nose.

He smiled. Danny didn't remember his mother's terriers being like that. They yapped a lot and carried on peeing in the house when they were mad. This dog had a deeper connection. She was more partner than pet; he could see it in her gaze. When he finished, he called the other dog in. "You must be Wilbur. Taller than Trudy, but thinner, he looked younger. He had a playful side but followed Trudy's lead as though she made the final decisions.

Danny emptied the water and dried Trudy off before starting the process over with Wilbur. Wilbur didn't much care for Danny putting him into the tub, and Danny had to struggle with him. Wilbur stiffened as though a porcelain figurine; a bath was punishment. "Wilbur, you have to get in. I can't have you looking like you've been beaten. It bothers me." Wilbur stayed stone still as Danny scrubbed him down. When Danny turned his attention, Wilbur sprang to life and attempted to bolt from the tub. "Stay!" Danny raised his voice and Trudy put her head over the tub, checking on her sibling. "Sorry guys, I'm trying to be calm here. Work with me, I'm not much of a dog person."

His phone rang. He knew if he answered, Wilbur was out of there. He quickly pulled the drain plug and reached for his phone. When he stood, Wilbur climbed out and shook a spray of crimson bath water in all directions. Danny held the towel to block the smattering of wet, but the damage to the rest of the bathroom was apparent. He shook his head and answered. "Hello."

"Mr. Gates?"

"Yes."

"I'm investigator Antonetti. We met earlier."

"Which one are you, the old one or the young one?"

The person on the other end paused. "The older one."

"What's your buddy's name?"

"Investigator Dobritt."

"Tell him I'm sorry I was unpleasant. That goes for you too."

"Mr. Gates, after what you've been through tonight, I'd be pretty much the same way."

Stoic and unmoved, he asked, "How can I help you?"

"May we come see you?"

"When?"

"Tonight."

The day had tired Danny. He wanted to go to bed and get up in the morning to continue plowing the field. He considered that option. Chances were, with three local deaths and one stranger dead, work would be suspended for a few days. "Yeah, come on over." He continued, "You two need coffee?"

"You don't have to bother."

Danny grunted. "It's not a bother, it's for me. If you want some, I'll make a full pot."

"Very well, that would be fine."

"Is John coming?"

"He'll be there."

Danny made coffee and waited for the authorities to show up. He still had that uneasy feeling. This had to be the work of more than one person. Jack and Pat might have been old, but getting the jump on them, especially for that attorney, couldn't be possible. Tom was a different story. He'd trip over his own tongue if a pretty woman came into the store. Did the person belonging to the car he saw at Jack and Pat's know who he was, and if so, know where he lived? He could be next on the target list. He turned the lights off so outside had more visibility than inside. The dogs laid their heads on his lap, ears pricked to the noise around them.

When he saw headlights of two cars pull in, he snapped the living room light back on and opened the porch door. Coming up the walkway, Sheriff Scott and the other two looked exhausted. "What did you do with the bodies?"

Antonetti stepped up. "We have teams there right now. I think we doubled your population."

Danny said in disgust, "Well that's good, because someone's trying to cut it in half." He welcomed everyone in and locked the door.

John commented. "That's not like you Dan. Big man like you tends to invite trouble."

"Well, John, when you don't know what trouble looks like, it's best to practice caution." He looked out the shades and scanned the field beyond the dull yellow light of the pole lamps. "Let's take this into the kitchen."

They sat at the kitchen table, Trudy and Wilbur lying at Danny's feet. Antonetti shot his questions straight. The Henricksens are dividing up their land, are you aware of who's getting what?"

Danny nodded. "Yeah."

"We understand you are inheriting a lion's share of that property."

Danny nodded again. "Yeah."

Dobritt interrupted. "Is it possible the contractors were upset about not getting more land?"

Danny hadn't considered anyone other than the attorney and her brother, or maybe the attorney and another accomplice, and the idea of a contractor going on a rampage over less land than they hoped for was ridiculous. Jack had coordinated the building. "I don't know. I never spoke to the contractors." Danny sipped of his coffee. "I didn't know they were leaving until a couple of days ago, and didn't know I was getting nearly half their land until a couple of days ago."

Dobritt continued. "How about you, do you feel slighted?"

Danny cocked his head and leaned into the table. His size, the height at which his upper body met with the table's edge allowed him to lean forward and meet the investigator halfway across the table. His hands were big, his shoulders were broad; he imposed himself. He jammed a stump of a finger down onto the table, a loud bang echoed in the kitchen. "They were my second parents." He narrowed his gaze and suggested, "You make that remark again and these other two won't be able to pull me off you." He snared Dobritt in his gaze. "Are we on the same page?"

"May I remind you—"

"No, you may not." He turned to Antonetti. "If you came here to accuse me, you might as well leave."

Antonetti calmed the room. "We did not. Tasteless questions in times of grief are part of our job. Offending you wasn't our goal. The truth is, these murders don't make sense."

Danny agreed. "No, they don't."

"We have to start somewhere."

Danny turned his attention to John. "Really?"

John apologized. "They are doing their jobs, Dan. I told them to clear you tonight and move on with suspects tomorrow. I said the first people they should call was the law firm handling the parties involved. They can give us a better idea of who is who."

Danny smiled. He wondered how that conversation would go. Would that pretty blonde chatter away how the contractor was shady? "Yeah, you should do that."

The night hadn't gone well for Danny. Being told to write down everything he saw at both locations, as the midnight hour approached, was misery. He obliged the two investigators and gave them his view of things. John had to hurry back to town for questions of his own, so he left Danny with the two investigators. Danny wrote down most everything he knew in their report. He failed; however, to mention the smell of Jasmine or his encounter with the attorney's brother. Danny had his own plan for that.

Chapter 28

Lyle woke next to Cindy for the second morning in a row. The week ended and there wasn't any reason to get up. He checked his phone and no one called. He worried over not receiving a call from his sister and relieved he didn't receive one from his employer.

He drifted off, comfortable enough to sleep past his internal clock. When he woke a second time, Cindy had risen; he could hear her in the other room. He donned some clothes and made his way to the front room.

"Good morning, Sunshine." Cindy cooked breakfast. "Over easy or scrambled?"

Lyle smiled. "Scrambled."

She turned and laughed. With the spatula in her hand, she said, "Now that surprises me. I would have guessed you for a purest kind of guy."

He laughed. "I suppose I am, but I never liked the taste of yolk."

Cindy did a workman's job in the kitchen, making Lyle a breakfast of eggs, toast, and bacon. She delivered it to his spot at the table. "What would you like to do today?"

As a controlling person, he should have heard that remark a lot, but he realized he never heard that from Lauren, who usually said,

"Let's…," and followed it with something she thought they should do. He controlled their moments with "Yes" or "No."

"Can we go see your mother?"

Cindy put a hand to her chest. "You want to see my mother."

"I would, I think time is of the essence." He took her hand and motioned for her to sit. "Chances are, unless you have a doctor who is willing to risk his license sticking chemicals he has no idea about into his patient, you are going to have to do this yourself."

Cindy said. "But what if it doesn't work?"

Lyle wanted to scold her. No one doubted his research. "We don't know each other well enough for you to put your faith in me, but there will come a time when you are willing to try anything, a time when the doctors tell you there's nothing more they can do. That's your window, but I caution you," Lyle stared at Cindy. "That is a very narrow window." He felt disappointed but agreed. "I wouldn't want you to worry I'm wrong, so let's work it that way, okay."

Lyle could tell Cindy wanted to believe him, like every test subject he'd ever saved, or lost, they all wanted to believe. That faith against faith expression on the face of every person was identical. They looked as though one more snake charmer entered their life, there to prove the last one was a charlatan, and yet, he had more than proved them wrong, time and time again. Still, they always moved forward because hope is a powerful thing, and when death is the prognosis, people will try anything.

"So, if we get to that point, can you do the injections?"

Lyle suspected bad things for his future. "I can, but let's teach you as well in case something should happen to me."

She frowned. "Nothing's going to happen to you."

His phone rang, Lauren called. She'd made it through the night. "Hold that thought." He stood from the table and excused himself to the bedroom before answering. "Sister?"

"I got another car last night."

Lyle knew his sister wasn't a thief, so if she had a car, the chances are, someone occupied it when she acquired it. "Are you still in Dirtwater?"

"Yes I am!" Her spirits had picked up, and she spoke with excitement.

"Dirtwater is a small place and you've caused quite a scene there, perhaps you should not be driving around."

"Oh, it's okay, this car has really cool stuff in it. It has a radio that tells me where everyone is. Someone has been calling it all morning."

"All the more reason to not drive around."

She sounded dejected. "I know. I have it hidden in the brush by another big pond. This one's off the road in the woods."

"Have you gotten over your urge?"

Lauren sighed. "I don't know. I really want to visit this man I have my eye on."

"What man would that be?"

Lauren erupted. "You would like to know, wouldn't you? You would just act jealous and march out here to stop me. Maybe if you paid a little more attention to me instead of those whores you run around with, you wouldn't have a need to be jealous."

"You're right, Sister. I wasn't thinking of you. Don't cheat on me, and I will come pick you up. We can move to the desert like you suggested."

"No! We can do that after I find out how much this man likes me."

"Okay, Sister. I won't stop you. I hope you don't have far to drive to see him." Lyle tried to pry her location out of her. Maybe he could find her.

"I am on his property."

"Does he know you're there?"

"No, but I see him. He's an early riser, earlier than you, Brother." She sounded shocked. "He woke up with the sun and started his tractor up, went out and started driving around his fields."

"And he can't see you?"

"No. He has big fields, and I'm in his woods."

Lyle tried to remember the big farmer's name. David? Donald, Dan…Dan! "Are you at Dan's house?"

An irritated response surged through the phone, "How do you know Mr. Gates?"

Dan Gates. That's what he needed. "Well, I trust you will be nice to Mr. Gates when you two get together."

"Oh yes, Brother. I'm going to give him everything he deserves."

Lyle cautioned her. "Make sure you don't move that car, okay. Don't drive it."

She started to cry. "What should I do? I need you here to help me."

"It's okay, Sister. I'll be there when you are through. Just call me."

"Should I put this car in the pond?"

"Is it deep enough?"

She boasted. "It's huge! It's got cliff walls."

That meant a gravel pit. There couldn't be many of those in Dirtwater. As he talked, he brought up his phone's aerial map and started zooming down. "Well, that would be the safest place for it." He had a bad feeling. "Is the driver of the car still with you?"

"Of course, who do you think kept me warm last night?"

He feared asking. "Well, you might want to ask him if it's okay to dump his car."

She was blunt. "He won't mind, trust me."

Chapter 29

Danny woke and cursed habits. "Damn it, you would think being up so late past my bedtime would have afforded me the opportunity to sleep in!" He looked at the clock—five a.m. The two spaniels had wormed their way onto his bed. "Hey, you two! I thought I told you to sleep on the floor."

The boy stretched and the girl crawled her way forward so she could have the attention of a petting hand on her head.

"Yeah, yeah, you are a good girl." He scratched her ear and thought about the details of the day before. "Where's that sister of yours?" He nuzzled Trudy.

The dogs didn't move as he rolled out of bed and went to the shower to wash the grime of horror away from his soul. He hadn't planned on plowing that day, but why the hell not. He knew the town crawled with police, camera crews, and crime chasers. It must be a zoo on Main Street. Besides, he felt sure, before the day ended, trouble would be knocking on his door.

He used the steam of the shower to trace the razor over his face, shaving in the shower was a ritual, and catching the hard spots no longer troubled him. He ran his palm over his face, smooth. He tapped the razor and ran it under the jets to remove the stubble. Another day in Paradise.

"Kids!" He called for the spaniels as they made their way into the bathroom. Wilbur wouldn't come all the way in, skittish to be around the tub. "Let's get you fed."

He made breakfast for himself and poured dry food for them; however, they had more interest in what he ate. "Let me guess, "Pat treated you guys like humans?" They sat at attention, one of Trudy's eyebrows lifting. Danny tossed a piece of ham and Wilbur caught it midair and swallowed without chewing. "Damn, Boy, enjoy that first."

Danny retrieved two more pieces of ham from the skillet. He cut them up and mixed it in with the dry food. Those dogs may not have had fingers, but it amazed Danny how they picked out the ham and barely touched the dry food. He shook his head. "You two could get pretty expensive if you only eat human food." He smiled. "That's okay, I got beef in the barn. We'll do okay."

Danny pulled his phone off the charger and left for the fields. He noticed a single call from John, but he didn't leave a message. If he had something he wanted to tell him, he'd call back. "You two want to stay here, or go with me?" He turned to the dogs as he opened the back door. They bolted for outside, and Danny realized they'd been in all night. The first thing they did was crap in the yard. Danny locked the door and watched in amazement. "Hey, you two, shit in the field with the cows, not in my yard!" It didn't help, they weren't listening. Danny slapped the bed of the truck and the spaniels jumped in, more comfortable than the day before.

He pulled out and studied the property, careful of any changes. Nothing appeared disturbed. He drove down Swaheenie at a snail's pace, scanning the fields for anything amiss. When they made it to the tractor, Danny carted his rifle with him. A precaution, he wanted it near him. The dogs followed, used to walking the fields when Jack plowed his property. Danny picked up where he left off, working farther and farther south on his fields. At eight in the morning, the dogs scrambled into bark mode, John arrived. Danny shut the tractor down and hollered to his friend as he made his way up a row, "What now?"

"Did the investigators spend the night?"

Danny smirked. "Hardly."

"What time did they leave after me?"

Danny shrugged. "I don't know, maybe one. Why?"

"They never made it back to Olympia."

"Maybe they're in Huggins."

John stood in between rows, his posture shaking. "They haven't answered their phones or their radios."

Danny wiped his face and stepped off the tractor. If two seasoned officers went missing, and they met with foul play, Danny knew it would take more than a pretty, innocent looking woman to pull it off. "Wow, missing?"

"Yep." John shivered. "You don't believe in vampire shit or anything like that do you?"

Danny stared at his friend. "You didn't really just ask that did you?"

"Okay, not vampire shit but like supernatural stuff."

"Or that! Are you Okay?" Danny put his arm on his friend's shoulder and squeezed. "No, John, I don't. This is the real world. God damn, I can't believe you're a sheriff."

"Dan, look around you, four people have been killed in less than twenty-four hours and two more are missing. That's not normal shit."

"No, but it isn't supernatural shit either. Catching someone by surprise isn't as hard as you think." Danny continued, "You find out about that body in the creek?"

"Like what?"

"Was he shot?"

"Nope. Neither was Jack or Tom."

Danny wondered how someone could get the upper hand on a man who carried a gun with him everywhere. Jack wasn't a fool, and even though he was up there in years, he could fire a pistol as quick as anyone. It stumped him. "Hmm. Keep on your toes, John."

"I was going to tell you the same thing."

"Well, if Jack and Pat willed me anything of value, you're standing next to them." He pointed to the spaniels. "They are keener than I am when there's danger around. Maybe you better start doing a ride along with that hound of yours."

Sheriff Scott grinned. "He's in the car right now!"

"Who's with your wife?"

"I sent her to Bradenton to hang out with her parents, along with my shotgun."

Danny pulled his rifle from the tractor and raised it. "Good idea."

"Chances are if those fellas don't show up, a whole new set of investigators are going to be out here in the next couple of hours."

Danny nodded. "Well, the more the merrier I guess."

John motioned toward the pits. "They may want to check those out."

"I'll dive down today to see what's down there, okay?"

"Fair enough, you need my help?"

Danny waved him off. "No, I can do it alone."

As the sheriff walked away, Danny worried.

That attorney is starting to piss me off.

Chapter 30

Lyle put his sister to the furthest reaches of thought so he could concentrate on Cindy. Cindy asked if he wanted to drop by his place to change before they left, and he suspected that might not be a good idea. He had no clue how close the cards were to collapsing. He used her bathrobe while he washed the clothes on his back and insisted she drive when they were ready to go.

They headed south to Corvallis, a rural college town and made their way to the Samaritan hospital. "I thought you said your mother was in pretty good shape."

"She is, but they've been radiating her pretty heavily and she's not handled it well."

Lyle shook his head in disgust. "I don't know what to say."

"What's on your mind, Lyle?"

He smiled. "It's not my place to say anything. Let's see her and see how she's feeling."

They stopped by the floral department, and Lyle picked up flowers.

"Thank you for this."

In truth, Lyle knew Cindy must not make much working as a bartender, there must be a lot of things she wished she could do for her mother, nice things, expensive things that she probably couldn't afford.

"It's okay, every woman loves flowers."

Cindy grabbed Lyle's elbow. "Yes, yes they do."

When they made it to the room, Cindy's mother's condition shocked Lyle. Gaunt in appearance and hair thinned and falling out; she looked like death. She had hollow sockets for eyes but her spirits were high.

"Cindy, sweetheart." She sat up and held her arms out for her daughter. As they embraced, she smiled. "Is this that wonderful man you glowed about yesterday?"

Cindy turned and beamed. "Yes it is."

Cindy's mom waved Lyle to her. "Come let Doris take a look at you!"

Lyle stepped forward and bowed his head. "Pleased to meet you."

Lyle sat and gathered in what position Doris felt about radiation. He discovered she wanted to quit. "If I'm not going to get better, but just live a little longer, wouldn't it be better to feel well for a shorter time?"

Cindy treated her like any loved one would, wanting quantity over quality, because quantity gave the greatest chance to extend time for a cure. "Let the doctors work their magic."

Lyle joined the conversation. "I hate to say this, but I think I agree with your mother." He'd caught a rebuke from Cindy. He nodded and went back to observing.

When they brought Doris her lunch, Lyle suggested he and Cindy do the same. "How about we go get something to eat while your mother does the same?"

Doris insisted, "Yes, you two go enjoy a nice lunch away from this place. Please."

When Lyle cleared the room, he said, "I know you aren't happy with me suggesting she go off of radiation, but you have to trust me. She can't go on my treatments until she goes off radiation. The sooner the better. Let her make that decision."

"I don't know, Lyle. You are asking for a huge leap of faith." She rested her head on his shoulder as they descended floors in the elevator.

"Your mother is further along than you know. I don't know if she's been telling you she has a year or if the doctor has, but I've seen a lot of subjects, and I am pretty aware of the stages of cancer, she won't make it another two months. Your mom needs treatments now." He looked at Cindy and saw resignation.

"I suppose." She stared back. "She doesn't look well does she?"

Lyle remained quiet. They understood the truth.

After lunch, when they made it back to the room, in a fit of bold acceptance, Cindy uttered, "Mom, if you want to leave here, to quit the radiation, I will support you."

Doris cautioned her. "You know your sister?"

"So what, this is your life, not hers." Cindy had gone through a complete change of belief because she put faith in Lyle, a tall order for Lyle, but he had practice filling tall orders on past subjects, and with a sister who'd put as tall a demand on someone as anyone could. Cindy pulled a chair next to her mother and whispered. "Lyle is a kind of scientist, and he has a drug that will help with the transition if you are willing to allow him."

She rubbed her daughter's hand. "Anything is better than this stuff." She looked past her daughter at Lyle. "So, are you going to promise me a year as well?"

Lyle gained his arrogance, something he nearly forgot. "I don't promise time, I promise cures."

Doris laughed. "Will I feel sick while you are 'curing' me?" She teased him.

"No, you won't feel sick, and I don't expect you to believe me. Too many people have lied to you in this process already. You just follow the treatments and we will let the results speak for themselves. How about that?"

"Well, I don't want to be in this hell hole one more day, so help me get dressed, Cindy."

"Mom, I think you need to consult with the doctors."

Doris waved her daughter off. "The hell I do. They already said I could quit whenever I wanted to, and I wanted to a month ago."

She nodded to Lyle. "That nice young man just convinced me I waited too long, so get me my clothes."

Unwilling to yank her mother out without approval, Cindy pushed the nurse light. When the nurse came in, she said, "My mother would like to leave the facility. Is that okay with you?"

The nurse shrugged. "I think she needs to talk to her physician, and since it's the weekend, she might have to wait."

Doris already pulled up her dress behind the curtain. She yelled passed the sheet, "The hell I do! You tell Dr. Paylor, if he needs to speak with me, he knows my number."

The nurse's eyes widened as the three of them walked out, Cindy and Lyle helping a weak Doris walk. "Would you like a wheelchair?"

Lyle intervened, "That would be wonderful."

Doris interrupted, "Nope. I walked in this place; I will walk out."

No one stopped them, although everyone watched. When they made it to the parking lot, Doris noted, "It's good to smell fresh air."

Lyle smiled. "Are you through with radiation?"

Doris said, "Hell yes."

Lyle sought clarity. "And you won't go back on that?"

"Nope!"

He whispered to Cindy, "I will teach you how to administer the shots…today."

Cindy grabbed his arm. "Lyle, I'm putting all my hopes into you."

Lyle winked. "Smart move."

Chapter 31

When Danny put on his wet suit, he looked like a black bear. He had his suit specially made because men his size didn't often go into diving shops looking for gear. He pulled the truck up to the edge of McCleary and released the winch line a few feet. The spaniels looked on, their heads peeking over the cab as they stood on their hind legs. Danny smiled and let them know. "I'm going for swim, you two hold down the fort."

Scaling down wouldn't be hard, he had a remote winch control and if he pushed off as he descended the cliff face, he'd be fine. Coming up created more issues. He had to walk up the wall as the winch line slowly pulled him. He hooked the line to a rock-climbing harness around his thigh, held the remote, and leaned back as he released the winch. His scuba gear weighted his angle and pulled him slightly back. He had a bag with his other equipment slung over his shoulder. A few minutes later, he bobbed in the water and put on his fins and mask.

Danny knew he'd find the biker and the bank robber in this pond, and the magazine salesman and the two cattle rustlers in the other. He just hoped that was all. He turned on his underwater light; the murky water came to life, dense particles and hues of green. He swam straight down, the further he went the cleaner the water became, the easier to see. The motorcycle was below him. The bike and body had traveled straight down; Danny figured the cars slid south a few yards as they sank. He followed the floor of the pit until he came to the bank robber's car, but it wasn't alone. Stacked on top of it in perfect alignment was another vehicle. Danny ran the light next to the sedan and swam around the car to the front. When he shined the light in the front window, he found the investigators; their bodies buoyant and tapping the inside top of the roof. Whoever killed the two lurked about the property the night before. He tapped the flashlight onto the hood in disgust. This day had long trouble written all over it.

Danny dropped down to the bank robber's car and opened a back door, the robber much in the same position as the others, only decomposition had set in and the elements had taken a toll on his body, bloated, patches of flesh eaten away. His window had been open and the leeches had found their way to the body. In the back was the bag of money. Danny thought about taking it and handing it to John to keep his mouth shut but decided against a bribe. He knew of a better way to keep the authorities out of his pond. In truth, this pond didn't worry him. The other pond and the amount of cars dumped by kids over the years would be a different story. Right now, he needed to do the work of ten men.

Danny winched himself out, and as he popped up over the cliff, the dogs barked with surprise. Danny pulled his mask off and paid attention to his surroundings. "We have company on the property somewhere. Keep your ears opened." He made it to the cab and called John.

"Hello."

"They're here, in the pit."

"I'll get people over there."

Danny said, "I'm bringing the cat out and will chain it up. You get here first and help me. I want it out when they get here."

John sounded suspicious. "You want to do this all by yourself?"

"Yeah, I do. Are we good?"

"Fair enough."

Danny drove back to the barn and started up the Caterpillar. He retrieved his logging cables and pulled his rifle out of the truck. He knew someone skulked about. The spaniels followed him back to the pit and for a second time Danny winched himself over the edge, this time he hauled a cable. He wrapped it several times through the back seats before hooking it to the rear axle. He put the car in neutral, surfaced and waited until John stared down from above. He shouted, "You still know how to run a cat?"

The sheriff shook his head with disappointment. "Of course I do, but why don't you winch up and do it yourself?"

Danny didn't want to snag the other car below the investigator's and have it come up too. "I'll ride it up in case it gets hitched on the cliff."

"Suit yourself." John stepped back and a moment later the cable tightened as the slack disappeared. Danny released the winch holding him and held the hook. He didn't want to get dragged off the car and pinned between the cliff and the vehicle. He waited until the car surfaced and stood on the trunk as it lifted butt end first. The car crept up the cliff as though in reverse, water spilling out through unsealed creases in a cascading rush until nothing but two bodies lay recklessly against the front windshield. Danny rode the vehicle to the cliff's edge and scrambled to the safety of flat ground. The cat pulled the car hard against the lip of the cliff and she tilted up and bounced onto the surface. Danny noticed a series of cars racing down Swaheenie. They would fly right past the dirt road, everyone did. John cut the engine and Danny yelled, "You better tell them where we are."

They found the road and, one by one, were on the scene like wasps to sugar. They piled out of cars, some running back the way they came to keep the horde of news reporters following them from entering the dirt path, while the remaining group descended on the car like a Christmas present. Danny had had enough time to do his own inspection underwater. Neither body appeared to have gunshot wounds. In fact, none of the bodies he'd seen so far had gunshots. Only Tom had puncture marks and those were from a pair of scissors. Danny doubted two seasoned investigators were killed with scissors.

The team of investigators covered the car with a sheet and proceeded to do their investigation in private. A woman detective approached Danny. "Are you the one who found them?"

Danny nodded. "Yep."

"Why did you look in this pond and not the other?"

"My plan was to check them both, I just happened to start here first."

"Why check the ponds at all?"

Danny smiled. He wasn't happy with her accusation. "You've never lived near a gravel pit, have you?"

She smiled back. "As a matter of fact, I have, Mr—"

"Gates." He continued, "Then you know if people turn up missing, these are great places to search, and I figured if your two investigators disappeared leaving my house, this would be a good place to start."

She looked back toward the road. "But why this one first?" She turned and looked up. "Wouldn't the other one make more sense?"

Danny stared down at the detective. "If they drove off the other one, I'd have seen tracks in the gravel."

She nodded. "Good point, Mr. Gates." She continued, "What else did you see down there?"

"Not much, it's pretty murky. I'm sure there are some old cars down there from kids dumping them. I don't know if the sheriff told you, they fished a local kid and his car out of there this winter."

"He mentioned a lot of kids dump cars here." She walked to the edge and looked over. Turning back, she raised her voice, "We will send a team out in the next few days to take a look, okay?"

Danny wasn't sure if she asked for approval or told him her intent, he suspected the latter. He didn't comment.

John joined the conversation. "Anything you need from me, Detective Zimmerman?"

She looked at John. "Not unless you're a trained dive investigator."

John grinned. "As a matter of fact, I am."

She waved him off. "Never mind."

Danny pulled John aside as he backed up to the cat. He needed to enlist the sheriff's help. "You want that bank money, it's down there. I saw it."

The sheriff whispered, "No shit?"

"He must have gotten lost out here and taken a wrong turn." Danny looked around. "You better get her confidence, and fast."

John looked determined. "You leave it up to me."

Danny wiped the stress from his brow.

What am I going to do?

He looked down at the two spaniels, "Let's take the cat back to the barn."

He hopped on the Caterpillar and the detective caught up to him. "Don't go far, we have some more questions." She noticed the rifle. "Can we have that?"

Danny was frank. "No."

"Excuse me," She rested her hand on her holster.

"Two men are dead on my property. My second parents and grocer friend are also dead." I'll hold on to my weapons. If your boys were shot by a .308, you come on over to the house and we can talk." Danny stared down at her. "You're on my property, treat me like it." He started up the engine and made his own path around the vehicles and to the barn.

Chapter 32

Lyle helped Doris find a comfortable position. "Now, you don't have to do this treatment. I don't want you to be uncomfortable with a strange man telling you he can cure you. Your daughter has known me all of two days."

She patted Lyle's hand. "I trust my daughter's intuition."

Lyle didn't want to tell her, her daughter had her doubts about his remedy. "Well, you won't be disappointed." She smiled, and he said what he truly believed, "You will probably be alive a lot longer than I will be."

Lyle lifted Doris' top to just below her breasts. "Cindy, we only have to be localized with the shots; however, the one location cannot be the stomach."

"Why?"

"Because the majority of the chemicals will be expelled. We need to make sure we hit an organ around the pancreas, of course, if we get the pancreas itself, that's fantastic, but it isn't vital." He placed his finger in the spot just below where the last ribs came together below the sternum. "If you push the needle in and up from here, you will be safe." He sighed, "It's not a pleasant feeling, and there is an alternative, which also isn't pleasant." He coaxed Doris to roll over. He pointed to the flesh halfway up her back, using two fingers on either side of the spine. "You can enter from either side of here as well, but this is tough muscle tissue, and it isn't a pleasant experience."

Cindy drew back, her face paling. "Oh God, I don't know if I can do this. Please tell me you will be here every step of the way."

Lyle found enough courage to paint on a smile. "Of course, but just in case."

She grabbed his arm and squeezed it. "Thank you so much."

Lyle rolled Doris to her back. "You ready for your first shot?"

"She shook her head. "No, but let's get it done." She reached across the bed and grabbed her daughter's hand. Everyone in the room knew, when Lyle pulled out a thick long needle and syringe, this wasn't going to be fun.

He stuck the needle down into the vial and pulled the plunger upward, drawing the fluid into the cylinder of the syringe. He tapped the bubbles and pushed a drop out the tip. When he readied his patient, Doris sucked a breath and closed her eyes. "Try not to think about this, Doris."

"Get it over with." Her eyes squeezed shut.

Lyle wiped alcohol over the pocket under the sternum and pushed the needle in and up, two, three, four inches in.

Doris screamed, "Oh, Dear God!" Cindy wept and Lyle pushed the plunger until the fluid disappeared.

He extracted the needle and patted her arm. "Done."

Doris gave a faint laugh. "And I thought childbirth was rough."

Cindy laughed and wiped tears.

"How many more of those do I have?"

Lyle nodded. "Twenty-five more."

She opened her eyes and insisted, "Let's try the back next time."

Lyle smiled. "Fair enough."

They remained in her room, Lyle monitoring her reaction to the drug.

"I don't feel anything."

Lyle assured her, "That's a good thing. I don't want you to feel sick. That could be a sign of your body rejecting the chemicals."

His phone rang. Lauren called. "My sister. Can I take this in the other room?"

Cindy smiled, and Lyle stood to leave. "I'll be right back." He bent down and gave Cindy a kiss. He'd never felt compelled to do that to a woman before.

In the other room, he said, "Sister, are you okay?"

"Yes!" Lyle could hear her opening something. "I had a wonderful morning."

"Did you get rid of the car?"

"I did. The two gentlemen were such good sports to stay with me through the night. One made a great pillow and the other, well, he was rather stiff." Her hysterical laugh echoed into the phone.

"Where are you now?"

"I just finished taking a shower. The man I came to see has been working all day long. I can't wait until he comes home to see me. He is something else. Mr. Rugged!"

"You're in his house?" Lyle looked at his watch, it was two o'clock. He could get there in four hours, maybe three. "I'll come get you."

"I haven't had anything to eat yet."

Lyle had to know. "Lauren, I need you to answer me something, and I don't want you to think less of me for asking."

Lauren sounded put off. "What is it?"

"Is the man you are seeing, the big man we met that day at the farmer's house?"

She was coy. "Maybe."

"Do you have some of my drugs?"

She whispered in disgust. "Brother, I have run out of that one you said is from a purple flower."

She meant Aconite, a poison, something that killed. "So what will you say to him if you don't have the purple flower drug?"

"I have more of the liquid Zolpidem." She snickered. "By the way, how did that feel when I gave it to you yesterday?"

Zolpidem was a sedative. "It was effective, but if I were you, I would just leave. I can come get you by five or six. Just leave his house. Please."

She screamed, "Oh, I see. You get to fuck some girl and I don't get a man. Is that it?"

"Lauren, I apologized, and you've had several men over the last couple of days." He could hardly believe he discussed this as though any parallel existed.

"Last one, I promise." She disconnected.

He tried to call her back. If she wasn't going to leave she needed to know something. She needed to understand the drug. He left a message, "Call me, immediately." She didn't.

Lyle walked back into the room and announced, "I need to get back to Portland. My sister needs a ride."

Cindy sat with her mother. "I think I should stay with her. "Take my car and the two of you come back here when you get her."

Lyle knew that would not happen, but he smiled. "Are you sure?"

Cindy stood and walked Lyle out of the room to her mother's front door. "Lyle, you are like a dream come true, a man I can be proud of, smart, loyal. Go get your sister. I'll be here waiting."

Lyle tipped his head to the ground, wondering if he would make it back. He straightened and faced Cindy. He put his arm around her and hugged tightly, his soul gripped with fear of losing. Releasing emotions he wished he could have shown Jackie all those years ago, releasing emotions he never allowed himself to show to anyone. "Thank you." He pulled away and studied her eyes. "I think a guy could fall in love with you." He kissed her and stepped out the door.

Chapter 33

The sun lowered over the horizon. Authorities set up lights at McCleary as a unit prepared to remove the bodies and send them to Olympia. Danny parked the cat at the barn and the two spaniels tagged along, comfortable being in his presence. He brought the water hose out and washed down both rigs—the tractor and cat. He parked the rifle back in the cab of his truck, honked the horn three times and when his girls started coming in, he said to Trudy and Wilbur, "Go get the rest of em'." They obliged and ran out to the field. He worked alone and tossed hay into the stalls.

"Is that Timothy?"

A voice shot up Danny's back and he turned, startled.

"What the—" It was Detective Zimmerman. "How about knockin'? You might get shot next time."

She made her way in and offered, "Probably not, you left your weapon in your truck."

He spoke up, "It better be there when I leave."

She smiled. "It is."

Danny put his pitchfork down. "So, what's on your mind, Detective?"

"If I'm to believe that you killed those two men out there, and I don't, I'd have to believe you overpowered two men and poisoned them. Something about you," She walked to him and craned her neck skyward. "Tells me you would rather beat someone to death, and probably could."

Danny rubbed his neck; the particles of hay had formed grime on his skin that irritated against the cotton of his shirt. "Poison, huh?

"Yeah."

"That's a pretty fast diagnosis."

"It's not proven yet, but your friend was poisoned, and I'm guessing the two needle marks on our men are poison as well."

"Needle marks?"

"Right here." She turned slightly and bent her head, pointing to the neck. "Antonetti on the right side, Dobritt on the left."

Danny said, "Antonetti drove that night."

She smiled. "I like your thinking. Are you thinking what I'm thinking?"

"That whoever did it was in the car?" He questioned, "Would they have picked someone up?"

She laughed. "After what'd happened? Without calling it in?" she shook her head. "No, they would have called it in. They were good investigators. They reported they were leaving your residence and that's the last we heard from them."

"I'm guessing you're cutting me some slack because hiding in their car might be hard for me."

"Pretty much." She wanted to know. "Sheriff Scott said the attorney wasn't very big."

"Also a woman, not that it matters. However, I understand Pat's body hasn't been found, and I was in the house, there wasn't any drag marks of a body leaving, so whoever took her carried her. I don't see that little attorney carrying her out."

"How tall was she?"

Danny grinned. "Detective, everyone is short to me. I'd guess she was about your height. How tall are you?"

"I'm five six."

"No offense, she was a little bonier than you."

She teased him, "I'm in a vest!"

"Fair enough, but she didn't weigh over a buck."

Detective Zimmerman smiled. "Okay, so I have a dime on her."

"Dime?"

"Geez, a quarter then."

Danny complimented her. "You look good in what you got."

The two spaniels trotted in, the last of the girls made their way to the barn, anxious to be grained. Danny continued as he went about his business. "So, if you think the attorney was involved, do you think her brother was involved?"

"Brother?"

Danny stopped and turned. "Didn't John tell you she had a brother?"

"No."

He came with her the first day she came out to Jack's house. Real odd dude, but not scary, more nerdy."

"The truth is they might both be victims as well. We haven't identified the body at the creek, which could be the brother; as for her, she hasn't been heard from."

Danny wasn't so sure she hadn't been heard from. He was quite sure the spaniels heard from her. "Pat said another attorney came out with her the next day."

"That one could be the creek body. He's missing as well."

"Detective Zimmerman—"

"Call me Karen."

Danny smiled. "Okay, Karen, if I'm being honest, none of this makes sense. Suppose the cute little attorney and her brother, or the other attorney, or all three of them, started killing people. What purpose was there?"

"You said she was cute?"

"Honestly? She was magnetic. There was something about how white her hair was; even her eyebrows were white, and her eyes were almost chatoyant, going from pale blue to a richer blue the closer she got to you. Same with her brother, but he looked odd; she looked appealing."

"I can't answer why these murders took place. We have no motive, but we'll find one, and when we do, we'll narrow it down to who did this."

"Well, I suspect you will."

She stared down at the barn floor, hesitating before asking, "I have one more favor to ask."

"And that is?"

"Can I park my cruiser in your driveway and camp in my vehicle?"

"Why?"

"The perpetrators may still be here, and I have taken the assignment to protect you."

Danny laughed. "Protect me, you?"

She winked, "Size isn't everything. Sometimes it's how you handle your gun."

Danny wanted to say something but thought better. He pivoted back around to the cows and grinned. "Suit yourself." She turned and walked away, but before she cleared the door, Danny shouted, "But you don't have to sleep in your car. If your husband doesn't mind, you can bunk up at my house. There are plenty of empty rooms."

She said, "Much obliged, and my husband won't mind at all because I don't have one." She turned the corner and Danny watched her drive back toward McCleary Pit.

He reprimanded the dogs. "Hey you two, what are you guys looking at?" They stood at the door of the barn and watched the car drive off. "Just another cop. Don't get too close to her; she might bite worse than you two do."

Danny finished with the cows and stood out under the evening sky, wondering if he should run home and shower or maybe go see what the detective and John had discovered.

Chapter 34

Lyle stopped by his condominium but noticed lights in the window. Someone was there and he doubted it was Lauren. He pulled into the parking lot and called his sister. "Lauren."

She sounded irritated. "What?"

"Where are you?"

"At my boyfriend's."

Lyle investigated. "Are you two doing okay?"

Lauren said matter of fact, "No we are not!"

Lyle continued as he pulled out and headed to the Fisherman's Reef. "What's going on?"

"He's got a bunch of friends over and they are partying at the lake. I thought he would be home by now, but no, he has to entertain others."

"Lauren, that's not a very attentive boyfriend. Maybe you should leave. I can be there in an hour and a half."

"Leave? He's got the truck. I'm so pissed right now. He's never been rude like this before." She changed the subject. "I think I'm ovulating. I feel like it. I hope I'm not coming across bitchy."

It was Lyle's nature to go into a dissertation about biology, about the difference between ovulating and discharging, but knew better. "I don't think you sound bitchy, but I would just put on your walking shoes and start walking. Is there a way to avoid the party?"

"I'm not going anywhere. No one treats me like this. I'm a pretty damn good fiancée."

"Lauren?"

"Yes, Brother."

"I want you to listen to me, okay. I need you to be in the real world for just a moment."

Lauren was put off. "You are so mean sometimes. Can't I just have a normal relationship with a guy I'm married to? Do you always have to get in the middle of it?"

Lyle shouted, "Lauren!"

"What?" Lauren shouted back.

"Make sure, with that drug that you—"

Lauren cut him off. "Sorry Brother, my honey's here, got to go."

"Lauren? Lauren? Hello." The connection went dead.

Lyle made it to the Fisherman's Reef and to his car. He went to the trunk and took out a kit of drugs. Lauren had taken all the killing drugs of Aconite and Belladonna vials. He wanted the Zolpidem, but she'd taken it as well. He could have saved everyone with that. All he had that could be of any use was Tetrodotoxin and a small amount of Benzodiazepine. Not the most ideal of drugs, but they'd have to do. He grabbed a flashlight, his tranquilizer gun and the shovel he'd come to despise. He packed Cindy's car and hurried north. He'd mapped out a way to get to the farmhouse with the pits without going through town. He'd guessed with the size of Dirtwater, and the activity Lauren said took place, Main Street would be crawling with authorities looking for someone out of place, and Lyle definitely looked out of place.

Before he left the city limits of Portland, he stopped by a camera store. He purchased a professional model, a pair of binoculars and a lanyard with a placard attachment. He placed his company badge inside and held it from a distance, his picture and a bold indiscernible print made it look worthy of a newspaper photographer. Lyle doubted it would work, but if someone stopped him, at least he had something to fall back on.

Six o'clock rolled over before he made it to the valley, dark, and surprisingly quiet. There were several news trucks coming and going down the country highway but not much else. He imagined the authorities hunkered down, viewing everything that came and went into the area.

Lyle drove past the Seefer Valley entrance and into Bradenton. From Bradenton, Lyle found a pass road that went over a hilltop and dropped down into the north end of the Seefer Valley. On the map it looked like the road had once been a highway; however, the map made it more generous in usability than it actually was.

They call this Swaheenie? Should be called, Dirt-road-do-not-travel road.

His lights on high, his speed risky at a paltry ten miles per hour, Lyle inched his way over the hilltop. It wasn't until he reached

Seefer that Swaheenie turned into a true road. He doubted anything but logging trucks used the road he'd traveled.

In the distance he saw a farmhouse. He located it on his GPS and realized he'd found the house his sister holed up in. Six o'clock turned into seven. Lyle didn't know what to expect so he turned off his lights and left the car a mile back of the farm. With a cool night and slight slope downward, the walk was easy. With the breeze in this face, his scent stayed behind him. At about two hundred yards he settled in to a ditch and pulled his binoculars. He spotted two dogs, busy, uneasy, pacing the porch. The driveway had a parked truck and large black SUV, like a government vehicle.

Lyle checked his backpack; he had the vials of Tetrodotoxin, a risky drug, but if he administered it properly, he could retrieve his sister and not kill anyone. The real problem would be the dogs, and the fact there were probably at least two adults already in the place, and with Lauren, that wouldn't last very long.

Lyle loaded his gun with quarter dose dart of his mixed Tetro and Benz, and made a second one ready to shoot. That much would probably still kill the dogs, but better them than his sister. He readied himself to march when he heard a gunshot ring out. The dogs went crazy and Lyle ran toward the house. As he made his way to the yard, the two dogs caught scent of him and approached in attack mode. Lyle aimed and dropped the first one, he reloaded, shot, and the second one staggered, stiffened up and fell in its tracks. He jumped up onto the porch and found a window to stare through. Someone lay on the ground; Lauren had an ax in her hand but struggled with the big burly farmer. He could tell his sister had staggered the farmer with something, his guess was the Zolpidem. What Lyle tried to tell his sister, what she failed to learn, a man his size would require a lot of Zolpidem to keep him down for very long. It looks like she'd miscalculated her dosage. Lyle counted to three, he was going in.

Chapter 35

Danny made his way over to the pit. Most of the officials had left, but a steady diet of news types hung around like vultures after a kill. Someone asked him if he owned the property, a mic in his face and camera rolling. "No, just passing through." They moved on. Detective Zimmerman and Sheriff Scott stood under the glow of a bright lamp, answering questions for the media. They wrapped up the day's events, giving a detailed account of what they planned to do in the following days.

"We will catch the perpetrators, whoever they are." Detective Zimmerman raised her hand as the noise spiked. "We have some very solid leads; leads I'm not going to discuss. Just wait and you will get your story very soon. Until then, we are done for the day." She sounded irritated. "Go home."

"Someone shouted, "Is it safe to walk around Dirtwater?"

Sheriff Scott spoke up, "Are you from Dirtwater?" The crowd tittered. "Then go home."

Danny waited as the generator powering all the equipment shut down, the lights turned off, and the to reporters scramble down the trail like cockroaches. "Turn the lights out and they aren't so tough." Danny spoke to Detective Zimmerman.

"You don't seem to be too scared."

"It's my property." Danny shrugged. "Besides, I have warning sirens." He motioned to the spaniels. Trudy and Wilbur hugged Danny's hip as though chained to it.

Sheriff Scott worried. "You going to be okay tonight?"

Danny gathered Detective Zimmerman didn't divulge her plans. "Yeah, I'm a big boy."

The sheriff laughed. "Yes, yes you are."

Danny had walked from the barn. "Would you like a ride back to your truck, Mr. Gates?" Detective Zimmerman stood on a makeshift platform, lifted high enough to not have to crane her neck when talking to him.

Danny nodded. "That'd be nice of you. I hope you don't mind the dogs?"

"They're more than welcome."

When they packed everything up and the only three left were Sheriff Scott, Detective Zimmerman, and Danny, Sheriff Scott finalized everything. "So Detective, you have everything covered?" The sheriff paid attention to his watch. "I promised my wife I'd get over to Bradenton and ease her fears."

She smiled. "Go ahead and go. I have Mr. Gates, who I believe is a pretty good man to have on my side."

John winked. "That he is."

The sheriff left the two of them on the lonely dirt road by the pit. Danny warned her, "Detective—"

"I told you, please call me Karen."

Danny obliged. "Karen, watch where you walk. It's a long drop."

She lightly took Danny's elbow. "That's why you're leading us out." They walked to the road. "This area is getting a reputation."

"With six deaths in twenty-four hours, I would guess so."

She echoed out into the darkness. "It's has been on our radar for a little longer than that."

Danny had a distant thought. "How so?"

Several months ago, a couple in Bradenton were killed and the killer was never found."

Danny reminded her. "That's Bradenton."

She reminded him, "It's this area." She continued. "Then a bank robber robs a bank and he disappears too."

Danny nodded. "Again in Bradenton.

She said, "Again, this area."

He said, "I heard about that. They never caught the guy?"

She delivered, "No, no they didn't." They walked carefully over ruts in the dirt. "And of course, you know all about the biker. The Bakersfield police said they camped on your property."

Danny nodded. "Yes they did. Seemed like a nice bunch. I especially liked their leader, Duke."

She sighed. "And there were a couple of cattle rustlers who mysteriously disappeared without taking their kill." They made it to the road. "They didn't get any of your cows did they?"

"Nope."

"So you can see this area is a rather interesting area."

Danny recalled every one of those people. "A pleasant valley may not be a good place for unpleasant people."

They separated and went to opposite doors. As Detective Zimmerman climbed in, she commented, "No, it may not be."

Danny opened the back door and the spaniels jumped in. Danny took the seat next to the detective.

They drove up to the farmhouse and Danny let the two dogs out. They ran for the yard and Danny hollered, "You two can stay out here and protect the outside." He was irritated they continued to use his yard as their own private restroom."

Detective Zimmerman noted. "You don't know a lot about dogs, do you?"

"Nope."

"Isn't that odd for a farmer?"

"Could be, but my dad didn't much care for dogs, and my mother had this love affair with ratty little dogs that did nothing but bark, so I wasn't around dogs like those." He pointed to the spaniels.

"They're good dogs."

"So I'm learning." Danny unlocked the door and told the spaniels, "You two protect the perimeter." He locked the door behind him. "I hope you don't mind, but in a life like mine, you take showers at odd times."

Detective Zimmerman grinned. "Don't let me stop you."

He frowned. "That bad, huh?"

She laughed. "No, but I understand." She stopped him. "I wasn't always a cop. I grew up on a farm."

That caught Danny unprepared. "Really, where?"

"In Eastern Washington."

He nodded. "Hmm." He made it to the bathroom door and hollered, "Make yourself comfortable."

Danny stripped down and turned on the shower. He wanted to hurry; he enjoyed his time with Karen. He soaped up and rinsed off. He felt his face to see if any growth had pushed up onto chin. He didn't want to look too brutish. He picked up the razor and something caught his eye. His razor had fine blonde hairs tucked between the blades. Danny jumped out of the shower, ran for the door and shouted, "Karen, look out!"

Detective Zimmerman yelled back, "What?"

Danny exited naked as the day he was born. He bounded down the hallway headed to the front room, knowing something was afoot. Before he rounded into the front room, something pricked him in the hip. He yanked at it and pulled a syringe out. "What the hell." He felt woozy and someone pushed past him. He shook the dizziness off and continued into the front room. Detective Zimmerman staggered backwards, a needle sticking in her shoulder. She reached for her side arm when a shot rang out, hitting the detective in the center of her chest. Danny watched as she fell back, lifeless.

The room spun and a manic voice spoke to him, spilling in his ears with the noise of a warped record, a vermiculate of movement and undulating sounds. "How could you? I trusted you. You bastard, and to bring her in our house when I was preparing a home!" She dropped the gun and fell to her knees, crying as though someone had wronged her.

"What are you talking about?" Danny jostled his head trying to grab hold of his senses. "You crazy bitch."

"Oh, now you're calling me names? You cheat on me; you bring this harlot home to our house and you call me a crazy bitch? I don't know how they do things in your neck of the woods, but where I'm from we cut that neck in two!" She stood and pushed Danny onto the couch. Looking over him, she muttered, "I guess that's going to be your fate. And to think we were going to have a baby! I can't stand you anymore. The honeymoon is over." She began crying. "I guess these weren't good enough for you? She opened her shirt and exposed her bra, the cut off hands of one of her victims stuffed inside. "I did this for you! That filthy man Hamilton wanted to touch my breasts. She looked around and found a bag, "This man here!" she reached inside and pulled Hamilton's head out, his tongue dangling from the mouth. She French kissed the head. "You like it when you see me with another man? Huh? Do you?" she bent over Danny as he ingested slow steady breaths, trying to gather his faculties.

Danny tried to maintain focus. "I have a question for you."

"For me?" she seethed. "What could you possibly want to ask me?"

"Did you kill my friends?"

"That old man tried to make love to me, and his wife watched."

Danny's head may have spun but he knew that was her delusion. He laughed.

"You think it's funny? Someone tries to rape your wife and you laugh?" She picked up an ax, Danny's fireplace wood ax, and carried it over to the couch. "Why you good for nothing man, we need to get Daddy out of you!" She raised the ax and brought it down, but Danny had worked enough reality into his head to reach up and catch the handle. With one arm he yanked at the ax and with the other he shoved her hard in the chest. She fell back and released the ax. She landed on the hearth and reached for the syringe. Danny slapped the blade of the ax down and severed her hand from her wrist.

Blood exploded from the stump, and she shrieked. "I will kill you; I will kill you." She raised her arms and lunged.

He stumbled sideways and pushed her to the ground. She reached for the gun but there was no hand on the arm she reached with, still, she kept trying, a look of bewilderment on her face as she tried over and over, the tendons strung out the end of her arm, just streamers slapping against the hard wood floor like crimson wet strings.

"This is for my friends." He gripped the ax and used 300 pounds of farmer to bring it down onto the attorney's neck with the force of a freight train. Her head fell to the ground, beautiful snow-white hair, a paint brush dabbing up the crimson as it tumbled to a stop.

It was over.

Chapter 36

Lyle ran for the door but couldn't believe what he saw through another window as he came around the corner of the porch. From that angle, he saw his sister, lovely Lauren, his twin, the girl he promised he would watch over forever, fall to the ground and her head separated from her body. He stopped; his tears were real. All the years he held her, stopped the moments from haunting her, ended. How could a man who didn't even know her treat her so cruel? Lyle stepped off the porch and ran for the road. When he made it to his car, he called his sister's cell phone. He hoped the farmer would answer. He did.

He said, "Who is this?"

Lyle answered, "You have my sister."

"Tough shit, you have my friend's body."

Lyle tried to reason. "I didn't do anything to anyone."

"Oh really, but you happen to know I have your sister. I bet you even know what shapes she's in."

"I want her back and I will leave you alone."

"I'll tell you what, I'll give her a better burial than you two gave my friends."

Lyle grew angrier. "I didn't do anything to your friends. My sister was sick, she's been sick for a long time."

"And you were aware of that and did nothing?"

"I did my best to keep her from hurting anyone." Lyle panted from running.

"Well, you did a shitty job." The farmer calmly asked, "You want her cremated or buried?"

"I swear to God if you don't give my sister back, you will regret the day you met me."

"Too late, I already do."

The phone went dead. Lyle called back but the farmer didn't answer. He watched as he saw him step out onto the porch. He must have seen the dogs because Lyle's phone rang. "I see you want to talk now?"

"You must be nearby. I see you killed my dogs."

"You should have let my sister go." Lyle only wanted his sister back. He wanted to grieve for a life confused, a woman who never knew who she was.

"Letting your sister go wasn't an option. We didn't have her, she had us."

Lyle apologized. "Mister, I'm sorry, I truly am. Can I please come take her home?"

The voice on the other end sighed. "Your sister is home. I'll make sure she doesn't get paraded through the streets; I'll give her a good place to rest her bones."

"Give me my sister!"

"I'm getting my gun and coming back outside. I'll be carrying a rifle that shoots a hundred yards without dropping more than a foot. I'm an excellent shot, so I'd be gone by the time I get back. Unless you want to join your sister?"

The phone went dead a second time and Lyle decided to regroup and come back the next day. He drove south down Swaheenie and through town, vans with numbers and satellites dotted the street like fairground roadies. He passed them looking like a reporter finding a story. He drove out the valley and worked his way down I-5, intermittently crying and cursing. "How could that bastard kill her? He could have let her go. He was so big; she couldn't hurt him." He wept and screamed, "Sissssssterrrrrr! God, why?"

By the time he hit Corvallis, his tears had dried and his anger exhausted to numbness. His head pounded with the reality life somehow crashed around him. He felt a weak joy when he rounded the corner of Cindy's mom's house. It neared midnight; a light rain owned the better half of his trip. Lyle made it to the front entrance and tapped lightly. Cindy came to the door and peered over his shoulder. "I thought you would have your sister with you?"

"It's a long story."

She reached out and pulled him in, pulled him to her and held him tight. She whispered, "You want to talk about it?"

He wanted to but knew he couldn't. This secret would explode in the next few days, but for now he wanted to pretend it didn't exist. Lyle could see the life Cindy promised wasn't one he would ever enjoy. "I have to go get her tomorrow."

They walked in and sat on the couch. "You want me to go with you?"

Lyle smiled. "No, I should go alone. The man she's with isn't very nice. He's treated her pretty badly and I think it would be best if I just quietly picked her up and took care of the disaster."

"That bad, huh?"

"Worse."

"Well, if it makes you feel better, Mom said for the first time she didn't feel sick."

Lyle smiled; that consolation felt better than nothing. "Well, that wouldn't be my drugs. That would be her going off the hospital's." He added, "But she will start to feel better each day."

Cindy kissed Lyle, first on the forehead, then the cheek, then passionately on the lips. Lyle felt guilty feeling so good. He kissed her back. They embraced and rolled from the couch onto the carpet. Lyle escaped his life and worked Cindy's sweater off as she unhooked his belt. They were quiet, they were involved, they entwined in love making through the night. She helped him leave the real world, if but for a brief moment, all he thought about was this raven-haired runner from Portland, so attractive in a way not like Lauren.

Cindy whispered, "I think we should take this to the bedroom. It's getting cold out here. Their chests pinned against each other.

The glow of a streetlamp shined on her face, and he smiled. "I'm glad you suggested it."

She whispered again, "I suggested it because you are shivering!" She laughed, "Shhh." She laughed harder. They stood, and together they tracked down all the clothing strewn across the family room floor. She giggled. "Did you see my underwear?"

He rifled through the stack he had and pulled them out. "Here."

She kissed him as they moved to the bedroom. "Thanks."

They crawled under the sheets and made love again. Lyle didn't want the night to end because he knew the next day was a day he might not like. He kissed Cindy and he held her tight. "Thank you."

They fell asleep to the sound of an increasing rainstorm, and another storm on the horizon.

Chapter 37

Danny sat there dazed. Sickness engulfed him like he drank too much. Karen lie face up, her arms out. He staggered over to her. He thought he could see her breathing. She wasn't bleeding. He dropped to a knee and put his hand onto her chest. Her vest was on. "Hallelujah, you're alive, darling." She slept off the drug the attorney had given her. He hoisted her up in his arms and carried her to his room and laid her down on his bed. "I'll be back to check up on you after I clean up the mess." He pulled on a pair of pants and a top.

Danny heard something ringing. He walked down the hall and realized something rang in the guest room. He opened the door and found a bag, inside a phone. Danny answered it. "Who is this?"

A voice said, "You have my sister."

Danny didn't care. "Tough shit, you have my friend's body."

"I didn't do anything to anyone."

Danny didn't believe him, that geeky little shit was just like his sister. "Oh really, but you happen to know I have your sister. I bet you even know what shapes she's in."

"I want her back, and I will leave you alone."

Danny offered. "I'll tell you what, I'll give her a better burial than you two gave my friends."

The voice shouted, "I didn't do anything to your friends. My sister was sick, she's been sick for a long time."

Danny had no sympathy. "And you were aware of that and did nothing?"

"I did my best to keep her from hurting anyone."

"Well, you did a shitty job." He calmed. "You want her cremated or buried?"

"I swear to God if you don't give my sister back, you will regret the day you met me."

"Too late, I already do." Danny disconnected the phone. The phone rang again, and Danny let it go.

He walked through the rooms, looking out windows with care. In the yard, he saw the spaniels and ran outside, reckless of who might be there, unafraid, his two guardians lying dead on the ground; their eyes open as though they'd seen a ghost. "Fuck me." Danny hit redial.

"I see you want to talk now?"

"You must be nearby. I see you killed my dogs." Danny felt rage. Why the dogs? They were just stupid animals that didn't hurt anyone.

"You should have let my sister go."

Danny tried to make her brother understand. "Letting your sister go wasn't an option. We didn't have her, she had us."

"Mister, I'm sorry, I truly am. Can I please come take her home?"

Danny sighed. "Your sister is home. I'll make sure she doesn't get paraded through the streets; I'll give her a good place to rest her bones."

"Give me my sister!"

Danny went in and retrieved his rifle. "I'm getting my gun and coming back outside. I'll be carrying a rifle that shoots a hundred yards without dropping more than a foot. I'm an excellent shot, so I'd be gone by the time I get out there. Unless you want to join your sister."

Danny marched out the house, the fresh air, cleaning up his system, his senses coming back to him. Whoever was out there hopefully heeded his warning. He picked up the boy, still warm, and placed him comfortably on a cushioned bench on the porch. He did the same for the girl. She was his favorite, the boss. "Sorry I didn't let you two in the house." He shed a tear; he shed a tear over two dumb animals.

Danny gritted his teeth. This wasn't over. He needed to bait that brother into coming back.

Give her back?

Hardly. In fact, no one would even know she was dead. Not even Karen. He grabbed his keys and jumped in the truck. In the barn, Danny's dad taught him to make cattle crates for discarding bones before they went to the glue factory. They were quite a bit larger than a casket; something Danny always thought would be perfect, with his size, to be buried in. He slid one out to the front of the barn and hooked the backhoe up to the tractor. He placed the crate into the bucket and drove over to the house. He went in and gathered up the pieces of the attorney. "Lauren, huh? I'm flattered you wanted to marry me, but I don't do bat shit crazy very well, and you my dear, were out there." He tossed the body over his shoulder and held her head by the hair. He tossed it in the crate and went back for the hand and her purse. He left the other head and hands behind. Karen would need those. "Damn woman, what do you have in this purse?" He took a brief look, besides a second hand gun she had just about everything a woman needs to survive, from food to toilet paper. He tossed her belongings in as well.

He continued on his way, driving out behind the house, to the dense brush and forest he left as a wall between him and the farm to the south. When he reached a fair middle of the woods, he stopped and found a clearing large enough to backhoe a hole with enough depth and width to fit the crate. When he finished, he yanked the crate off the bucket and laid it down in the hole. Plenty deep enough, the lid would be three, maybe four feet down. He buried the box and even said a few words on her behalf. "You tormented bitch, may you rot in hell." His watch rounded over to eleven p.m. He wondered if the detective had awoken yet. He took the tractor back to the barn and hosed it down.

By midnight, he safely made it back to the house. He checked in on the detective. When he bent down to get a look, she opened her eyes. "We're alive!"

"Yep."

She coughed. "I don't know what hurts worse, my head or my chest."

"You took a .9mm at close range. Thank that jacket."

She reached up and rubbed her chest. "Where's the vest?"

"I took it off, I needed to see how bad the bruising was."

The shot was mid cleavage. "You saw the bruise."

Danny smiled. "Yeah, nice bruise by the way."

She sat up. "What happened to the crazy blonde bitch?"

Danny frowned. "She got away."

"How?"

"Hello, I was able to take the gun away, but I was pretty drugged up too. I started waving the gun, and she ran out the front door."

"So you saved my life. Wasn't I supposed to save yours?"

"You kind of did. She wasted most of that drug on you."

Karen sat up. "We need to get dogs out here; we can track her."

Danny didn't like that idea at all. "She hopped in a car, someone picked her up. They drove north over the old logging road."

"How long ago?"

"Five hours ago,"

"Did you call anyone?"

"John, but his phone went to answering machine." He helped her up. "Don't worry, they'll be caught; they are long gone, they aren't coming back here."

Karen scowled. "I want this collar, this is personal." She started to walk but her legs gave out.

Danny caught her and wrapped his arm around her.

"Thank you again." She grinned. "Do I recall you being buck naked when you came into the front room?"

"Nothing gets past a drugged-up detective."

She smiled, "No nothing…"

"Huh um, let's get some food in you."

They walked past the gunny sack the attorney had carried. "What's in there?"

"Your John Doe's head and hands."

She peeked inside, flinched slightly, and then shook her head. "You got a drink?"

"Whiskey."

"That'd do nicely."

They sat up for a few hours; Danny mentioned the spaniels, and Karen told him she was sorry. They commiserated; they entertained each other with a few crude laughs. By two they knew morning comes early and Danny gave her the guest room, and he went to his. About an hour went by when a scream woke him. He jumped out of bed and grabbed a rifle. He turned on the hall light and heard the scream again. It came from Karen. He didn't dare enter or he might get shot. He hollered, "You all right?"

She yelled back, "Yeah."

She came to the door and her face dripped with sweat. "Can I sleep in the same room with you?"

"Excuse me?"

"Bad dreams. I don't know if it's the drugs or getting shot in the chest, but I don't want to be alone."

Danny frowned. "I thought you were a bad ass cop?"

She smiled. "Not tonight."

Danny brought her into his room, tucked her in and he slept on top of the covers next to her. When he woke the next morning, she had her arm over his stomach and her chest snug against his.

Chapter 38

When Lyle woke the next morning, Cindy's had her arm across his stomach and her chest snug against his. He'd slept restlessly and wanted to make it back for his sister. It had nothing to do with right or wrong, it was about duty, loyalty, and his promise. He needed to bring her home.

Cindy stirred. Her eyes opened and she whispered. "You looked concerned."

He shifted his weight and rolled into her, face to face, he confided, "Things aren't good."

Cindy propped her head up with her arm. "What kind of not good?"

"My sister's done some bad things." He sighed. He had to remove this from his mind, even if Cindy didn't forgive him, he couldn't have her learn this from someone else. This would make it on every news station in the Pacific Northwest.

Cindy hesitated, her stare penetrated Lyle. "What has she done?" Lyle stiffened. "Has she hurt someone?" Lyle drifted off into his own world. "Lyle?"

Lyle started slowly, "My sister is a troubled woman. She's pretty, she's smart, she's everything a guy would want in a woman except for one small detail."

Cindy gained Lyle's attention, staring eye to eye. "And that would be?"

"She's psychotic."

Cindy started to laugh but suppressed it. "You're serious."

"Very."

"What kind of psychotic."

"The kind that boils over every once in a while."

She leaned into Lyle. "Is that the reason you don't want to bring her here?"

Lyle closed his eyes, visualizing the image of her dismembered body. "No, it's deeper than that."

Cindy put her hand to her chest. "Does it have something to do with the wine bottle she sent to me?"

Lyle sighed. "You're not gathering what I'm telling you. My sister is about to be front page news."

"Is she dead?"

"Yeah."

Cindy put her hand to her mouth. "Please tell me you didn't have anything to do with it?"

Lyle shook his head. "Of course not."

"Did the guy she's with do it?"

He nodded. "But it's not his fault."

Cindy sat up in the bed, the sheet falling to her waist, comfortable sitting before him bare-chested. "I don't understand."

"My sister is going to be front page news, not because she's dead but because she went on a killing spree."

Speechless, Cindy held a hand over her mouth.

"I told you I had a lot on my mind."

She reached out. "What are you going to do?"

Lyle took a deep breath. "Well, I'm going to get up and draw some blood from your mother and label it."

"We have to do that too?" Cindy cringed.

"Just a couple of times. We will know the progression immediately. The white blood cell count will change within the first couple of injections." He inhaled, pulled the sheet back, rolled away and stood. "Shower?"

She grinned. "Are you asking me where it is, or if I want to take one with you?"

"Where it is, but please do join me." Lyle lost his inhibitions.

Cindy crawled out of bed and took his hand. She peeked out the door and put her finger to her lips. They tiptoed across the hall and into the bathroom.

Lyle held Cindy tight as they lost themselves in a warm shower, resting on each other; Lyle sure their time together came to an end. He could have stayed a lifetime in that shower, but duty called. They exited and dressed in silence.

When they prepped Doris, Lyle gave Cindy another lesson, this time he had Doris lie on her back, and he found a spot in the muscle where he could run the needle through. It went much farther in, farther because the Pancreas was farther away. Doris groaned in a low moaning sob. "Unbelievable," she huffed as it went in. "I didn't think it was possible to hurt worse than yesterday's shot."

Lyle bent down and whispered, "Just hang in there."

She insisted, "You better save my damn life after these things."

Lyle worked in silence. He rolled Doris over and wrapped a rubber tourniquet on her arm. He slid the needle into the crux of her arm and hit the vein. He extracted blood into a blood tube and pulled the needle. He labeled the first tube #1. "Tonight, when I get back, I will bring some equipment to get a reading. In the meantime, keep this refrigerated."

Cindy took the tube and headed for the kitchen. Doris spoke up, "I don't know whether to thank you or punch you." She sighed. "Do these shots get easier?"

"Not really. The more you get the more you realize they're coming." He admitted. "The first ones are always the easiest. You don't believe it's going to hurt that much."

She frowned. "Thanks for cheering me up."

Lyle offered, "Well look at the bright side. In six months, you're going to be the talk of the community."

"Do I have to take these shots every day?"

He smiled. "Nope. You have to take four in the first four days, and then one a week for the next twenty-two weeks.

"When will I feel like I'm improving?"

Lyle sat next to her bed. "You'll start feeling better much quicker than you will be better. It's vitally important that you don't skip or stop the treatments. Promise me you'll take them right up to the end, no matter how great you feel."

She said, "As much as it pains me, I promise."

Lyle patted her arm and stood to leave.

"My daughter likes you; I can see it. She has always been attracted to intelligent men."

He paused. "I like her too." Lyle realized the story of his life amounted to being in the wrong place at the wrong time. "I like her too." He left the room so Doris could rest.

His phone rang.

Who now?

He studied the number; it was his sister's phone. He stepped into the bathroom and answered, "Hello?"

The farmer spoke. "I still have your sister. I'm not turning her over until tomorrow."

Lyle felt the game. "Do I get her?"

"Only if you can take her."

"I'll be there."

The farmer hung up after saying, "I hoped you would."

Lyle lost his temper, but the line went dead. "You asshole." He looked in the mirror and attempted to calm himself. "Keep it together, Lyle." He pushed a strand of hair back over his head and checked his anger. He stepped into the hall and listened for Cindy.

He walked into the kitchen.

Cindy made breakfast and offered, "I don't have to work until tomorrow night. You can take my car again."

Lyle gave a somber nod. "Thanks."

"Thinking about your sister?"

"Constantly." He came up behind her and stole a piece of bacon from the counter.

She playfully slapped his hand. "You want me to go with you?"

Lyle shook his head. "You're kidding."

"I'll go if you want."

"No. I don't want you to go." He lied about the possible situation. "There'll be reporters and police, and I'm going to have a lot of explaining to do."

"You have nothing to be worried about, you didn't do anything."

Lyle minimized his involvement. "But I knew who she was and I didn't stop her."

"You didn't murder anyone."

Lyle may not have murdered anyone, but he covered all of them up, he gave his sister the opportunity to continue, and her upbringing was as much his responsibility as it was his parents'. He shrugged. "Keep your mother off the television. I would really like to not have her know about this too soon. Just what I don't need is her thinking mad scientist and Frankenstein's sister."

"Even if she saw the news, she wouldn't put two and two together."

Lyle laughed. First off, I'm sure I'll be mentioned, second, if you saw my sister, you would put two and two together. We share many of the same features." Lyle pinched a white eyebrow.

"Lyle, maybe you shouldn't go."

Lyle wanted to agree, but that farmer wasn't getting the best of him, he wasn't getting his sister.

Chapter 39

Danny rose from bed and made coffee. It was early for a detective but late for a farmer. He figured he'd get started on burying the spaniels. He'd nearly forgotten Detective Zimmerman mentioned growing up on a farm until she made her way out to the table at six thirty and sat. "You normally get four hours of sleep, Mr. Gates."

He frowned. "Mr. Gates?"

She smiled. "Danny boy?"

He slid a cup to her and poured coffee into it. "That beats being called my father."

She spoke to herself. "I need to get forensics out here. This is going to be a zoo."

Danny requested, "Can they possibly not spend all damn day here?" He stared at her. "Get them in, make them leave."

"This is a crime scene, Dan."

"I don't give a shit. The attorney bailed on out of here, that's where everyone needs to be, searching for her and her accomplice."

She stared. "You think it's her brother?"

"Nope."

His ideas drew her attention. "Why not?"

"Gut feeling."

"That's the reason you don't think it was him, gut feeling?"

Danny nodded. "Yep."

"So you think if we saw him today, we should just let him know his sister is on the loose and wave to him."

"I reckon that's what I'm saying."

She smiled. "And if he came here, you'd point him up the hill and tell him, 'look over there' and not worry about him? Because you don't know where she is?"

"Yep."

"Interesting." She sipped on her coffee. "You know, if my second parents were brutally murdered and I suspected someone, I might bait them to come back."

"You lost two members of your team. The same could be said for you."

"Damn straight, and that's exactly how I feel."

Danny raised his eyebrows. "Then maybe you should appeal to her on television, maybe tell her she didn't finish the job and that she should come back to see you."

She stared at Danny. "You think she'd do it?"

"Maybe."

"Better yet, you think she's capable of doing it?"

"What are you driving at Detective?"

"Well, the fact that we're alive, which I thank you for, means she didn't get what she came for, and I might have been pretty drugged up, but what I saw was a woman who was killing us or would die trying." She looked hard at Danny. "And I'm sitting here sure as shit, alive and breathing, and so are you."

Danny nodded his head and drank his coffee.

"So, if I drain those two pits, I won't find her in there will I?"

"That would be a pointless endeavor."

She winked. "I agree." She stood from the table. "Nonetheless, I'd like to keep the security detail for another day or two."

Danny bristled. "Do what you must." He needed to keep her and her team away from the back woods. His grave digging left an obvious mound out there and even covered with all the brush in the world, it wasn't fooling anyone. "I need to bury the dogs. Gonna take em' under the oak and lay them down.

She inquired, "Where's the head and hands?"

He motioned to the refrigerator. "In the freezer."

She pointed her finger. "That's a food freezer. That doesn't unnerve you?"

He expressed little concern. "Where else would you like me to keep it?"

"What about your meat freezer in the barn?"

"I wasn't going out there at two in the morning." He reasoned. "It's in a bag, besides, I haven't heard a peep out of him all morning, so he isn't complaining."

She laughed. "I'm sorry," she winked. "That was so wrong."

Danny laughed back. "But it was funny." They touched their cups and saluted.

They had a second cup and then a third, followed by a fourth. Danny asked if she shouldn't get the show started and get her forensic group out there for 'Johnny Headroom' in the freezer but she said it could wait. They both enjoyed each other's company. He feared it wouldn't last if she did her job well. Sooner or later, when the attorney didn't appear somewhere, they would come back and inspect the pits and even though they wouldn't find her, he would have a lot of explaining to do. Last time he checked, the law didn't hold too kindly to vigilantism.

Karen excused herself. "It's been a day, a shooting, and a nervous night. Would it be okay to take a shower?"

"Sure, towels are in the bottom drawer."

She smiled. "Thanks."

Danny marveled at her build; she had a callipygian shape. Take the vest off and she had a solid but not heavy frame—a shapely farm girl. When she left, he pulled the attorney's phone out and redialed the last number.

Lauren's brother answered, "Hello?"

Danny said with a cold bite, "I still have your sister. I'm not turning her over until tomorrow."

Her brother sounded nervous. "Do I get her?"

Danny manipulated him. "Only if you can take her."

"I'll be there."

Satisfied, Danny said, "I hoped you would," and pushed the phone off. He might not be able to dish up Lauren for Karen to get her revenge, but he could give her the next best thing.

Karen hurried into the kitchen, her blouse covered a braless bosom, and the tails of the material hung down over bare legs. "Did you hear that?" She carried her pants. She heard something again, "That?"

Danny paid attention. He heard a thump. "I heard that!"

Karen sat and threw her pants on. It sounds like a dog."

They made it to the front room and Danny opened the door. The boy had fallen off the love seat; his head rocked like a bobble head.

Karen wept. "He's alive."

Danny went over to Trudy. Her tongue hung out and she panted. "She's alive too." Danny looked up. "How is that possible? They didn't have a heartbeat."

Karen pulled a small flashlight from her utility belt and shined it in Wilbur's eyes. "Apparently they did have a heartbeat, slow but a heartbeat." She rubbed the dog on the nose. "Whoever did this used a high-profile drug. This isn't dime store stuff. This is a paralytic."

They each picked a dog up and carried them inside.

Karen insisted. "I need to call in the team." She looked at Danny. "I'll get them in and out, and I'll get a vet in here too."

Danny eased up. "Thanks." He shook his head. "In and out."

"Don't worry, I can make that happen."

Danny winked. "Good."

Karen stared back. "Something tells me it will be good."

Chapter 40

Lyle left the house on a mission. Before he drove off, he inspected his bag. He had plenty of poison cartridges. If the farmer still had Lauren, who was the dead woman on the floor and how was the farmer going to keep that a secret? Lyle considered his opponent. The farmer had size on his side and the only advantage Lyle had was that he was smarter, a lot smarter. Even with the farmer knowing he would arrive, even though the game took place on the farmer's property, Lyle guessed he could still have the element of surprise.

Lyle pulled up maps on his phone and zoomed in on the property. He could see on the southeast side, a set of woods stood between the farmer's property and the next farmhouse. If he could make it to that land, he could hide out in the dense trees. The main road ran on the other side, the farmer would be waiting for him there.

Lyle drove up I-5 and found a hunting store. Big screens carried the news and a story crackled with reports of multiple homicides in Dirtwater, Washington. Lyle found it curious that no one mentioned anything about his sister. The farmer stayed true to his word, because had he given that body up, they would have splashed Lauren's name across the screen as the Lizzy Borden of the next century. None of the faces of the deceased showed Lauren, and they didn't list her as a person of interest. Curious, there wasn't a woman other than the old lady. The woman on the floor wasn't among the dead, and they hadn't tied Lauren to Ms. Newberry yet.

"Can I help you?"

Lyle pulled away from the screen long enough to answer the clerk. "Yeah, you have rubber shoes?"

The young man laughed. "We are a hunting store in Oregon; of course we have duck shoes.

"Duck shoes?"

"That's what they're called. Right this way." He took Lyle to a section of boots that had a leather rise with rubber from the ankle on down.

"Perfect. How about camouflage gear?"

The guy spotted Lyle wasn't a hunter. Lyle's questions made that obvious. "Right this way." He led Lyle to the clothing section.

Lyle pulled clothes that would conceal him, make him look like the nature he walked through. When he finished, if he hurried, he could get to Dirtwater around noon. Lyle could see from the map, he needed to travel on a road even more primitive than the one he traveled on the night before. He found a car rental store right past Portland, across the river in Vancouver, and stopped. He parked Cindy's sedan and rented a rugged four-wheel-drive SUV. He rumbled onto the freeway and hurried to the Dirtwater exit.

Twenty miles in, he located the abysmal logging road that skirted a cliff, his destination around that hill. He turned onto the no trespassing road and headed up. Still before noon, and his plan remained ahead of schedule. Even better, the rains in Oregon hadn't penetrated Washington and he didn't fight mud. His road provided less trouble than he expected. When he reached the summit, he found a western slope that ran down into the valley the farmer lived in. From his vantage point, Lyle could see the farmhouse miles away. If he stayed on the logging road, he could get within a half mile of the forest behind his house. It may not have rained but the valley glistened with moisture, damp, saturated fields of puddles. When Lyle traveled as far as he could go, he parked the SUV, hoping it'd be there when he returned and not swept off the road by a logging truck. It was his only option. Lyle traded his clothes for camouflage gear, strapped on the boots, and pulled his backpack from the seat. Armed with a shovel to bury the farmer, Lyle headed to make his first kill, to avenge his sister from the man who killed her; right or wrong, this was about family.

He should have asked for a brush whacker. He had no idea some of the brush would be so heavy. He swung the shovel like an ax to lop some off the dense growth. He high stepped and jumped when he could and followed a shallow creek for part of the way, wet up to his knees. When he reached the property line, he had to negotiate an old barbed-wire fence and leaning wooden posts covered in lichen.

Farmers, what a crappy life.

Lyle made his way into the farmer's forest, working his way to a closer view. He took his binoculars out and noticed a bevy of activity, police cars, news vehicles, ants on an anthill, every one of them. He shook his head, that lousy ass hadn't kept his word. They swarmed his house, ecstatic they had stopped the hundred-pound troubled woman. Lyle hoped they were proud of themselves. He bowed his head and cried. He sat there and wept, sitting on a dirt mound, hoping they at least would give her a decent burial. Who was he kidding, she would be cremated; her crimes too gruesome; she couldn't have a grave without it being desecrated. It was over. He turned to leave, walked a few paces and spun back around.

Fresh dirt.

He pulled his phone out and hit redial. "Come on, don't let me down."

"Are you here?"

Lyle lied. "Not yet, do you have my sister?"

"I do."

"I don't know. I'm watching the news and I see a lot of cars at your farmhouse."

"They're not here for her body. I said she ran off. They are taking the head your sister brought with her. Is he a friend of yours?"

Lyle guessed the head belonged to Hamilton. "Didn't know him."

"She's safely buried. You show up and we can discuss it."

"Oh I'm sure. Trust me, I'll be there. But I hope you are alone."

"Don't worry about it." The phone went dead.

Lyle hated that the farmer always had the last word.

Damn him.

He turned to the sky as though thanking God for a prayer answered. He threw his shovel into the soft packed dirt and started digging. Two o'clock, three o'clock, halfway to four and Lyle hit wood. He had blistered hands and a soiled face. He'd reached the lid. "What do we have in here?" He wiped away the dirt, made the lid accessible. In his tool kit he had a hammer. He worked the claw between the lid and box, cranked on it and popped nails down the row until he could wedge it open. Inside, his sister lay haphazardly strewn about the box. Lyle wept. He stepped in and pulled her body close to him and hugged her torso. "I'm so sorry I wasn't there for you." He picked up her head and stroked her beautiful blonde hair. Her face looked tortured. He held her cheek to cheek. "Goodbye, sister." He rearranged her so she was anatomical. He placed her bag next to her head to keep her from rolling away. She looked whole, she looked settled. "All right farmer, you picked her grave, now I'm going to pick yours." He could have gathered her up, he should have gathered her up, but this was personal. He left the box open; he would let the farmer spend eternity with his sister.

Chapter 41

The official cars started arriving around ten and Danny felt nervous, like unwelcomed relatives inviting themselves over for the holidays. The lone visitor he appreciated was a veterinarian from Huggins, Dr. Parrish. When you live in a farming community, a vet is an important professional, and he and his partner, Dr. Larzarz, were like gods. Dr. Parrish took care of everyone's dogs and Dr. Larzarz, everyone's cows.

"Mornin' Daniel." Dr. Parrish raised his head and peeked over the rim of his glasses at the big farmer. "You're looking especially tall today."

Danny joked, "Tall enough to touch the ground."

As he passed Danny to see the dogs, he cited, "Lincoln."

Danny followed behind and worried. "They're starting to move, but they seem real stiff."

The doctor grabbed Trudy's leg and squeezed it. "Muscles are constricted."

"Are they going to be okay?"

He turned and shrugged. "Don't know. Let's draw some blood and find out what they've been hit with." He sat a bag on the table and pulled out a syringe. "This Jack and Pat's spaniels?"

"Yeah."

"Where's the other one?" He rolled Trudy to her back and found a vein in the soft skin just behind the knee.

"She bolted out the door the day when I found Jack and Pat."

"Hmmm, hope the coyotes didn't get her."

Danny watched, unsure why he felt so protective over two dogs he didn't care about a few days before, whom now he would give anything to see jump up and wag the nubs at the end of their butts. "Can you help them?"

"Dan, I just drew blood. You think I now know what they were poisoned with?"

Danny's impatience grew. "Sorry."

Dr. Parrish opened up a kit with several chambers in it, each with clear fluid in them. He put drops of blood in to each one, a total of twenty fluid filled chambers. He capped them and started shaking it. Danny watched as two of them turned colors, one a pink and one a light blue. The rest stayed clear. "What does that mean?" Danny stepped closer and bent down to take a better look.

Dr. Parrish pointed to the blue chamber; this is a fast-acting sleeping agent. The dogs probably dropped inside of ten seconds from this one."

"And the pink one?" Danny stared at the doctor.

"This one is a paralytic. Probably something derived from shellfish."

"What does that mean?" Danny remained attentive.

"Well, it didn't kill them, and they are slowly recovering. I have antidotes at the office. I'm going to pack them up, get them IVs and start them on a regimen. Two, three days, they will be good as new."

Danny beamed. "Really?"

The doctor smiled. "Really."

Danny grabbed Doctor Parrish's hand and mauled him with a hearty hug. "Detective Zimmerman, you hear that? They're gonna' make it."

Detective Zimmerman shared her time with canvassing the approaching cars and taking in what the doctor said. "Fantastic news."

Doctor Parrish stood and reminded Danny, "I'm an old man and I'm not carrying these dogs out to the car. Maybe you and one of those police officers walking around this house can help?" He stared at Danny.

Danny waved off a young man willing to help. "I'll take them both. They are alert and know who I am. I want them to feel comfortable." He nodded to Karen. "Can you sit with Trudy while I take Wilbur?"

She came and replaced his position as he carefully picked Wilbur up. He nestled into the dog's neck and whispered, "We'll get you fixed up, boy." Wilbur's eyes scanned the room, and he moved his legs slowly. "Just relax; you did a great job last night."

When he returned, he swept Trudy up and found himself with a tear in his eye. She whimpered in pain. "You'll be okay, I'll come get you in a couple of days, I promise."

Karen followed behind, and as Danny put Trudy in the vet's dog holder, the vet said, "Whoever did this was a pro."

Karen stared at the twitching dog. "What do you mean?" These shots were meant for the dogs. Human doses would have killed them. This wasn't meant to kill."

Danny didn't care, he knew who did this, and this was unacceptable. "Maybe, but disabling the dogs meant something more grave."

The vet nodded. "Yeah, no dog, no burglar alarm."

Danny watched as the vet drove down Swaheenie road. Danny waved as though the dogs could see him. He turned and his front area teemed with cars. News vehicles had caught wind of the activity and they lined Swaheenie. Danny whispered to Karen, "You promised, in and out."

"Don't worry, I have it taken care of."

The forensic team scoured the house, every room the attorney had put a foot in they picked over; they scrutinized the freezer for any hairs that might have fallen off the corpse's head.

One of the team said, "This area around the fireplace looks like it was cleaned up. Mr. Gates, you didn't wipe away any evidence, any blood, did you?"

Karen intervened. "I was here and of course he didn't. Did you, Dan?" She smiled.

"No, of course not."

They stayed insufferably long. Noon became one and Danny feared the attorney's brother wouldn't come. He wanted that son of bitch to come. He knew that attorney didn't cart off Pat's body, and he doubted she killed all those people by herself. Danny wanted the accomplice. Karen pulled Danny aside. "There's quite a shine on the wooden floor."

Danny played it off. "Where?"

She tilted her head to the area by the fireplace. "I don't remember it being that clean."

"I'm a clean guy."

"Yes you are. I just don't remember it that clean." She winked as though she helped hide something. What exactly did she suspect?

Detective Zimmerman stepped out to address the media. Whatever she said, several members hurried out as though the action took place somewhere else. Danny milled about the house, stayed out of the way, but kept an interest in the activity. When his phone rang, he looked at the caller—the attorney's brother. He stepped outside and responded with cold anger. "Are you here?"

"Not yet, do you have my sister?"

"I do." Danny's bated breath deadpanned.

"I don't know. I'm watching the news and I see a lot of cars at your farmhouse."

Danny offered, "They're not here for her body. I said she ran off. They are taking the head your sister brought with her. Is he a friend of yours?"

"Didn't know him."

Danny admitted, "She's safely buried. You show up and we can discuss it."

The attorney's brother snapped. "Oh I'm sure. Trust me, I'll be there, but I hope you are alone."

"Don't worry about it." Danny disconnected. He hoped the nit wit had more to say and that it steamed him being hung up on.

He stood on the back porch alone, waiting for the parade to die down, die down so he could get on with his meeting.

Karen came around the corner. "Here you are. The forensic team is ready to go. The other detectives want to know about what you saw last night when the attorney 'left.'"

Danny followed her back in and gave an account of how she hurried out of there with an unknown accomplice. Karen backed up Danny and before the hour ended, the team had packed up and left the scene. With a few news reporters still hovering about, Karen asked Sheriff Scott, who'd been quiet the entire afternoon, to assist her in shooing away the last of the stragglers.

By four, only Detective Zimmerman and Danny remained.

Chapter 42

Lyle watched as, one by one, cars left the scene of the farmhouse. When five o'clock rolled around and the sun hung low in the sky, the sheriff's car pulled out and left the farmer's truck and one black official looking vehicle, the same black vehicle from the night before. Lyle saw the body on the ground. Were the authorities there for her? Had his sister killed someone in that house, and if so, why wasn't that one of the victims he saw on the screen? It was a woman, of that he was sure. Nightfall approached and Lyle's plan neared. He loaded his dart gun, enough paralytic drugs to stop the farmer in a living coma-like-state, long enough to bury him with his sister. He worked his way toward the farm when he saw a second figure, a woman. Apparently, his sister didn't kill her. He pulled his binoculars out and looked closely. She was bulky. He focused the lens. She wore a vest. "So that's why you didn't die. I apologize for my sister; she's a bit crazy toward other women." He smiled. "Who am I kidding, she's crazy toward men too." Lyle had to change his plans. He looked in his backpack. He had dozens of syringes. He started loading each one with tetrodotoxin. He had a ball of kite string and started tying each syringe with twelve-inch lengths. He hung them like model airplanes from branches leading into the forest, tying them off around six feet up. He put dozens hanging from tree branches along the trail, each one six feet up, and one he could grab if he needed to. Lyle crept his way to the farmhouse. He had a loaded cartridge in the chamber of his dart gun and a plan. He wasn't sure the plan would work but had a suspicion a man the farmer's size was of the belief weapons were not needed. The night covered over in a shroud of clouds, and the lack of city lights left the area as dark as lifeless dreams. Lyle stumbled over uneven ground, unable to see the earth below him. He turned around and noted a lone light from a farmhouse beyond the forest, nestled halfway up the ridge. He paid attention to the angle for the way back; it was to the right of that light. He checked his bag, made sure he had a working flashlight. When he made it to a woodpile, he found an ax and carried it with him. Close enough to smell the pleasant odor of beef cooking, the sounds of idle conversation, the warmth of radiating heat from a brick fireplace, he made a call. He could hear his sister's phone ring.

"I take it you're here?"

Lyle whispered, "Just about." He heard the table move in the kitchen, someone stirred. Lyle's heart raced. Whatever adrenaline rush his sister experienced, he didn't understand. He felt terror and conflict. He wanted to turn back. He could take his sister and leave. That's what he should have done. Was loyalty and family so important he could avenge the death of someone who had killed indiscriminately? He loved his sister; that was the point. That was always the point, the point that his father instilled in all the kids.

You don't turn your back on family. He found resolve and lifted the dart gun. He heard the screen from the front door creak open, he heard a voice.

"I don't see lights yet?"

It wasn't the farmer; it was the woman. He watched as she came into view, the lights of the porch giving him a view she didn't have. He heard a second set of steps on the porch, heavier, louder. In his line of sight, the farmer came into view. They stood twenty yards from him, the black of night camouflaging his position. So close he could hear their words.

"So you should turn off the lights." She told him. "I doubt he's coming here with his headlights on, and in this darkness, he will see us better than we see him."

The farmer agreed. "I'll shut em' off. Here take this." He handed her a flashlight. He walked away and she turned it on. She started to sweep the grounds and Lyle needed to act. He waited, waited for the farmer to disappear around the corner. As she swept the light in his direction, he fired a shot that caught the woman in the fleshy part of the thigh.

"Oh shit." She screamed, "Dan!"

The farmer made it back to her as she sat on the porch. "What is it?"

She had the dart in her hand. "Not again."

"How do you feel?"

"Not like last time, not as dizzy, but I sure feel sleepy."

Lyle rolled to his left and ducked behind the woodpile as the farmer grabbed the flashlight and shone it into the field. "I know you're out there. How about fighting like a man?"

Lyle shouted from behind the woodpile. "She's going to be out cold in about thirty seconds, maybe less."

He said something privately to her that Lyle couldn't hear. Lyle peeked over the pile, and they conversed until she went limp. "I'll be back for you, man to man." He picked her up and Lyle watched as he disappeared around the corner. He heard the screen open and close; then open again.

The farmer came back into the light carrying a knife in one hand and an ax in the other. He told Lyle, "There's an ax in that wood pile you are cowering behind. Why don't you find it?"

Lyle stood and shouted, "I already did." Lyle shined his flashlight on the farmer and the farmer shined his on Lyle. "Nice to see you again, Mr. Gates, wasn't it?"

The farmer nodded. "I don't recall your name and I doubt it's too important, seeing you aren't going to be using it too much longer."

"I'd worry about yourself."

The farmer laughed. "You are one brave little man. All this to get your sister?"

"No, not to get my sister, but to get revenge."

"I'm here, come and get it."

Lyle stepped out from the log pile and the farmer stepped off the porch, they were halfway to each other when Lyle took off running the other direction, toward the forest.

He could hear the farmer shout, "Really?" He looked back and the farmer followed in pursuit.

Chapter 43

Danny's heart raced, anger in his soul, as he bounded heavily over cold wet ground, farther out into the field, toward the man he found responsible. He neared, pushing branches out of the way, taking sharp hits from thickets and brush, breathing hard but determined, carrying his ax in one hand and knife in the other.

The attorney's brother stopped and turned, out of breath and holding his hand up for a truce. "You know you can't win?"

Danny carried the ax with ease, it was more of a hammer than an instrument the average man leveraged with all their might. He tucked it under his shoulder. "Really, and what makes you think so? I chased you out here—in the middle of my nowhere."

"You didn't chase me out here."

Danny tilted his head. "No?" Amused by the little man's bravado.

"You followed me out here."

"Well then!" Danny put his knife away and clutched the ax with both hands, holding it in case the brother had something waiting for him. "You look pretty scared for someone who led me out here."

"Scared? Not really," he caught his wind, "worried you would stop and go back, but not scared."

"Geez, I give you credit, you might be the boldest nitwit I have ever killed."

"I'm not your first?"

Danny looked up into the night sky, the moon had cracked the clouds and a glow beamed down upon him, the darkness had lifted. Sad to say, "No, mister, you are not my first, hopefully the last but not the first."

"I'm only sorry I didn't meet you sooner."

Danny stood over him. "Not a big lover of life, huh?" Danny tried to figure the guy out. Why come out here to die. He couldn't have loved a sister as awful as the attorney. All he could figure is this guy had to be worse.

"No, that's not it." He rolled over and sat on a log, looking up at Danny's face. "I just wish I had met you a long time ago so I could have stopped you sooner."

Danny held the ax and patted his chest with the flat side, an echo slapping between them. "Little ole' me? You think I needed stopping?" Danny shook his head.

"Yeah Danny, I think you do."

"Oh! You remember my name!" Danny sat on a stump opposite him. "I'm intrigued."

"I told you; you didn't chase me out here, you followed me."

"Look, you nitwit, this is my field, sits right out back of my house. You have no idea where you are."

"You think I don't know where I am? You think the logging roads behind your property are out of the way? You think I wasn't ready for something odd to happen? You think I got scared and decided to run instead of having an ax fight? Wow!" He pointed at Danny. "How unlucky were you?"

Danny squinted in interest. "You drove down the logging roads? So, you came in this way?"

"Of course I did."

"And you meant to get caught?" Danny tried to piece it together.

The attorney's brother fiddled with his shoelaces. "Yeah, I meant to get caught. I meant for you to follow me all the way out here."

"Why would you do something so stupid?" Danny bent over and stared at him.

"The answers written all over my face, can't you see it?" Danny closed the gap, the light of a full moon, the clouds dispersed, shining upon them through a clearing.

"What should I see?"

"My name is Lyle, my sister was everything to me, she was my twin, her name was Lauren, and we were connected in ways you would never understand, and yes, my face is her face."

Danny pulled a lighter from his pocket, struck it with his thumb and illuminated the space between them. "You two do look a lot alike."

"You didn't know Lauren; how could you kill her?" He wept.

"She had it coming to her." Danny nodded. "Just like you."

"Calm down, Danny, you'll get your chance if you were a careful man."

"Careful?" Danny laughed. "So why would you come out here? I'm twice your size; you can't possibly believe you can overpower me?"

"I found my sister out here. I'm guessing you buried her because you didn't want to get caught. I saw what you did. She fought you, and she was tough." Lyle focused his rage, "Then you separated her head with an ax."

"Pretty much, pretty much how this one's going down too."

"Are you sure, Danny?"

Danny took caution. "If you are anything like your sister, it is. You are dressed the part, but you don't have a weapon on you, you pea brain." Danny turned, canvassed the area, and gathered some bravado. "Oh wait, your sister is buried out here, let me guess, she's gonna' rise from the dead and exact revenge! Damn, sorry Little Lyle, that ain't happenin' and you know it."

"You're right, that's not going to happen. As much as I want my sister back, she's dead and she's not coming back."

"So, what's your surprise Lyle, you gonna' talk me to death?"

"You look a little sweaty, Danny." he continued, "You feel okay?"

Danny rubbed the back of his neck and tried to speak, "shhhh," He shook his head and tried to stand but fell back to a seated position. Stiff and dizzy, he remained seated.

"Ah, this must be part of that talking to death, huh?" Lyle nodded his head. "Right?"

Danny dropped his ax and swallowed hard, "Whaaaat's happpp…"

Danny's opponent screamed, "What's happening? Is that what's you're trying to ask?"

Danny couldn't hold his balance and fell off the log; his heart felt heavy. He shook and tried to roll over.

"Here let me help you, Danny." The attorney's brother rolled Danny over so they could see each other. He snapped his fingers. "Look at me, Danny."

Danny followed Lyle with the only working muscles he had left, his eyes.

The man sneered. "You can hear me, Danny, so let's have a conversation, okay?"

Danny was stiff but paid attention.

"I laced the trail with a drug called Tetrodotoxin. You probably were stuck by needles a half dozen times. I missed it. Good thing I'm so much smaller than you!" The man grabbed Danny's chin, picked up the lighter and flicked it on. He twisted Danny's face. "Oh yeah, look at those marks, you took a few good ones."

Danny was stiff but paid attention.

"You're probably wondering what Tetrodotoxin is?" He nodded Danny's head for him. "Yeah?"

Danny was stiff but paid attention.

"It's famous for coming from Puffer Fish. It's a neurotoxin and it puts you in a death state. Eventually it either kills you, or you slowly recover, really depends on how much you got. I hope you didn't get too much. But don't worry I have something to counteract it. I'll fix you up."

Danny was stiff but paid attention.

The attorney's brother stood and walked to a corner of the clearing. "So, now you want to know what we are doing out here?" Lyle looked back at Danny. "I will take your silence as a yes."

Danny was stiff but paid attention.

Danny's adversary cleared a patch of brush and located his shovel and flashlight. "I located my sister and asked her what she wanted me to do with you. She said she would like to spend some time with you, Danny. She really wants to get to know you, and I hope you will get to know her."

Danny was stiff but paid attention.

He came back over and shined the flashlight in Danny's pupils. "You are a large human, Danny; I hope you don't mind getting a little wet? I have to roll your fat ass about twenty yards." He shined the light to an area not too far away. "I have a resting spot for you. You can handle that can't you?"

Danny was stiff but paid attention.

Arm by arm, he rolled Danny from back to stomach, from stomach to back, and over again. The flashlight illuminated a hole in the ground, a large wooden box at the bottom, his sister littered the box. "Danny, I wanted you to see where you will be spending the rest of your life." He wrestled with Danny's girth, managed to hoist him to a seated position, and held his head so Danny could see down in the hole. "That's my sister." A torso, a hand, and a head. "Don't worry, I will leave you with some light so you two can get to know each other a little better, for when you come back around. The ground isn't packed too tight and with the gravel content, and as long as it doesn't rain, you should be able to breathe." With that he slid Danny down and into the box. The attorney's brother jumped down and stuck a needle into Danny's hip. "An antidote, I want you to be awake." He placed the lid over the box; hammered dozens of nails so it was snug. Danny could hear him climb out and start whistling 'Kumbaya' as dirt fell on the lid like sand through an hourglass. Danny listened to the whistling until it sounded only like muffled memories. The loneliness of being shut in; the desperation of being entombed.

Danny was stiff but paid attention.

Chapter 44

Lyle had a problem. He hadn't counted on the woman. He wanted the farmer to stay with his sister forever, they were meant for each other, but if the woman knew about the rendezvous, she must know about the grave, and Lyle knew the farmer would spend quite a few days alive before he expired, madness being entombed in a box with his sister. Lyle only wanted to hurt the person who killed his sister. He had nothing against that woman, but she was an accomplice.

Lyle grabbed his backpack. He pulled his dart gun out. He made a decision to cross the line. If the law thought his sister roamed the countryside, on the loose, they would suspect her of further deaths. She would take the blame for this. He loaded the cartridge with enough paralytic to kill an elephant. The clouds closed up as quickly as they opened, and he again found himself in a night painted black. He followed the light of the house. Each step, a little closer to the inevitable, the crossing of a line he watched for twenty years develop. When he reached the house, an eerie quiet covered the moment. Nothing stirred; the porch light, a beacon to the ocean of darkness around it.

Lyle stepped up and walked across creaking boards, a lone coyote in the distant calling, the cattle still in the fields coming home, a subtle sound of the country. He made it to the door. The farmer was so sure of himself; he left the door wide open, the screen protecting the woman from the elements. Lyle entered and approached a couch where she lay unconscious from the sleeping additive Lyle had mixed to her dose of paralytic. Lyle thought the woman had a beauty to her, soft dark hair of subtle red hues in the light. She looked innocent, even with the badge on her hip and the gun in her holster. She wound up in the wrong place at the wrong time. The farmer did this to her. He invited her to this meeting, and collateral damage was his fault. Lyle noticed a keychain peeking out of her pocket. He reached down and pulled it up and out. He pushed the lock button and the dark car out front chirped. Lyle had a change of plan. Stupid he thought, but killing this woman wasn't right. He sat her up and hoisted her up to his shoulders. He took her to her car and opened the hatch. He laid her down and tucked her in, closed the back and hopped in the front seat. Lyle went to the farmer's truck and opened the door. As he suspected, the farmer kept tow chains and a tow bar. Lyle drove the woman's vehicle south on Swaheenie, a quiet night considering all that had happened. He went through town and out to the main country road and headed east. When he made it to the logging road on the ridge, he turned in and headed back to where he parked his vehicle. When his car turned and hooked up, he towed his vehicle around to ridge. If he could make it appear someone kidnapped the farmer and the woman, the authorities would continue their search in another area, he hoped. Lyle couldn't justify killing this woman. As much as he realized this could be his undoing, his sense of right and wrong wouldn't let him go through with it. Why didn't he just kill them both and be done with it? Lyle spent the rest of the evening battling his own demons. With a poor road and loose tow, Lyle crawled around the ridge. As the sun rose from the east, and the break of day brought orange skies and morning songs of nestling birds, Lyle finally made it. He brought her car to the other side of the ridge and concealed it behind a row of alders on the east side, the opposite side of Seefer Valley. With her vehicle missing, any manhunt they had wouldn't be in the field.

Lyle opened the hatch. He pulled the woman out and repositioned her inside her vehicle. If she came to, she would be in a paralyzed state, but at least she'd be in familiar surroundings. Lyle felt exhausted. He wanted to rest but had to press on. Doris would need a procedure and Cindy needed a few more lessons before she could conduct them. His work expected him back that day, but it was only a matter of time before the authorities started snooping around, and even though the farmer had concealed Lauren's identity, they'd lift finger prints sooner or later that led back to her, and when they did, they would lead inevitably to him. Few people could have access to the poisons and chemicals she had. He alone had that sort of clearance, so he couldn't deny his involvement.

On his commute, he monitored the stations. Every station covered the deaths of Dirtwater. Around six, someone finally mentioned his sister.

Lyle made his way back down to Corvallis; he pulled into the driveway of Cindy's mom's house and shut the engine off. He closed his eyes and rested his thoughts. He sat, nodded off between horrible thoughts, woken when Cindy knocked on the window. Lyle's eyes snapped open, startled. Through the window his eyes widened. "You scared me."

She opened his door and knelt beside him. "Did you get your sister?"

Lyle shook his head. "No."

"Did you see her?"

Lyle rested his head against the backrest. "Yeah."

"Lyle, I'm so sorry." She mentioned, "It was on the news last night and your sister has been mentioned as someone they are looking for."

"I heard on the radio." He found it surprising his name hadn't come up.

"But I don't understand. How did you see her?"

Lyle paused. Rather than tell the truth he said, "It's a long story." He changed the subject. "Let's take care of your mother."

Cindy walked behind Lyle as his gait slowed, wilting up the sidewalk to the house. He turned and Cindy looked at him with a wary eye, as though her deep thoughts troubled her. "Cindy, I'll tell you all about it after we take care of your mother and I get a little rest."

Cindy crossed her arms and walked past him. "If you say so."

Lyle caught her arm. "You mean more to me now than you'll ever know."

She frowned. "Then I wish you could be honest with me. I'm a big girl I can handle to truth."

Lyle doubted that. "I understand."

Chapter 45

Danny's arm moved. "Shit!" His heart started to pick up. He labored to breathe, the darkness overwhelmed him, his breath gave the box an uncomfortable warmth and a stale smell of blood from the corpse filled the space. His leg kicked. He met the wall of the box with his torso and used an arm like a stroke victim to push off. The body of the attorney had him pinched in. He felt cramped; being in the box horrified him. "Oh my God!" He concentrated on getting his thoughts back, getting them functioning with the movement of his body. He touched his finger to his thumb, his middle finger to this thumb, his ring finger, and then his pinkie. Over and over, he demonstrated the skill: one, two, three, four, four, three, two, one. He bent his arms and straightened them back out, up and back, up and back. When he had his faculties, he screamed, "Let me out!" He pounded the lid and could feel the weight of dirt against it. That shithead brother had buried him alive. He fumbled around, feeling for something he could use to try and poke through the wood, it was pine, it wasn't that strong. He found something cylindrical; he pulled it to him, a flashlight. He turned it on. The first image he saw was the attorney's face, her eyes penetrating; her mouth agape. "Damn, not you again." He grabbed her by the hair and flung her to his feet. He shoved her body as far to his feet as possible. That last thing he needed was her reminding him of his direction. Next to where her head had been, her purse rested against the wall. He opened it and her belongings tumbled out, save the gun and knife he took out before burying her. "I am such a nitwit."

Time stands still when you can't see it running.

It felt like eternity, but he guessed only minutes passed, maybe only seconds went by between his sudden attacks of panic. Danny had to control his fear, fear couldn't help him. If that punk didn't go back and finish Karen off, maybe when she recovered she'd bring hounds onto the property and find him, surely they would find him. How long would she be under? Had he done to her what he did to Danny? Did he go back and silence her? If he left her on his property, they still may bring the hounds. He had to believe he had a chance. He didn't want to lose hope.

His thoughts raced; every moment he concentrated on his predicament. It was suffocating, he wanted out and he couldn't get past the horror. He searched her bag again, something to draw his mind away from the moment, away from the coffin, something that could transport his thoughts to somewhere free, open, away. Inside the lining of her purse, someone had sewn something in. He inspected the walls of the bag carefully and found a secret compartment; the hard lining was a book, or rather a diary, thick and many years old. He opened it up and thumbed through the pages, the writing chronicled her life from a young girl to the present. He marveled over the handwriting, cursive and beautiful. It was the journal of Lauren Beatrix Thibodeaux. The last entry, written the day before, in the hours that Danny plowed the fields, read this:

"I wait for him to come home. It is the calling of my father's voice I hear. He has asked me to stay pure for the Thibodeaux name, to be a bride of a Thibodeaux. He has no idea how many times I have killed him before. It is with regret that I am forced to do this, but he gives me no choice, he looked at me, and looking at me is something he shouldn't have done. My father is in that man, he is hiding inside them all. It has been a bad week for me, I fear I am losing my sanity, and everything is appearing from my childhood nightmares. I feel as though I am becoming the bride of the very monster I kill, as though I am no better than he is, and that I should let myself go to him, let him have me for his very own. I hear someone coming; I must put him to rest one more time, Daddy, I hear you coming."

Danny worked backwards to the day she killed Jack and Pat:

"Daddy was everywhere today. He was in Hamilton, he always was. I knew it the first time I saw him. I discovered he was in the old man the day he told me I was lovely. Daddy had a wife who

knew the truth. How a woman could wed a man not her brother or father is beyond me, how I can live among them is worse yet. Daddy was charming as Hamilton. He offered me lunch and he was the gentleman he sometimes appears to be. Thank you, brother, for your years of service in the world of chemistry. You and Daddy always had the best treatments for the removal of stains. Daddy was a stain. He barely cringed when he drank the coffee. He smiled and while we drove away from the farmhouse, Daddy must have guessed too, because he suspected something and wanted to touch me. I was so disgusted with Daddy, I needed to show him his evil ways. Those furtive glances were way out of line. I separated his head from his body to give him time to think about what he did. Going back to the farmhouse was a mistake. That body had a wife and she suspected I'd done something. Her years of unholy marriage to Daddy had given her the Devil's view, and she was ranting at me when I came to the house, wanting to know what I'd done to her husband. I could see she was the reincarnation of Jackie. When I told her I was releasing her from her bondage she slapped me. She slapped me! Her head needed to be put in a position so she could see her body was corrupt. I hit an artery and I've never seen someone bleed like that. It was beautiful. I bathed in it; I stripped down naked and made the most beautiful angel on the kitchen floor and then combed her fluids through my hair and soaked in her essence. I did her a favor. She's in a better place. I went to get a drink. Daddy was tricking me as a clerk. He looked at me as though I was dirty. He asked if that was blood on me. I was taken aback that he could be so rude. All I wanted was a drink. He said he was calling the police. For what? I picked up the scissors when I realized he wanted to see the 'me' underneath the mask. He was longing for me. He turned his back on me when I pleaded he not call and when that failed, I made him stop. He staggered to the backroom, and I helped him end that incarnation. He didn't want to live in that body, I could see it. He was in pain and I did everything I could to take it away. The mouth screams for a pain it thinks it feels. I got my meat saw and stopped his pain. We enjoyed a beer together and I left him with the understanding I am not a woman of easy ways."

Chapter 46

Lyle entered, and the morning news broadcasted on television. It embarrassed him to see a picture of his sister on the blotter report. "Your mom hasn't seen this has she."

Cindy shook her head. "No." She moved around him and turned off the TV. "But you can't keep this news from spreading."

"I know." He needed to buy enough time to get Cindy ready to administer shots if she had to. "Let's give you a lesson."

She winced. "I am really afraid."

The two hadn't touched emotionally since he returned and they weren't going to. Lyle put his hands on her shoulders and spoke frankly. "You have to suck it up. This is your family, and family is everything."

Cindy nodded. "Okay."

"Good, let's do this." He wiped the sleep away from his face and put on a gleeful expression as they entered Doris' room.

"Mom, are you ready for your shot?"

Doris bellowed, "Hell no, but we're going to do it anyway."

Lyle nodded and handed her daughter the needle.

"Good Lord, two lessons and she's going to do this?"

Lyle stated, "No time like the present." He smiled. "You never know when you might be stuck in a box."

Doris responded, "Well I think we are working to keep me out of one, I hope."

279

"That we are." He turned to Cindy. "You ready?"

"Not really, but I'll try."

"Where do you want the shot, Doris?" Lyle leaned over the bed.

"The stomach I guess."

"That's actually the solar plexus."

"Yeah well, it hurts like hell so call it what you want."

Cindy used her index finger to locate the indentation below the sternum. She looked at Lyle. "Here?"

"Yep."

She wiped the spot with alcohol and apologized. "I'm so sorry, Mom."

She opened her eyes and smiled. "Honey, don't be sorry. If this works, you saved my life."

As Cindy brought the needle down, Lyle instructed her to push up under the sternum and slightly to the back, and to go in three inches and inject. Cindy flinched as she broke skin and Lyle put his arm on her shoulder. "It's going to be okay."

She slowly pushed it in and at three inches she pushed the plunger and released the chemicals. Doris groaned, not letting out a death scream. When the plunger had pushed everything out, Cindy slowly backed the needle out.

"You don't, and shouldn't, pull it out slowly. The faster you are, the less pain your mother will feel."

Cindy had a layer of panic sweat. "I didn't like that."

"You did great."

Lyle smiled at Doris. "Your daughter is a natural. She's going to be a great alternative if something should happen to me."

She shook her head. "Boy, you are a pessimist. You plan on disaster?"

Lyle hid his thoughts. "You never know."

Lyle and Cindy left Doris to rest and they went to Cindy's room to talk. "Would it be okay if I slept for a little while?"

Cindy lightened up. "Would it be okay if I lay down with you?"

Lyle smiled. "I would like that very much."

As they lay side by side, Lyle gazed into Cindy's eyes. He didn't feel like he stared at himself, as he had so many nights before, across from Lauren. Her eyes were dark and not pale blue like his and Lauren's. The lines on her face told a story so different than a Thibodeaux. She had peace across her forehead and innocence danced on her cheeks. She had a strong jaw, a full smile, but her worry stood out, the penetration of her gaze spoke volumes for her thoughts. Lyle reached up and traced the bridge of her nose, simple, button, pleasant. She snapped at the end of his finger and giggled when she caught it.

"I seem to have a lot of regrets for my timing lately." He pursed his lips and lost his emotion, just a steady stream of chiseled stillness. He blinked, felt comfort in her presence and closed his eyes.

When he woke, Cindy had long since risen. His watch had circled around to four o'clock. He jumped off the bed and came around the corner. Outside, he could see Cindy carrying his backpack. He met her at the door, a possessive panic about him. "I'll take that."

"Man, that's heavy, what do you have in it?"

"Well, you saw me when I showed up today. I was in hunting gear. I was spying on the guy who had Lauren. I have binoculars, and a sundry of spying stuff." He passed it off. He didn't want her checking and finding the cartridges, gun, syringes, and chemicals for something more than spying.

"Are you going to want to go up to Portland with me?"

"Why?"

She sighed. "I have to work."

"Would you be okay with me watching over your mother?"

She exhaled, a heavy burden in her eyes. "That would be great. Are you worried about going back to your place?"

"Yeah."

She told him, "Your phone rang several times today. I looked at the caller ID and it was your work."

"I left a message this morning I wasn't feeling well. I'm sure they were calling to make sure I'm okay." He realized they had probably put two and two together. If Lauren had poisoned Ms. Newberry and the police plastered her face all over the news as a person of interest, he could bet the police looked everywhere for him. "I have a favor to ask."

Cindy winced. "To keep my mouth shut if someone should stroll in and ask if I've seen you?"

Lyle frowned. "Yeah."

Cindy admitted, "I have an awful feeling you're in way deeper than you're admitting, but I want to believe you when you say you haven't hurt anyone."

The day before, Lyle could have answered that honestly, but now he couldn't. He sighed. "Thank you."

She turned to go to the kitchen but stopped. "Why don't you leave the US? You could cross the border and disappear."

"Would you go with me?"

If we get my mother well, we could take her and all go."

Lyle smiled. He knew that would never happen. The idea came from someone who hadn't thought through the idea very well. "Sure, let's discuss it when you get back. I think you're on to something."

Lyle knew Cindy's allegiance to him grew because of his work with her mother, but he wasn't about to involve her in the mess he'd created, created over the last thirty years.

Chapter 47

Danny did everything he could to keep his mind off of his situation. He wondered if a day had passed, but judging the amount of reading he'd done, he guessed maybe he'd killed an hour. It was the end of March and still cold outside, but in the confines of the box, being underground with his body radiating heat, the temperature felt unbearable. The air stagnated and the lack of good ventilation left him a little dizzy. He returned to the diary, turning instead to page one:

"I am Lauren Beatrix Thibodeaux, and I am twelve years old. I am the oldest, or I should say, my brother and I are the oldest of a growing family. Lyle Lawrence Thibodeaux is my twin, and he has me beat by four minutes. It's four minutes I will never live down, but it's four minutes he's earned. He's the bestest brother a sister could ever have."

Saturday: "My father is older than my mother, or at least he looks a lot older. He won't admit it, but we all kid he could be Momma's dad. He doesn't like to be teased, at least not about family. Momma recently had a baby and that brings our family to nine kids. After Lyle and me, there is Rebecca, the only child not the color of snow, Michael, Angela, Walter, Daniel, Helen, and the baby Clarice. I like being in a big family, but I don't like where we live. Daddy and Momma were originally from New Orleans, and they moved to the mountains of Arkansas, where Daddy retired from his medical practice, even though he still travels back to Louisiana every so often and does volunteer work. We live in as rural a place as you can imagine. Daddy and Momma educate us at home, and we aren't allowed to watch TV. We aren't a church family, but we are a bible family, and Daddy is insistent that family unity is part of that religion. He believes the only allies we have in life are our brothers and sisters, and that we should never trust anyone outside the family."

Sunday: "We live in a big, beautiful house, overlooking our own lake. The folks around here are scared of Daddy; they are sort of scared of us all. They don't see many people who are blonde like us. Daddy says they're jealous, but I hear them talking, they think we are strange. I wish we could go to school so they could get to know us. I think they would like us."

Monday: *"Daddy is nicer to Rebecca than he is to me. I am so mad sometimes. He will take her places and spend time with her, but he always tells me that he has other plans for me and that I'm special because I'm a twin. Daddy says he was a twin also, but that his sister Lucretia passed away giving birth. Rebecca with the dark hair is what Daddy calls a throwback, a child with strong genes, good to strengthen a bloodline. I don't know what that means, but it sure gives her precious time with Daddy that I wish I had. Lyle tells me to leave it alone, that I have him. Then he laughs and says he's better for me than Daddy anyway. I love Lyle; it's like looking at me every time I look in his eyes."*

Tuesday: *"Momma looks sad. She looks tired. She has baby after baby, year after year. She never talks back to Daddy; she's like one of us when he lectures. I don't ever remember her being very motherly to me, but I guess when you have to nurse the next one down and then the next one after that, older kids like me get left without the attention we seek. I look at mother holding Clarice and wish I could be held like that. Sometimes I hold Michael and Walter because they need it; they feel like me, left out. Lyle never feels that way. He's so strong.*

He listens to what Daddy says and follows it every time. I don't think he's ever been punished."

Monday: "We started our classes today. The summer of the Ozarks are winding down, the warm evenings are winding down and the cool air is pushing in from the north. Daddy is teaching us English and science today. He says we can never be too well spoken and if we know the way of science, we can never be too far behind the universe. Daddy expects a lot. We study for eight hours a day. Tomorrow we will do our math and history. Lyle is the best student in our class, but he is four minutes older, so I sort of expect that. Rebecca is the worst student, but Daddy doesn't push her very hard. She's his favorite. He never yells at her."

Saturday: "The weekend, and I am so happy. The summer is lasting and Momma is letting us play in the lake. Daddy is home so Momma and Daddy can let us swim. Daddy says it isn't an all-play day, that Lyle and I have to give Angela, Walter, and Daniel swimming lessons. It figures, just when I thought it was a play day, I am working. I'm glad Lyle is with me; he will make sure the lessons run smoothly. He is my better half; he keeps me on track."

Wednesday: "I had a nightmare last night. I think it was a nightmare. I heard Rebecca crying and I walked across the hallway to see why. It was dark but I could hear her begging him to stop. She sounded so horrified. When I woke up today, I found her and hugged her. I told her I had a bad dream about her, and Daddy looked concerned. He said not to worry, that sometimes nightmares are about the things we are doing wrong. He asked me if I had thought bad things about Rebecca. I suppose I am jealous, and he scolded me, he took his belt off and punished me. He said I must always put family ahead of everything else, that all loyalty must be to the family and to never trust anyone outside the family. He forced me to apologize for the horrible thoughts I had about Rebecca. I will never have another bad thought about my brothers and sisters. None of us will."

Chapter 48

Lyle let Doris rest. The first few days of therapy would drain her as the chemicals repaired damage. She would sweat, she would feel a dull ache, but her overall health would improve. He sat on the couch and flipped through the news stations, following the events of Dirtwater. His sister their lone focus. One station even had his picture, the brother missing and a possible victim as well. He doubted the police thought that. He figured they worked the angles in hopes he'd waltz into a station somewhere and say, "I'm not dead," and be arrested as an accomplice. What concerned him most was the woman. Half a day had gone by and they weren't reporting anything. Did they not know yet or were they keeping it a secret? If they found her, the farmer might escape his fate.

Secrets have a strange way of coming back to haunt you. He remembered the secret of his family. It didn't damage him as much as it damaged Lauren. It destroyed her. She went on the path of striking out at anyone not part of the family. He wished he'd been stronger, that he'd been able to help her. Lyle picked up his phone and dialed home.

"Hello?"

"Rebecca?"

"Lyle? Is that you?"

"Yes, Sister. I have some bad news."

His sister waited, a long pause before asking, "Is she having moments?"

Lyle sighed. "I wish it was that simple."

"Has she been caught?"

"She was killed."

Rebecca said, "Oh God, not Lauren." She huffed. "Daddy would have been very disappointed in you, Lyle."

"I'm sure he would, but he's not here to deal with it now is he."

"How did it happen?"

"She had a moment like no other."

Rebecca spoke in a nurtured soft voice, "Did you play a role in her going over the edge?"

"Perhaps, but she'd been unstable for months. I was trying to chemically treat her, but she was on to me, she wasn't taking them."

"Are you okay?"

"No."

"Do you need to come home?"

"I fear it's not that simple." Lyle bent over and whispered into the phone. "I've avenged her death."

"As you should."

Lyle took a deep breath. "I'm not so sure I should have." Lyle offered, "We have covered up for her ever since New Orleans, ever since the night of the dream. I think we were wrong."

"She was your twin; you know what Daddy said about you two."

"I know." His family still lived under the spell of a father who'd been dead too many years to remember. Lyle changed the subject. "How is everyone?"

Rebecca operated ground zero for the family, the hub of unity. "Good." She itemized her tone. "Have you called the boys to see if they can help?"

Lyle sighed. "I don't want to involve anyone. This is quicksand and I'm in it."

"Brother you are the patriarch of the family; we will do whatever you ask us to do."

"Good, then do nothing." Lyle wanted to hear Rebecca's voice, her motherly voice—so family. "It was good hearing you."

"You sound desperate, Lyle. I don't like hearing you like this."

Lyle thought perhaps desperation or perhaps reality, a reality that he'd been wrong all these years, and his behavior led to the death of more than a half dozen people in the last seventy-two hours. "Well, I just thought I'd let you know. I wanted to tell you I love you and tell everyone I love them as well."

"Hey! Don't be so defeated. We will see you soon."

They'd see him again, of that he knew, but he wasn't so sure he'd see them. "Take care."

"Will do, you take care and we love you." The phone disconnected and caught an aerial shot of a vehicle on the television screen. He sat up and followed the sight. The caption said, "Missing detective found, alive." They found her too quickly, but he took solace she was alive. It would take them another day to bring her up out of her comatose condition. He turned up the sound.

"We thought she was dead." A logger spoke to a reporter. "She didn't have a heartbeat. We called the cops and when the paramedics came in, they said she was alive. I still don't get how. She didn't have a heartbeat."

The reporter cut away to a news release where a pathologist addressed a crowd outside a hospital in Seattle. "The patient was rendered immobile by a neurotoxin that is a paralytic drug. She's in critical condition and has been unresponsive to any treatment." He stared down at the dais and viewed the cameras over his glasses, "and her prognosis is grim. We are doing everything we can, but we are facing a difficult battle." The cameras shifted to a detective who offered, "The resident of Dirtwater that she was in charge of protecting is missing. At this time, we don't have any leads, but we believe he was transferred from our agent's car to a waiting vehicle. We found a second set of tire tracks at the scene, and they lead to the highway. The person of interest is Lauren Thibodeaux." He held a headshot of Lyle's sister up for the cameras to take in. There is a chance she is being aided by her brother Lyle Thibodeaux." They had his picture from his job.

That explained why his work tried to get a hold of him. Lyle was sad to see the addition of Ms. Newberry as a victim of the killing spree, a nice woman, never paid much attention to Lyle other than her initial interview.

His phone rang, he looked down and Cindy's number popped up. He answered but didn't say anything.

"Are you there, Lyle?"

"Are you alone?"

"Yes. You are all over the news." Her voice shook, "If your sister is dead, did you do that to the police officer?"

"Cindy, I promise you, she's fine. I needed to get her and the farmer far enough away so I could get to my sister."

"You need to run. Everything you are doing for my mother puts me in debt to you, but if I help you hide away until you can find some place safe, we're even."

Lyle was on his own. The woman he'd fallen for knew this was more than a sister who went crazy, this had history written notoriety all over it, and she wanted none of that. "Make it back here tonight and tomorrow you'll get one last lesson, and then I will be gone."

"Lyle, I am so sorry. I'm sorry you got mixed up in your sister's business." Lyle didn't get mixed up in it; he lived it his entire life.

Chapter 49

Danny occupied his time by reading the diary, his only escape from imprisonment, his only salvation to what may be his final thoughts, his resting place. If fate dictated he spend the remainder of his days in a box with another human he owed her the respect to understand her. The diary was his only outlet to something outside his own mind. He continued reading:

Black Friday: "I have witnessed Daddy doing something I don't think is right. He is hurting Rebecca, even though she won't admit it. When I asked her about it, she told Daddy and he reprimanded me for not understanding the importance of family, he reprimanded me hard. He told me that relationships which involve family are not wrong, are not unholy, but are how relationships should be. He said my focus should be on family. I think I understand him, he sees Lyle as my perfect match, because as he was whipping me, I was strong enough to ask him why he thought that; he said his first wife was Lucretia. I don't understand but he said this is the way of the

Thibodeaux and that it was a secret I must not share with my siblings.

"Daddy sat me down on the bed after he was done beating me, he said he was so disappointed that I made him hit me, and that if I was a better girl, it would never happen again, but that I would be better off for it. He said he would do better at letting me be the secret keeper and as a sign of our bond, he told me another secret, the child's birth that caused his first wife to die, was the birth of Momma, his second wife, our mother. I don't know what to think. He assured me that the only way to keep the Thibodeaux pure, and without the ills of other people, was to make sure we kept our loyalty to the Thibodeauxes. He has said that I must resist any urges of the flesh and that I should prevent any of my siblings from doing the same. Daddy has entrusted me with this secret, Daddy has made me part of his inner circle. I feel so privileged to have Daddy all to myself on this."

Tuesday: "Today I told Daddy that I thought Lyle had affection for a girl on our mountain. He smiled at me. He was very happy I informed him and told me he would spend time with me tonight. He allows me to come into his private room late at night when I am a good girl. I am so happy he approves."

Wednesday: "Daddy punished Lyle for the first time that I remember. Lyle didn't understand Daddy. Even though Daddy has always told me that I am meant for Lyle, I had to side with Daddy. It is important that we remain family first. I tried to talk to Lyle but he said that I had ruined everything, that if Daddy knew he liked that girl, I think her name is Jackie, that he would put an end to it. I saw Lyle cry and I felt bad. When I told Daddy, he said, Lyle was weak and he needed time to think about what he'd done."

Saturday: "I haven't seen Lyle for two days. Daddy has locked him in the cellar; he says time shut in will give him time to reflect on what he's done. It will make him understand the loyalty of family."

Tuesday: "Today after five days in the cellar, Daddy let Lyle come out. Lyle said he understood and that he would not see that girl again. I was sad because today was our birthday, but Lyle didn't feel like celebrating. He stayed in our room for the entire day. When I went to spend time with him, he told me to leave him alone. I told Daddy and Daddy

*said that girl had influence on him. Daddy wanted
me to find out more about her. He wants me to
make sure they are never together again."*

*Friday: "I discovered the girl named Jackie is
going to Mardi Gras next month. I came home and
told Daddy, and he suggested we should go. He says
it would be good for the family to see his old home
and to celebrate what he called 'Fat Tuesday.' He
was so happy with me that he invited me to come to
his private room tonight. I am his special girl today.
I'm so happy I have pleased Daddy. I hope that Lyle
will be pleased when this is all over."*

*Saturday: "Daddy told me last night that I must
put an end to Lyle's feelings for that girl. He wants
me to concentrate on being a better sister to him, to
make him feel more like family. Daddy wants me to
love him the way I love Daddy. If this is what
Daddy wants, I know I am to obey. I will miss my
time with Daddy."*

Danny stopped reading. He felt antsy, restless. He pounded on
the lid. Why hadn't anyone noticed the grave? Shouldn't
somebody be coming? He needed to go to the bathroom, he was
hungry. Everything intensified in that box. He shut off the
flashlight and closed his eyes, picturing his bedroom as a boy on
nights when darkness reigned and you could see nothing in front

of you. He pictured himself there, as though transported away from the confines of the tomb he lay in. Where was John? Shouldn't he be snooping around the property? Any fool should see a mound of dirt that looks fresh. With him missing, why hasn't anyone come looking for him?" Danny sighed. He went stir crazy. He pounded on the lid and screamed, "Hey! Is anyone out there?" the dirt had no give and the echo of his voice stayed confined to the box. Danny quit thinking of the dead woman as the attorney. He wondered if Lauren had anything useful in her purse. "Lauren, you have any Snickerdoodles in your bag?" He turned on the flashlight and rummaged through her belongings, a pile of mints scattered across the bottom along with a couple sticks of gum. He found a picture of her and her brother. It looked like they were teenagers. Danny started to realize who Lyle and Lauren were. Lyle didn't look happy, he looked like he carried a weight, and from reading Lauren's diary, he understood why.

Chapter 50

Lyle thought about his years growing up in the Ozarks. How the boys escaped their father's wrath, and how his sisters didn't. Even though the boys escaped his punishment, save the times they spent locked in the cellar, he indoctrinated them all with the belief that family stays together. Only now did he come to realize how wrong that was. Lauren may have suffered greatly at their father's twisted beliefs, but no one suffered his father abuse more than their mother and Rebecca, both daughters of his, both mothers of his children. The reason why all the sons moved away was to escape the fate their father had for them, to marry a sister. Only Lyle remained stuck, stuck with a sister their father had convinced was matched through divine intervention to be with Lyle. Maybe it was sympathy for her moments, something he tried over the years to prevent, or maybe he too had come to see her as his perfect match, after all, he'd sat in the cellar many times reconsidering the idea that loving someone outside the family was acceptable.

Lyle's father gave him that life, and Lyle didn't do anything in the years after he broke away to change it; he was accountable for his own behavior once he made it to adulthood. He lived with the fact his stoic intellect and duplicity of values showed he did not value the life of others. He told himself his sister had issues and he only acted as her keeper, and for the thirteen years since they left the family home, it worked. Her occasional moments were so well crafted that he only needed to help clean up and give her the collusion she needed to escape suspicion. He convinced himself those actions were not sinister, were not calculating, but rather after the fact. Now he realized his assurance to his sister that he would always be there gave her entitlement to continue when she felt the urge to kill at her leisure. He not only enabled her, he encouraged her. Her method of poisoning to execute her victims, and the chemicals to do so, were at his disposal, and he never kept them from her. He trained her in their applications.

He sat on the couch and knew he had to do the right thing. Helping Cindy's mother was his attempt to balance the scale of injustice he'd participated in. However, as much as he felt the farmer had the right to kill his sister, something he said about her not being the first person he'd killed left him with no remorse for letting him die in that box with his sister. He might believe his father was wrong about the things he did and said, about the unity the family was supposed to have, the loyalty at all cost, but he did have loyalty to Lauren; she was his twin, and he did have responsibility once he'd crossed that line to continue crossing it. He watched that man cut her head off when she had no more fight in her, her hand severed, bleeding, overmatched. He could have stopped and put an end to her madness, instead, he put an end to her life. That was unforgiveable.

His phone rang—a number he didn't recognize. That would be the police. They closed in. He didn't answer, letting it go to voice mail. He hit one and retrieved it. "This is detective Vichinski from the Thurston County Sheriff's department. Mr. Thibodeaux it is imperative we speak with you. Could you please give us a call?" He left his number and extension as though he provided a courtesy call.

Lyle knew he couldn't go back to the condo, but he kept nothing of importance there. His car however, did have things he needed, not to mention, evidence that a body had been in the trunk. He also kept a storage unit with the truly important things, the chemicals he used to control Lauren, the chemicals he used for his own theoretical experiments. Lyle had had plans to change the world for the better; too bad he hadn't worked on his own life first.

His phone rang again, this one from a Portland number. He waited it out and checked the voice mail. "Mr. Thibodeaux, this is Detective Osment from the Portland police department, we would like to speak with you when you have the opportunity." He too left a number and extension. With two states looking for him, he could bet the FBI wouldn't be far behind.

Lyle stood and went to Doris' door. He lightly tapped. "Excuse me, Doris, are you awake?"

"Come in, Lyle." Her voice had more weight to it.

He peeked his head in. "How are you feeling?"

"Better. I can't believe three shots later and I have appetite and strength."

Lyle stepped in and cautioned her. "Remember what I said, just because you feel better, don't quit taking those shots."

She changed the subject. "Son, you look worried about something."

Lyle paused. "I am." He hated to impose. "Do you have a car?"

"In the garage, do you need to use it?"

"Can I?"

"Absolutely." She frowned. "Would you like to talk to me?"

He hesitated, committed to walking out and saying nothing, but chose to speak candidly. "You won't be seeing me again." He held his hand up. "But I promise you, you will get your car back."

She laughed, "I think I owe you at least a car, but thank you for assuring me." She sat up and patted the bed. "Come here and talk to me."

Lyle spent the next hour telling her as much of his life story as he thought she could handle. He didn't spare the abusive and despicable things his father did, but he left his sister's activities prior to the last four days out, only that she'd snapped and was the person responsible for a string of murders. He even admitted to trying to help her, that he felt he had to. When he finished, he said, "Because you need to maintain these shots, and because they are going to be coming after me, I have to leave. I would love to see Cindy one more time, but it isn't safe for anyone if I do, and seeing her will only make this harder. I can tell you this; you have nothing to fear from me."

She patted Lyle's hand. "Lyle, I'm truly sorry for the life you were dealt. My thoughts go with you, and if you need to speak to me, call. She jotted down the house phone number and handed it to him. "Do you need money?"

"He smiled. "No, I've done well, and money isn't an issue." He pulled out his wallet and handed her a debit card. "I have a few accounts, and I would like for Cindy to have this." He wrote down a number. "This is the pin number. There is probably twenty-five thousand in it. I want her to have it."

"Lyle, are you sure?"

"It's fine. My sister and I have other accounts and I have plenty." Lyle gave Doris a hug and straightened up. "Thanks for letting me use your car."

"The keys are on the wall by the door to the garage."

"Thanks." Lyle grabbed his bag and left the house in Doris' car.

He drove north.

Chapter 51

Danny wasn't sure if his nerves made him feel nausea or if maybe it started to rain. Rainwater would fill the holes in the porous dirt and start the process of suffocating him. The more he worried about it, the more panicked he became over being in that fucking box, "Damn it!" He screamed over and over, "Get me out of here!" He pounded on the lid. "Please, please, please." Growing up a big child, his father raised him to believe boys shouldn't cry, and Danny definitely fit that mold, but gosh, he sure wanted to cry. He started thinking about the time he couldn't find his way home from his own property, how he couldn't remember which way was back to the house. It had rained and he had taken a hike along the back side of the property, toward the western ridge, into the trees and the river, cold and the day grew dark, at seven years old he panicked. He went the way he thought he came but worked his way into more and more forest. He was seven years old, but because of his size, everyone treated him like he was twelve, a big boy, one who couldn't get lost, who couldn't get scared. Danny was scared. That cold and wet day frightened him. He had cried, "I want to go home." One of his mother's terriers had tagged along but did nothing. He didn't guide him out, just acted as though Danny would eventually walk home. So, he sat, sure he would never be found. Even though it must not have been too cold, and he hadn't been very far from home, to the unknown, the fear surfaced like no other in his life. He wound up sitting under a tree and falling asleep.

It was dark when his dad lifted him up into his arms and gave him the comfort of a father. "We've been looking for you."

Danny had opened his eyes and smiled. "I've been waiting for you to come." He put his arms around his father and fell back to sleep. That was the dad he had.

Danny wished his father was there to pick him up right then. He didn't feel like a man, he felt like that lost boy all those years ago.

He turned on the flashlight and continued Lauren's diary:

"I have sworn to secrecy the greatest secret of all. We went to New Orleans for the Mardi Gras festival, and Daddy and I went to find the mountain girl, Jackie. My secret is something Daddy says can never be told to anyone, especially not to Lyle, but I have two secrets, because I lied to Daddy and did show Lyle, but I kept Daddy's secret from Lyle. Daddy took me with him, and we found Jackie and he told me what to say to get her to follow me. I told her Lyle was over there and she could come with me. I talked her into following me to where Daddy was, and he gave her some sort of shot, and she went to

sleep. Daddy took her down by the river and he said
I must perform the sacred ritual of ridding the
monster from the body. He handed me a saw and
said the head must be separated from the body. I
was so scared, but Daddy said it was the only way.
There was a lot of blood, and I didn't feel like we
had gotten rid of something evil, it almost felt like I
released something evil in me, but Daddy said it
would all feel normal someday. We left her by the
river, but I was so worried about what I'd done that
I needed to know if Lyle felt the same way, so after
Daddy and I left, I came back and retrieved her
head. I took it to Lyle and told him I'd done it alone.
Daddy had said I must never tell anyone, but as he
said, family is family. Lyle was shocked but he said
he understood. He went back to the river with me,
and we buried her in a mausoleum. What I don't
understand is he told Daddy and Daddy acted as
though he had nothing to do with it. He told Lyle I
would have to be watched over and that it would be
Lyle's job from then on. Daddy won't admit he
made me do it, and I will never tell Lyle otherwise."*

Danny put the diary down. "What sort of Dad did you have?"
His words echoed off the pine walls speaking to a dead woman
he'd killed when she attacked him, her madness like nothing he'd

ever seen. Danny felt regret. "I'm so sorry for the life you lived." He remembered when his mom's cousin Louie passed away, how everyone said he was a no-good drunk, ran his farm over in Huggins to the ground. Danny liked Louie. He drank a lot, but he was a happy drunk and nobody could say, other than being lazy, he was a bad man. Louie had three daughters, one who committed suicide, now he wondered why. Did Louie have the kind of demons in him that Lauren's father had in him? None of Louie's daughters were particularly close to Louie. Danny felt jaded, as though he didn't really know the average person on the street. When he first saw Lauren, he saw a beautiful woman, not one with more baggage than Samsonite. He shut the flashlight off. He wondered about the time. He had no bearing on how long he'd been in the box. His hunger grew, but that wasn't unusual, at six-foot-ten, a three-hundred-pound man's constant hunger was pretty much standard twenty-four seven fare; having to go to the bathroom concerned him more. He held it in, the last thing he wanted to do was make the smell worse than the growing stench of death. He huffed. There might come a time when relieving himself might wind up smelling better than the smell of a rotting corpse. He figured he could hold it in a little longer. He yelled one more time, "Help!" A pointless endeavor. He closed his eyes and thought about happier times.

Chapter 52

Lyle drove into Portland and waited out the day's light. When darkness fell, he parked across the street and viewed his car. The parking lot had few cars, with his to the back, parked discreetly against the river's edge. Like usual, the lounge didn't attract much of a clientele in the later hours. The weeknights were a courtesy for the busy weekends. The few patrons, the casual residents who found a home away from home in the dark lighted cavern of booths inside the Fisherman's Reef, kept the place afloat Monday through Thursday. Lyle locked Doris' car and made his way across the street. He cut through to the walkway along the river and came up the back side of the parking lot. He hesitated, scanned the area and made his way to the trunk of his car as quiet as a shadow. He pushed the trunk lock on his keychain, and it popped open. He grabbed a briefcase and the plastic liner he'd laid in the car when he put Mrs. Henricksen in. The beating in his chest overwhelmed him. He rolled the liner into a ball and trembled as a person approached, walking up the sidewalk. He closed his eyes when the man asked, "Excuse me?"

"Yes?" Lyle waited.

"Do you have a lighter?"

Lyle wiped his face, the sweat beading up on his temples. "No, I'm sorry." He froze as the gentleman continued on his way. Lyle waited for anything suspicious, but the man continued and never looked back. Lyle stepped around the car and unlocked the passenger door, pulled the pink slip out, slipped the car key off his key ring and put the key and remote up under the inside of the bumper. He turned and walked away at a brisk pace and found the nearest trash receptacle to dump the liner. He carried the briefcase and pink slip back to Doris' car and drove off. Lyle wouldn't try to evade capture; just to evade capture at that moment. He had things he needed to do.

Lyle made it to his storage unit. No one knew about it, that he knew for sure, the one secure place he had all to himself. Not even Lauren knew of his storage unit. He'd rented it under another name. His offsite studies more valuable than any work he'd ever done, and his unit was his lab. Inside, he had experiments in process, aging in Petri dishes with agar and test tubes in motion. He had hoped it would be an augury of things to come in his studies. He had meticulous notes on several experiments he thought could move medicine forward many years. For all of Lyle's misgivings, he had the everlasting goal of helping the world live longer. He grabbed the extracts he had in a cabinet, the extracts he used to make the poisons and sedatives and the antidotes and cures. There wasn't much else of use. He sat at his research table and tore a sheet of paper from his research journal. He composed a long note of various issues with his research. He taped it to a beaker and left the storage unit for good.

He waited until he was just outside the gates of the unit and dialed the number to his co-worker Niraj.

"Hello?"

"Raj, before you hang up, hear me out."

"Are you crazy! The police were here looking for you. They say you are tied to the killings in Washington, and of Ms. Newberry." Panic streamed from his voice.

"All I can say is I wasn't, but that's beside the point right now."

"What possibly could you want calling me?" Niraj hyper vented in his temperament.

"I don't have time to argue with you, but if you want to advance your career, if you want to open a whole new world of medicine, listen to me." He'd caught Niraj's attention; He went silent on the other end. "Are you listening?"

Niraj sounded wary. "I am."

"I have a storage unit on Baker Street, at the U Store It storage building. I've been doing my own experiments, and they are still in progress, but more importantly the journal is on my desk in the unit. You and I have become friends, I hope."

"I think so."

"Then trust me. Get there tonight. The lock has the key in it and after you get the journal, and you see I'm telling the truth, you can make the decision as to what you want to do."

"They have told anyone who hears from you to call the authorities."

Lyle sighed. "I understand, just wait until you get the journal, and maybe you will want to take the experiments too." Lyle assured him. "There's nothing else here. My life was my work, and my sister."

Niraj's accent came through the receiver. "Your sister is a bad woman."

Lyle hadn't the fight to disagree. "She was a lot of things, Raj." He whispered, "But most of all she was my sister."

"Where will you go? No, wait, don't tell me, I don't want to know. I don't want to have to tell on you."

"Thank you, Raj. You turned out to be a great lab partner."

Niraj calmed and admitted. "I was a lab assistant. We were nothing until we got you. You will be missed my friend."

"By the way, I didn't dump D1."

"I know that."

Lyle coughed in embarrassment. "Does the boss know?"

"Nope, I covered."

I left a name of the person receiving the D1 shots. It's on page 1, line D. Her address is listed; one letter at a time in the upper right corner, and the street name is the name of the last entry. It's in the town of Corvallis."

"Why are you telling me?"

"Because you may have to help administer the shots. The woman doing it now, may not be able to handle it."

"Those solar plexus shots?"

"Yes." Lyle made him promise. "Don't let anyone find out until she is done with the shots. I don't want them taking the shots away from here." He continued. "Anyway, the calculations are perfect. It's a good drug."

Niraj ended with, "I will take care of your unit and I will find your subject. Don't worry and have a safe journey."

Lyle hung up. Funny Raj would mention a journey, because now Lyle's real journey could begin.

Chapter 53

Every second felt like a minute, every minute felt like an hour, and every hour like a day. Twenty-four hours, if he'd been there twenty four hours, felt like a lifetime. Danny had one outlet and it was the sickening descent of a young girl who chronicled the events of her tumultuous life. He could think of better things to read, but perhaps nothing more appropriate than reading the life of the corpse in the box with him.

He cracked another chapter:

"Sometimes I wonder who I am. Who is Lauren Beatrix Thibodeaux? I have tried to leave Daddy's teaching, but I am a member of the family Thibodeaux, and no one else will leave with me, and I would never leave Lyle. I celebrated my fifteenth birthday, or rather Lyle and I celebrated our fifteenth birthday by bending to father's will of consummating our relationship. I looked up consummate; it means to complete a relationship with sexual intercourse. I could see Lyle did not enjoy it, and for that, neither did I. Daddy promised me, this would be what was right, but seeing Lyle sickened by our act, broke my heart. I wanted to

undo what was done. I even made plans with a boy on the mountain to go on a date, something he'd ask me to do when I would go to the store for groceries with mother. We were to meet on the bridge across the Arbuckle Gorge, but Daddy stopped it. Daddy pushed him over the bridge and then told Lyle, Lyle's lack of caring for me was the reason I did it. He told Lyle I did it. To the community it was a tragic accident. Daddy locked me in the cellar for two days, convincing me I'd killed Kenny Hall. I'm writing in my diary, before I forget the truth, I did not push that boy over the edge. I did not, no matter what Daddy tells Lyle.

"I see the reason why Daddy said what he did. Lyle is much nicer to me now. Lyle apologized for what he did, for making me kill that boy, for how he treated me after we consummated. He is much happier now and we are one. Daddy isn't so bad after all. Daddy has moved Lyle and me to an upstairs room where we will have a bed to ourselves. It's good to be wanted.

"Lyle has been distant. We sleep together but that's all we do, is sleep. He says consummating drains his mental capabilities and he doesn't want to consummate. I threatened to tell Daddy and Lyle *gave in but he cried the entire time we consummated and he didn't please me, he was not how he was before, or how Daddy was. He was soft inside of me. I'm going to tell Daddy.*

"A few days in the cellar did nothing for Lyle's attitude. He returned and still cried when we consummated. I will stick Lyle in the cellar myself if he doesn't change his ways. I will do something to make him come around."

Danny shook his head. "Lauren, if ever a person was in a better place being dead, you are."

Danny recalled Bethany Stricker, a girl two years younger than him. Danny didn't have a lot of girlfriends, and in fact, with a school as small as theirs, you liked whoever liked you. Bethany was a pretty girl, but her parents forbid her to date an upperclassman, and as her father said, one who was built like a grown man. Bethany would sneak out from cheerleading practice and hang out with Danny after football and basketball practice, but not long into their courting, Mr. Stricker wound up at Danny's house speaking to his father, telling his dad a boy Danny's age shouldn't be with a child. Danny might have kissed Bethany a few times, and even might have reached second base, but they had an innocent relationship, two kids who liked each other. Danny's dad took in everything Mr. Stricker said with a study of seriousness. Danny sat on the top step of the stairs and heard it unfold. He couldn't believe he'd probably be grounded for liking a girl. When Mr. Stricker left, left with an 'I showed you' grin on his face, Danny's dad turned to him and demanded, "Come down here." As Danny came down the steps, his father smiled and his mother grinned. "That man is certified." He sat Danny down and gave him advice. "I'm not going to tell you to stop seeing that girl, but I am going to tell you this, that's a father who isn't going to put up with you soiling her. Do you understand what I mean?" His dad tried to give him a birds and bees conversation without using the word sex.

"Yes, I understand."

"Danny, I'm serious. You are of an age where your desires could get you in a lot of trouble. Our community isn't one where you can hide things and you could wind up a father, or worse in trouble with the law, because that dad's not playing.

Danny said, "So I can still see Bethany?"

"Yeah."

It delighted Danny that his parents backed him up. He had great parents, but it didn't matter because Bethany was under the control of her father, and she chose to obey him rather than follow her young heart. He watched her from afar, watching her by the lockers, rooting for the team as a cheerleader, always from afar. Danny went out with a few other girls, but he never felt the same connection as he did with Bethany. Bethany left the valley and married a guy from Olympia. The last time he saw her was the ten-year reunion and she arrived with a pregnant belly from her fourth child. Even with the years behind them and a mother of three and due with the next, she looked good. Danny regretted how it turned out. He was only in his thirties, if he could get out of that damn box, maybe there was still a life for him out there. He pounded on the lid, it cracked, a little dirt spilled through. Danny realized, another hit like that, and he could be buried in dirt before he could move. He decided to keep his anger to a minimum and shouted instead.

Chapter 54

Lyle crossed the river into Washington and found a seedy little motel along the interstate to hold up in. He carried in his extracts, set up several Bunsen burners, and filled Pyrex Beakers with liquids he'd stored in containers at the storage unit. He shut his phone off, he was now on his own and there would be no more calls he'd take. He started several liquids over small flames, took a shower, brushed his teeth, and went to bed.

When he woke, he prepared his first experiment. He poured a plant extract into a beaker and stirred the fluid until the liquid darkened to a brown and slowly congealed. When it had the thickness of syrup, Lyle took it to the bathroom and applied it to his hair. He combed it in and let it stand for ten minutes before washing his scalp. He toweled down and when he looked in the mirror, he laughed at the still downy colored eye brows. He applied more liquid to his brows and twenty minutes later, Lyle Thibodeaux was a brunette. In the mirror, a peculiar image of a man he didn't know stared back. He was a twin, and unlike other people, he saw himself every day when he looked at his sister. He seldom saw himself from the inside out, but rather the outside in.

Lyle had aided his sister all those years, but he never condoned what she did. With the detective lying in a hospital bed, fighting for her life, Lyle knew his culpability and it didn't sit well. Killing the farmer was one thing, he had it coming; an eye for an eye, but he only intended to disable and remove the detective, not kill her. If he could get to her, the amount of time for her to gain consciousness, coupled with rain in the forecast, there wouldn't be enough hours to save the farmer. As much as he knew he should flee and head back home to the mountain, he couldn't leave that woman to doctors who didn't know what to do with her condition. This plan amounted to an espionage script made for the movies, and Lyle knew in real life, these sorts of clandestine journeys didn't work. His chances of making it into a room where there were bound to be security was practically nil; yet he felt an overwhelming obligation to try.

Lyle gathered the antidote for the detective and completed his other experiments, filling several vials with various chemicals. He dismantled his makeshift lab, boxed up the supplies and emptied the room of his presence. He drove north, past Olympia and Tacoma, looking for the medical center mentioned in the news. When he made it to Seattle, he found a remote small quiet park to pull into. He had looked for a secluded one; the one he found would be the perfect spot. He turned on his phone and dialed 911.

"What's your emergency?" A steady beep behind the voice.

"I've had my car vandalized. Can I get a patrolman out here to look it over?"

"Where are you located?"

Lyle gave his location. They asked for a name, and he gave them one, "Daniel Gates."

How morbid.

He waited forty-five minutes, irritated how slow the police could be. He'd nearly given up when he saw a patrol car entering the lonely park. Lyle worried there would be two patrolmen, and there were. Either way, it wasn't too big an issue. He loaded his dart gun and tucked it in his coat, he stood on the opposite side of the car as they pulled up. Lyle pretended to investigate the damage. He turned to the patrol car, and an officer had his window rolled down.

He looked at Lyle with a policeman's caution. "Are you the person who called?"

"I am." Lyle straightened and held an indignant position. "I went for a walk, and when I came back someone had broken into my car." The driver stepped out while the other officer punched in numbers to a computer. Lyle moved around to the open window of the patrol car while the first officer inspected the vehicle. Lyle bent slightly and smiled through the window at the second officer. "Hello."

The officer acknowledged him but continued looking at his screen. When the first officer bent down to look at Lyle's car, he disappeared from view. Lyle causally pulled the dart gun from his coat and shot the officer in the passenger seat. The sedative acted swiftly, and as the officer called out, Lyle turned back to his car and shot a second dart at a surprised patrolman. That officer collapsed onto the ground.

Lyle walked around to the first officer, disappointed in what he saw. "Well, you are way too big for me." He returned to the police car and sized up the second officer, "You'll do." Lyle opened the passenger door and pulled the officer out. He disrobed him and put on the police uniform. He felt uncomfortable belting the sidearm, this meant he was armed and dangerous. He took a quick look at the computer screen the officer had preoccupied himself with and realized his car would be wanted as well. "In and out, Lyle."

Lyle drove off in a hurry, headed for the medical center. He wasn't sure how much time he had, but he doubted they'd put two and two together. All he really needed was to do his job and return south. He pulled into the hospital at eleven thirty a.m. He entered wearing the policeman's uniform and approached the front desk. "I'm on the poisoned detective detail. What floor is that?"

A security guard smiled and looked at a sheet of paper. "The fifth, west wing."

Lyle smiled, "Thank you."

Lyle felt out of character. He had always been sure of himself and always in control, but cloak and dagger stuff left him feeling naked and uncertain. He planned to pass a line of cops and get to another cop. He prepared for everything to end in a hail of bullets. It dumbfounded him he'd gone this far. He made it to the elevator and pushed five. When the doors opened, he crossed into an ICU ward, the pace of the floor was quiet, calm; nurses moved with patience in their steps. Lyle needed them to panic. He found a fire alarm and pulled it. As the motion around him went from serene to frantic, he made his way to the detective's room. An officer radioed in something from his shoulder mic.

Lyle hollered, "What do I do? This is my first day on the job?"

The officer sighed. "Stay here, I'll check the floor." He stepped forward. "Don't leave this spot!"

Lyle acted obedient. "You got it."

Lyle watched as the officer disappeared at a dead sprint down the hall and around a corner. With the commotion, nurses went into fire duty, a set pattern of rules. Lyle tipped his hat as a nurse passed him. Lyle stepped inside the room and felt disgusted the doctors hadn't figured this one out. He pulled the line into her shunt and deposited the contents of two syringes into her arm. "You'll be just fine in about twelve hours." He reinserted the line and checked her pupils. "Wake up, lady."

So far, so good.

Lyle slipped out of the room and the alarm stopped. He walked out the other direction, found a service elevator and took it down. He undid the shirt and tie, removed the holster, and bundled them up. He un-tucked his tee shirt and looked like any other visitor. On the ground floor he found a garbage can and quietly tossed the clothes and gun in, made it to the parking lot and breathed relief.

"No way." His heart raced to his throat. "Did I just get away with that?"

Chapter 55

Danny could hear the boards above him creak. Weight bore down and he suspected a rain had started. One of three things had a chance of happening, first, he would suffocate from the porous ground filling up with water and air having no way to reach him, second, a heavy enough rain to fill the box and drown him, or third, the weight of wet dirt becoming mud pushing through the pine and crushing him. All three were options that didn't appeal to him. He turned on the flashlight and ran the light along the boards above him, looking for the swelling of water. Worrying was worse than dealing with it. He turned to the diary, "Tell me more, Lauren." He occupied his thoughts with another chapter:

"Momma had our tenth sibling, a boy name Zachery. It is appropriate his name begin with the last letter of the alphabet, because it's the last child she will have. She passed away a few weeks after she gave birth. She seemed fine but she fell ill and never woke. Daddy took it very well, and he moved Rebecca into his room to take care of the baby. Rebecca is a good mother, even though she's only fourteen. I can see being Daddy's favorite is a curse and not a blessing. Zachery is a quiet baby, he

324

doesn't fuss much and Rebecca's milk must be rich because he is chubby. I asked Rebecca how she is producing milk and she said Daddy started her on a special pill about four months ago. How did he know she would need to produce milk? Did he know Momma was sick?"

Danny read through the daily life of a young girl, nothing extraordinary until he hit the eve of her seventeenth birthday.

October 30th, 1996: "It has been a while since I've written. Lyle and I are very independent, we live our own lives within the house, and yet we are only sixteen years old. Daddy has taken on full time responsibilities of teaching us, and he is heavy into the sciences. Momma was so much better with the humanities. I think Lyle will excel in the sciences, he such an intelligent man. Lyle and I are on the eve of our 17th birthday and Rebecca delivered the news that she is expecting a child. Zachery is barely two years old. I have applied to school in California, both Lyle and I have. Our scores for our junior year achievements are far ahead of students our age. Daddy has much money and has entertained the possibility of us enrolling at Stanford. He has stated that if only one of us gets in, the other will have to enroll nearby. He wants us to be together. He believes in family, that we must always be loyal to the Thibodeaux name."

Wednesday, 98': "I am Lauren Beatrix Thibodeaux and the birth of Rebecca's child has rocked my foundation. The child is a girl, downy white like our family, but with a cry that sounds like the hiss of a cat. Her fists clench and her face contorts as she screams with all her might but only manages an airy sound of agony, of which she seems to be in constantly. Daddy has committed us to family first but he has made his commitment extend to activities which are biologically unsound. His behavior appears to be very selfish, and yet, he is selfless in his commitment to family. He has chosen one of us rather than go out of the family. He is both dangerous and dedicated at the same time.

Friday, 98': "Today, I saw something I will never be able to forgive Daddy for. I saw him in the arms of a woman not a Thibodeaux. He did not see me, but I saw him. He was engaged in activity he swore us off of. He is a liar and not a champion of the Thibodeaux way. He has grown old, and his mind is

Danny started to see Lauren, the crazed woman he met in his front room, emerging from the little girl. He wished he could have gone back in time and stopped her father, but his atrocities started long before Lauren was born.

He put his hand up to the roof of the box and could feel the tension against the board, a slight bow in the center. "It's raining." He spoke to Lauren, "I don't have long; either I'm suffocating down here, drowning, or being crushed. Take your pick." Yelling about it wasn't going to do much good; pounding on the roof would be worse, so he calmly took a deep breath and turned off the light. He listened to the sounds around him. Even in the box, there were sounds of earth moving. The wood had a vibration, ever so slight, of shifting dirt, of dirt taking on new consistency.

One year, during a particularly bad flood, Danny went with his dad out to the field where one of the girls had attempted to make it back to the barn. She'd stepped into a depression, only lightly filled with water, but the ground saturated and water percolating upward. The mud she fell in acted like quicksand and she had kicked and struggled her way in deeper. By the time Danny and his dad made it out to her, they had to tie a chain around her shoulders and under her front legs and use the cat to pull her out. She slopped out like a wet cork, a gassy sound of wetness as she came unstuck from the mud. When they unchained her, they realized both her back legs were contorted and broken. Somehow before they had arrived, she'd twisted herself and the weight of her body snapped both hind legs. Danny found it amazing that the cow had so much determination to get out that she had struggled to the point of injury. It's what desperation looked like; it's what defeat looked like. In the end, with on-looking cows scattering in fear, his father pulled out the rifle and laid her to rest in the middle of a rain-soaked field. Nobody complained, and there was no remorse. It was the best option available. Better to not suffer. Danny could only hope his end would be as quick.

Chapter 56

Lyle worked his way down I-5, past Tacoma, past Olympia, stopping in the last major city before Longview, in the little town of Centralia. He dropped off the freeway and stopped in at a country restaurant with a painted rooster on the wall and a cock-a-doodle-doo recording when he entered. The place was dark.

"Can I have dinner in the lounge?"

A woman in a checkered skirt and an apron said, "Absolutely."

It was still daylight, the lounge TV blared, and Lyle stuffed himself in a back corner in case his image came up on the screen. He nursed a beer and had chicken fried steak with starchy mash potatoes. His mother used to make chicken fried steak. He remembered her death. She quit breathing one day. Daddy said it was from complication in childbirth, but the truth is, she was two weeks past childbirth. Knowing what he knew now, she was poisoned, and he had a good idea who poisoned her. Mother made Lauren jealous. She had Daddy's attention and that bugged Lauren. Daddy treated it with ambivalence because he couldn't turn away his daughter. Daddy had the strong belief in family, in the Thibodeaux code.

Lyle blended in as the late afternoon crowd started filing in. He knew better than to be too exposed, so he lifted his hand to the waitress as she passed and asked for the check. He laid two tens down and took leave before the stations started airing the news. He was close enough to Dirtwater; he knew the town folk were probably wary of strangers. Lyle pulled his cap down tight and stared at the ground as he quietly left. He pushed through the doors and came face to face with two patrolmen. He sensed they studied him, and his paranoia got the best of him, sure they recognized him. He nodded and let out a quiet titter. He placed his hands in his coat pockets and found his keys. He didn't give them a second look as he jumped in, pulled out of the parking lot, and hopped on the freeway.

Lyle felt more alone than in his entire life. Even during Lauren's 'moments' he didn't feel alone. He knew she needed him and even with her anger venting on some unsuspecting victim, she would return to being his sister when they came together. The killings were nothing more than white elephants, something they never discussed; never in all the years she actively killed did they mention the moments. They were as if they never existed. He wanted to go home.

Lyle pulled off in Longview and found a pay phone. His nervousness prevented him from using his cell phone, sure they could trace it. If the feds were involved, they had no restrictions in how they could find him, legal or otherwise. Lyle dialed the number to his brother, Michael.

"Hello?"

"Michael."

Michael paused. "Safe?" He spoke in code.

"I think so."

"Where are you?"

Lyle said, "In Washington."

Rebecca told us what happened to Sister. She said you weren't going to come home."

Lyle had resisted but had a change of heart. "I've changed my mind."

"A couple of detectives have already visited Rebecca."

"I need assistance."

"We can be there today."

"No, I don't need you here that quick, but I do need you to rent a vehicle large enough to bring a casket back."

"Are you going to bring Lauren home?"

Lyle bowed his head and admitted, "No, you are bringing me home."

Michael cursed, "Damn it, Lyle. You are not dying."

Lyle reminded his little brother, "I'm still the boss of the family. I have no other options."

Michael insisted, "A gunfight with the police is unnecessary."

Lyle laughed. "I'm not going to have a gun fight. I'm going to end my life."

Michael begged his brother, "Don't be like that. We can come get you, we can hide you out. They will never find you."

"Michael, it would be one more secret in a family of secrets, bad secrets. I'm tired of this life. If I'd been any kind of big brother, our family wouldn't be as screwed up as it is. I was weak. I didn't stand up to Lauren. I didn't stand up to Daddy. I was the first link in the disaster."

"And you think killing yourself is going to rectify our shitty life? Let me remind you, we might be as dysfunctional as they come, but we own half a mountain. We are pretty rich for being so messed up."

"And you think that makes it okay?"

"Hell no, but it makes it tolerable. Besides, not all of us turned out psychotic. Last I checked it was just one of us."

Lyle laughed. "Who is the mother of your children Michael?" Who is the mother of Walter's children?"

Michael fired back. "It's the Thibodeaux way. We are a special family with superior abilities."

Lyle said, "No we're not. You have been drinking the Kool-Aid all these years. We are nothing but inbred children of a twisted father. It's amazing we still have a gene pool left." Lyle wasn't going to change his brother's mind, but he wasn't going to turn him away either. His order to come get him would be followed because it was the Thibodeaux way. "You will have to pick me up at the morgue."

"Why the morgue?"

"Because if I kill myself and they don't find me, they will be all over you guys for the next hundred years and you don't need the authorities snooping around our lake. They are liable to take every child we have." Lyle had lived for the last ten years in the real world; his maturation was complete. He understood the right and wrong of his past. "All I ask, is you don't let them cut into me. I am of sound mind and I'm not Lauren, so I want my body left intact. Are we clear about that?"

Michael softly said, "Yes."

And I need you here within two days. If you have to fly up and rent a U-Haul, so be it, but don't be late. The later you are, the better chance they have of cutting into me."

"Where will you be?"

"I haven't a clue, but it will probably be in Longview, Washington. It'll be on the news, that much I'm sure. I will have a package for you at the Longview bus station, locker 39."

"We'll be there. Zachery, Daniel, and Walter will come with me." Michael paused. "I love you, Brother."

"I love you too."

Chapter 57

Danny grew tired, oxygen became scarce, and he feared a rainstorm had gripped the valley and sealed his fate. He would rather die entombed and not buried under a rush of mud, so he opted to leave the lid alone. He figured he could snap the wood, but he knew he would be met with dirt and mud filling the box to the brim. He accepted fate and decided to continue reading. He chose to read out loud:

November, 98': "Daddy has broken the Thibodeaux code, and I will have none of it. It has come to my attention that he may have also killed mother. Lyle passively accused me of killing mother and when I called him on it, he said she did not die of natural causes, she was poisoned. If that is the case, I blame Daddy, and if he has led Lyle to believe I have done so, I will have to have a talk with him."

December 98': "Daddy has taken ill. I think he knows what he's ill with, and thankfully for my listening to his lectures, I am aware he has suffered an ingestion of a drug for which there is no cure. Within him lies a monster that must be vanquished.

I will seek that monster out wherever he is, for I do believe he is the embodiment of something not Thibodeaux, and the Thibodeaux way is the only way."

Christmas day, 98': "Daddy died a rather painful death today. He was defiant to the end and peculiarly loyal. He knew who did this to him and yet, convinced Lyle his was a death at his own hands. If you ask me, he was not man enough to admit he'd been beat, and he was beat because he wasn't focused on the Thibodeaux way."

August, 99': "I am worried about the kids. Lyle and I are headed off to college, Stanford to be exact. (We scored very high on our entrance exams. I want to be an attorney. Lyle wants to be a genius) Rebecca has assumed guardianship of the rest of the siblings. I'm afraid she isn't the teacher Daddy was and the kids might suffer without him there. With Michael's help they should be fine. Michael is an exceptional sixteen-year-old man. He and Angela have taken our old room. I have nothing but fond memories of the room above the house.

"We will not hurt for money. Lyle said Daddy was very wise with money and had a large inheritance from his father in Louisiana. I'm sorry I

never met him. Both he and my grandmother died tragically in an accident. Their cause of death was never determined. They had just the two kids, and Daddy received the entire fortune upon Lucretia's death."

Friday: "I am filled with trepidation of this move. Lyle says we should live off campus, but we will be in different classrooms, and I have never been far from Lyle. I don't know if I will be able to function if I am separated from him. I am so angst by this that my awareness of Daddy's monster is all around me. I know when I see him. It's almost as though the fear in my heart gives me the vision of second sight. On our way to California, at a gas station, I saw Daddy in a clerk. While Lyle filled up with gas, I defeated Daddy again. I fear though that the reason why he keeps coming back is because he must have his head separated from his body. Daddy taught me that rule when he killed Jackie. He told me only when the body was separated from the head, would the monster within be defeated."

Danny interrupted his oration. "You went over the deep end little girl. I have no idea what became of your sanity, but I give you credit for surviving as long as you did." He rested his feet on her legs, her body twisted and stiff at the foot side of the box. He heard a noise that sounded as though it came from inside the box; he jumped a bit and shined the light where Lauren's head was. He wanted to make sure she hadn't come to life, or her eyes weren't open, or she wasn't laughing. Nothing had changed, except for the fact he really had to pee. "No scaring the shit out of me, okay?" He rubbed his face, the temperature felt as though it rose ten degrees.

Danny put the book down. It turned from a tragedy into a horror story. He recounted the summer his dad came in the house and said, "Grab some blankets. Someone has hit a tree up the rise of Swaheenie." Danny didn't understand why he had to bring blankets. It was a warm day. They jumped in the truck and hurried up the North Slope. There was a sharp turn on the primitive road and a station wagon had slid off the gravel embankment, probably traveling at least fifty. They'd hit a cedar flush, and it appeared no one wore seatbelts. The blankets weren't for comfort; they were to cover the bodies of the five family members. Two of them so small, one blanket engulfed them both. Danny had never seen a dead person, a person whose life had been cut short, not by disease, but rather by the instantaneous moment of fate. The expression on the mother's face was one divorced from surprise or shock, as though she never saw it coming. Her expression appeared as if in mid-sentence of a joke, a hint of smile on her face as though she planned to break out into laughter. Danny and his father sat with the bodies for a half hour before the sheriff made it to the crash site, all the while, Danny's father lectured him on the perils of the primitive road. His father feared when Danny came of age to drive, living that close to the North Slope, he'd have an odds-on-favorite to suffer the same fate. His father's voice buzzed unnecessary noise. All he could think about were the two children under the blanket. If fate slates someone for death, it should be by fault, not by accident. Unless you go looking for trouble, trouble shouldn't come looking for you.

Chapter 58

Lyle held his hand out and felt the dapple of a spring shower. He smiled and stated, "Farmer, your hour's at hand." He knew a hard shower would probably suffocate the farmer; the ground would turn to liquid above his coffin. He looked at his watch, day turned into night.

Lyle stopped at the local bus station and found locker 39. He put a bag inside and signed the key over to the front office for a Michael Thibodeaux. He left and located another sleepy motel and carried in his supplies for another experiment. While the burners boiled chemicals, Lyle paid attention to the news, breaking news out of Seattle.

"According to hospital officials, Detective Karen Zimmerman has awakened and is remarkably stable." The camera cut away to a doctor speaking on behalf of the hospital. "Small miracles in the field of medicine occasionally happen. All I can say is yesterday we were prepared to cut her life supports and today she is asking for a discharge." The doctor shook his head. "This is unexplainable."

Lyle scoffed, "No it's not!"

The reporter continued. "There were reports that someone staged a brazen attempt on Detective Zimmerman's life today."

The doctor disputed that. "That's not known for sure. We had an incident that is somewhat unexplainable. That's all."

Lyle again yelled with fury, "If you did a proper blood test, you would see someone slipped her the cure and it wasn't an attempt on her life it was her life redeemed! I am not a monster! I did that for her."

The camera cut to the reporter as she spoke directly to her audience. "Speculation is that the Thibodeaux twins may have visited this hospital. Police have surveillance of a dark-haired man who resembles Lyle Lawrence Thibodeaux dressed as a police officer. Further speculation is, wherever Mr. Thibodeaux is, his sister isn't far behind. That uniform came from an officer who they ambushed earlier today in a small park south of the city. The officer and his partner were inexplicably left alive and unharmed. The whereabouts of area farmer Daniel Gates, the man Detective Zimmerman was detailing, is still unknown. The Thibodeauxes are believed to have gone on a rampage through the town of Dirtwater after killing a secretary at Mr. Thibodeaux's place of business in Portland. The dead include two seasoned investigators, a fellow attorney with Ms. Thibodeaux, a store clerk, an elderly couple, and the possibility of Mr. Gates. The police are asking for citizens to be on the lookout for a late model Audi, a 1998 Audi A6 Quattro with an Oregon license plate. The Thibodeauxes are considered extremely dangerous." Lyle jumped off his bed and grabbed his keys. He stumbled out the door and down the stairs; rain pelted the pavement in the beat of a snare drum. He jumped in the car and pulled out of the parking lot, the hiss of water beneath the tires. Down the street was a used car lot. It was dark and the lot closed for the day. Lyle pulled in and parked the car to the rear of the property, in amongst other cars. He made sure he'd removed all his possessions and left the keys in the ignition. He stepped out into a pouring rain and casually walked back to the motel, his collar turned up and a cap shielding his view with a steady drip from the bill. Lyle's world shrank by the minute. He thought about Cindy, the car plates would lead right back to her, and she would be under scrutiny as well. He felt sorry he'd involved her in all this.

He stood dripping on the carpet of his room and peeled off his clothes, changing into the only clothes he had left, the camouflage from his night of hunting. He sat and composed a letter. 'To Whom It May Concern, I, Lyle Lawrence Thibodeaux did not participate or have anything to do with the murders committed by my sister.' He studied it and knew that would never be the Thibodeaux way. He crumpled the paper with a swipe of his hand and tossed it in the waste basket. He started another, 'It is with deepest regrets that I was unable to help my sister through her darkest hours.' Again, he rejected the opening. The Thibodeaux way was one for all. He closed his eyes and bowed his head, cursing the empty room, "I must fall upon the sword of my family's honor and accept I am just as guilty."

He looked over his shoulder and another report out of Seattle flashed across the screen. The earlier reporter made it past a crowd where Detective Zimmerman pushed her way through the throng of reporters. "Detective Zimmerman?" microphones overwhelmed her. "Is it safe for you to be up and out of bed?"

She looked stern. "I'm fine. I woke up and felt like a million bucks. I have work to do. It has come to my attention that Mr. Gates is still unaccounted for. It is my job to find him."

Lyle raised his eyebrows. "Good luck with that." She seemed feisty. Perhaps letting her recover so quickly wasn't such a smart move. She appeared to be someone who would not take finding the farmer dead very well.

He sat up and went to one of his experiments. He turned the Bunsen burner off and let it cool. He carried it to the bathroom and reversed his hair color, rubbing the viscous fluid onto his scalp, rubbing his eyebrows and letting it stand. Like magic the dark bled out off the strands. He rinsed his hair in the tub and towel dried his head. Looking in the mirror, he saw himself again. He hungered for something to eat but he knew a full stomach would be a bad idea. It was best if he made himself comfortable for the night and relaxed. It was still early; the news had rolled over into the Wheel of Fortune. He turned the volume down and marveled at the ferocity of the rain dancing off the roof above him. He'd read about the spring rains of the Pacific Northwest, and how they could bring floods with them, floods that saturated the ground. His thoughts drifted to the little girl who always followed his every move. He remembered a little sister, long before an illness jaded her and consumed everything she believed, and how she would laugh at the simple things in life, a fly landing on a window, the way birds dug for worms, the ripple of a rock skipping across the lake, footprints on a virgin lawn's dew covered morning, but nothing made her laugh more than when the rain would dance on the roof above their heads.

Chapter 59

Danny may not have had his bearings on how much time he'd been in the box, but he could guess it went on two days. He'd slept, lightly throughout his time in the box, off and on for what he guessed amounted to an hour here and there. He must have dozed off because he felt disoriented, as though surprised by his own awareness. He turned on the flashlight, it dimmed slightly. He slapped it and the light brightened. "Son of a bitch. If this light goes, I am going to freak." He shined it on Lauren, "I'm going to finish up your diary tonight, today, this morning. Whatever the time of day it is. I see you didn't write much after you went to college." He carried on a conversation with a corpse, but at least he knew he had some sort of audience, dead or alive.

"I vanquished Daddy today. I was shocked to find him in one of my classmates. He clearly followed us to California. Anyway, I was invited to Half Moon Bay for a study session with one of my classmates, a very nice boy name Gage. Gage, little did I know, had Daddy lurking around that head of his because Gage suggested we go swimming and while we were out there, he tried to touch me, he

violated the Thibodeaux way. I grabbed him by the neck, and he laughed and laughed the way Daddy would, until he realized I wasn't letting go and he was having a hard time staying afloat. Daddy isn't a very good swimmer when someone is holding him down. Sadly, I couldn't bring him to shore and separate his head. Now I must endure Daddy finding his way back to me in someone else. Daddy escapes and poor Gage drowns. I was so sorry Daddy got away."

Danny scanned a few pages, innocuous references to flying home for the holidays and special times with her brother. Danny looked for a death toll. He thumbed through ten years of quiet behavior. About a year before now, she picked up with a much faster pace.

"Jeff Lambert, I was so sorry he wanted to spend time with me. It was only a matter of time before Daddy entered him. Sure enough, at one of our Saturday night movies, even though I kept him at bay for fear Daddy would enter him, it happened anyway. Daddy can be so gullible. I led him out to the national park; in the massive fog of a late summer night and this time I did what I knew I had

to do. I separated Daddy's head from his body, and to make sure I did it right, I separated every limb too. When I was done, I had to call Lyle. I was too drained from a day with Daddy. I cried to Lyle, and he was so good about coming out to the park and helping me destroy the monster of Daddy. It was a good day for the Thibodeauxes. I took Lyle home and I consummated our family name, and he didn't cry once.

"Lyle has been giving me a drug. I hope he doesn't have Daddy in him. I need to be vigilant to the possibility Daddy jumped into Lyle when he helped me dispose of Daddy. I believe if I can keep Lyle away from passions outside the family, I can drive Daddy out. If not, Daddy will have to be vanquished."

Danny said to Lauren's head, "Seriously? You were seriously contemplating killing your brother? Good Lord, get a grip woman!" He continued reading.

"I learned today that Daddy is in women as well. I discovered a wine lady he entered. I didn't have time to separate her head, but I did make sure he wouldn't have that body to tease my sweet brother

with. I have no time for this, Daddy. Why do you insist on staying in this world? Stay gone!"

Danny nudged Lauren's torso. "Well, at least you opened up a dialogue with your dad again."

"Lyle and I went to a movie tonight. Daddy was there. I am not sure how to get him out of the women. He is more determined than ever to make Lyle fall from the Thibodeaux way. Why, Daddy? We followed you all our lives, why now? Lyle loves me, don't tempt his heart. I would like one day to have children, don't take over his body and cheat on me. I will not allow that."

Danny noticed the last few entries were only days old.

"Daddy has learned how to be in many places at once. He is in the woman Lyle works with, and he is with a woman I found on his Lyle's phone. I shall bring you out, Daddy. You have never been able to stop me from defeating you, and I will defeat you again.

"I defeated you, Daddy. The women you are in are no more. Now, I shall get you out of Hamilton."

Danny slammed the book closed. "Your brother is an ungrateful A hole. I actually saved his life, and this is the thanks I get?" Danny shouted, "Let me out!" a drop of water pelted his forehead. "Oh shit." He could hear the board groan. He ran his finger along the edges of the boards, they swelled with water. "Fuck, I'm dead." A board cracked and snapped in the middle of the lid; mud filtered in. He tucked his knees up and used his hands to push the dirt and mud to the far corner of the box, covering Lauren as he did. Water started spilling in, first muddy brown and then opaque dirty brown. Danny tried to make sense of that. Why wasn't the mud rolling in, why only water, with dirt above him, it should be muddier. He pushed on the wood directly over his head, the boards had no give, yet in the center, cleaner and cleaner water seeped in. The box filled up quickly. He lay in water about three inches deep and growing. He held the flashlight up so it would still give him light. He could hear something, the shifting of soil, as though a pool splashed above him, water filled the box at a quicker pace. "Well, Lauren, we took door number two, drowning." Danny didn't know what to do. If he hit hard enough, he could break the board above his head, but there was nearly four feet of dirt over him, mud or no mud, without the ability to sit up, he would be dead instantly. He watched in horror as the box reached ten inches of water. He lifted his head up to catch a breath of air.

Chapter 60

Lyle finished his experiments and put the distilled liquids in small vials. He disassembled his equipment, boxed them up, and took them out to the dumpster, unrelenting rain pounded the pavement. The sky had opened up and dumped the tears of a million hearts onto the land. He completed his job. If they hadn't found the farmer by now, they weren't finding him alive. Lyle returned to his room, took a warm shower and rested on his bed. If no one discovered Lyle for another twenty-four hours, he may have the opportunity to watch them find the farmer's body. The detective had the right attitude and probably the right idea. If anyone would find his grave, she would.

Most of his life, Lyle cleaned up after people, mostly his sister. His was not a life of initiating contact; the life his father gave them assured him of that. His action against the farmer was his first just act, or perhaps not, but it was the Thibodeaux way, and Lyle might have come to realize the Thibodeaux way had many flaws, but they were flaws he'd lived by for too long to let go of easily. This was about loyalty, about family. If someone killed a family member, they must pay.

He clutched a vial. He didn't want to go on, he wanted to ingest it now, but if he did, he wouldn't have the satisfaction of knowing he'd vanquished Lauren's last person she raged against. Maybe that killing would have brought her home from the other side of sanity. Maybe insanity would have left her for good. Lyle would never know; the farmer killed her.

Lyle turned on his phone. He checked his voice mail to see if anyone attempted to contact him. A half dozen calls from callers identifying themselves as authority figures, more hang ups than he received in a year, and one voice he recognized who said, "Call me." Lyle rubbed his forehead, wondered if it was a smart idea. As reluctant as he felt, the truth couldn't hide that when they located Doris' car, the police would know he was in the area, if this was a setup, the only thing they'd get a jump on was the area. He didn't plan on leaving the room, he, like the farmer, was in a tomb. He was in the place he planned on being found in. He called.

Cindy answered. "Lyle?"

Lyle whispered, "Yes."

"I was so worried. The police were here today. They asked me a million questions and then took your car."

"Where are they now?"

"They left and said they'd be back. Lyle they're treating me as if I had something to do with this."

Lyle sighed. "They're saying the same thing about me." He changed the subject, "Did you give your mother her shot today?"

She said. "Your coworker Niraj did."

Lyle smiled. "He already contacted you?"

She blurted, "He showed up at my mother's house at six in the morning. He said he would be administering the shots and taking data."

Lyle said. "Raj is a good man. He will make sure your mom stays on task."

Cindy apologized. "I am so sorry I said the things I did. I know this has to be hard on you. Raj said you are a focused man and thoughtful enough to give your research to him."

"That doesn't change anything. What is about to happen will be justified."

"I enjoyed our time together, even though it was brief, you entered my life and have saved my mother's." she choked back tears. "What are you going to do?"

"You don't want to know."

She asked. "You aren't going to do something rash are you?"

"Rash? No." Lyle cautioned her. "I'm going to do what's right."

Cindy followed Lyle's words. "What does that mean?"

"Just what it sounds like." He changed the subject. "You made me a happy man among all the turmoil. If not for my life, I could have spent a lifetime with you."

"Thank you. That's so kind of you to say." She insisted, "You were the blessing."

Lyle thought about those words. "I don't know about a blessing. One cannot dismiss the un-dismissible because of an act of generosity. However, if I was a blessing, it's because my thoughts were wrapped around you. I was taken in by your beauty," There was silence between them, a final goodbye. It was unexpected but Lyle cherished it. There wouldn't be more conversations with Cindy, this would end it. He choked on the words, "Goodbye," and disconnected. He turned the phone off and walked to the desk to write his thoughts about this woman, to lift the veil of Thibodeaux off his indoctrinated life. Lyle wrote poetry to this woman, he told her he loved her, he wished in another life he could meet her under better circumstance, but he never dwelt on the circumstances surrounding the life he had or the days leading up to this point. Lyle couldn't rationalize to anyone what happened, because it was irrational, likewise, blaming his sister, his father, or himself wasn't going to make a difference in the end. He wrote poetry. Page after page, he wrote words he never expressed, all about one woman. He poured his thoughts onto paper. With each stanza the words became lighter and filled with more destiny and spirit. Not the letter he'd expected to write, and not one the police would understand. Lyle laughed as he finished, they would certainly think he was mad.

He collected the thirty-six pages and placed them face up on dresser, retrieved his car's pink slip and signed it off to Cindy. He slipped it in between the pages and added a cover sheet that read, "To Cindy."

He turned on the ten o'clock news and surfed for more coverage of the Dirtwater massacre, but a program about a dysfunctional family dealing with an addicted family member sidetracked him. The trouble of the family enthralled him, how one member could destroy so much, and yet the family willingly participated in going to the ends of the earth for that one member who they deemed still part of the family. He realized the Thibodeaux code ran strong in a lot of families, and a lot of families paid the price. He bowed his head. He wasn't alone. The whole world had a form of the Thibodeaux code. The next day was only hours away and that day would be judgment day.

Chapter 61

Danny braced for a grim ending. The horror of the rising water met with confusion as he heard rapid scratching on the middle of the lid. "What is that?" Danny now floated a foot off the bottom as the water filled a third of the box. He twisted his frame and craned his neck as close to the crack in the lid as he could get, holding the flashlight up so he wouldn't die in darkness. He was a foot from the crack, the flashlight shedding light on the cascading water when a snout pushed through the hole and a dog barked. The image startled Danny and he reared back but realized something tried to get to him. Danny didn't know how big a space the dog had dug, but he lay back down, and with his head under water, bent his knees enough to tuck them snug against the lid. He strained and pushed against the opening and tore a gaping hole into the lid. Dirt and mud collapsed onto Danny, but the dog had dug a big enough opening that walls along the hole in the dirt fell in and not a total dump. Danny surfaced, gathered a breath and tried it again, another board snapped and more of the dirt cascaded in, but the hole grew bigger. Danny was now in a box full of dirt and mud, but he wasn't giving up. He dropped down a third time, the ooze of mud all around him, he kneed the boards again and the lid ripped open, and a spaniel landed on his lap. Danny surfaced, wiped his face and shined the light on a dirty wet spaniel. He laughed, "Tess, I assume?"

The spaniel that darted off the day Danny found Jack and Pat, came to his rescue and barked with excitement. He had no idea how or why this dog found him, but he hugged her as though she were human. It was the dead of night and water still streamed in and dirt collapsed around them. Danny stood and used a board to clear mud way from the walls of the hole. He tossed the spaniel out and dug a foot hold to lift himself out. The dirt gave way, and he slid back in. He tried again and still couldn't lift himself out. The earth began reclaiming the hole with mud. Danny stood waist deep, Tess barked, and the rain fell in sheets. Danny had nothing left, tall enough to see out of the hole, but he'd be buried up to his chest in mud in minutes. He looked at Tess, "Could be worse, I could be down there with Lauren right now."

Tess growled.

"Yeah, my sentiments too."

From the distance he saw a light bobbing up and down, then another. Someone yelled, "Danny!"

"Over here." Danny waved his arms. "Over here."

Peace settled with him when he saw John and Karen. "What took you so long?"

John said, "I looked for you in the pit and Sleeping Beauty was in bed."

Danny brushed mud and dirt off his chest. "How long have I been in this hole?"

John shined the flashlight on him, a mud covered giant. "I'd say since the dinosaurs."

Karen said, "Two days."

Danny reached out for a lift and stated, "God, I got to pee." The two of them locked onto the Danny's hand and braced themselves as though they played tug o war. "Pull, you two." He felt like the cow in the mud, and he hoped he didn't end up with the same ending. Danny kicked and braced a leg on the back wall, pushed and climbed his way out. He stood and raised his arms. "Yes!" John slapped him on the chest and Karen hugged him.

She exhaled. "I'm so happy to see you."

He placed a hand on her shoulder. "I'm happy to see you too. I was worried about you."

Karen directed her flashlight toward the hole. "Did they bury you in there?"

Danny started walking to the house, "No, they didn't, just the brother. She was in the hole with me."

Karen helped Danny steady his walk. "And how did she manage to get in the hole with you."

"She didn't, I managed to get in the hole with her."

Karen suggested, "We might want to talk about that before this goes to report."

Danny agreed. "That's probably a good idea." He turned his attention to his left where John propped up Danny's other side. "How about you, anything you want to talk about?"

John shrugged. "Nope, nothing I can think of." He hesitated, "Oh wait, I did come into some money while you were gone."

Danny said, "You don't say."

The sheriff shot back, "No, I don't say." He squeezed Danny's rib cage.

Danny was able to grin after two days in a hole. "Have you two met my other dog, Tess?

Karen said, "We heard her barking like she'd found a treasure."

Danny laughed. "She did." He teased his friends, "A dog saved me instead of you two."

Karen admitted, "I'm sorry, Dan."

Danny stopped her, "Are you kidding me. My two favorite people pulled me out of a hole someone destined me to spend the rest of my life in. You have nothing to be sorry about."

She said, "I'm talking about my lousy detail work."

Danny pointed out, "That boy's smart. You're lucky you didn't get killed too." He said, "He knocked me out alive, then sticks me in that hole and be damned if he doesn't wake my ass up with another shot." The brother had amazed Danny. "I couldn't move, but I could pay attention. I know what those dogs were hit with now, probably you too."

Karen thought out loud, "That explains yesterday."

Danny listened. "What?"

"Thirteen hours ago, I was about to have the plug pulled on my respirator, when Lyle breaks into my room. Everyone thought it was an attempt on my life that he backed out of, but an hour later, I'm up eating solid food, and three hours later, I'm walking out of the hospital."

Danny pictured his adversary. "Was he caught?"

"Nope, walked out without a problem."

Why would he save you?"

"Thanks a lot!"

"Not that I'm not grateful, but why?" They made it to the house and onto the porch; a full array of lights and not just a flashlight to direct his sight. Danny offered an explanation. "I think I know why he saved you."

He didn't say anything, and Karen prodded him, "And?"

"I think I was his first victim, and the only victim he was interested in."

Karen stepped to a hose and turned on the spigot. "Why do you think that?"

"What time is it?"

John said, "One a.m."

Danny pointed at Karen. "You are not spraying me with cold water on a cold March night."

She laughed, "It's April now!" She fired away with a jet of water, rinsing mud and dirt from Danny. Over the hiss of spraying, she hollered, "Why do you think you were his first?"

"I got to know Lauren pretty well down there in the hole."

Karen stopped spraying and looked horrified. "Was she alive?"

Danny laughed, "Sort of." He reached inside his shirt, wedge between his waist and pants, was a book. "I have her diary." He handed it to Karen. "You might be interested in reading it."

Karen winked. "I guess I will still have detail if you want me."

Danny grinned. "I'd like that."

John interrupted, "I think we have police business."

Karen agreed. "Let's get you showered and ready for an interview."

Chapter 62

Lyle woke up restless. The dreams outweighed the sleep. He rolled out from under the sheets and made his way to the restroom, showered, changed into the clothes hanging to dry and settled in front of the TV. He scanned the channels and made himself comfortable when he heard commotion outside. He slid his hand between two pieces of curtain and cracked them wide enough to view the scenery. The parking lot bustled with a convention of suspicious looking people. He sighed.

That was a little faster than I expected.

His room phone rang and with a gait of little concern he reached for it. "Hello?"

"Mr. Ketchum?" Lyle had given that as his name to the front desk clerk.

"And this is?"

"I'm Mr. Ahern, the manager. We have a package for you."

Lyle started laughing. "Can you bring it up?"

Mr. Ahern paused. "We're not allowed to, but I have it ready if you want to hurry up."

Lyle rubbed his face at the lack of transparency of Mr. Ahern's words. "Yeah, okay. I'll be down in a jiffy."

Lyle figured ten minutes would clue them in he wasn't coming down. He continued surfing the channels, hoping they'd made it to the farm and found the farmer dead. If they did, the news would be all over it. Weather reports were pretty prominent, as was a flood alert. He waited it out; hopefully something had developed over night. He held the vial and had another waiting by the sink.

The phone rang again. He reached across the bed and picked it up. "Yes?"

"Mr. Ketchum, we have this package, don't you want to come down and get it?"

Lyle was blunt. "Mr. Ahern, tell them I'm not coming down and coming in would be dangerous." Lyle didn't have a weapon, other than a dart gun, but they didn't know that.

The phone went dead.

A voice boomed through a megaphone. "Mr. Thibodeaux, we have your room surrounded, please surrender. Nobody else needs to get hurt."

Lyle shook his head. Nobody else was going to get hurt, the person who did all the killing died. He kept his attention on the TV. He had to know before he went, if he'd completed his final task.

The phone rang. Lyle was tired of the volley. "What?"

"Mr. Thibodeaux, this is the FBI, I'm agent Darbe. I'd like to settle this peacefully. Would it be all right if I came to your room so we could talk?"

"Agent Darbe, I'm quite capable of coming down on my own. If you wait until I am done with what I'm doing, I will come down, unarmed. If you insist on pressing me, this could get bloody. It's your call." Lyle sounded convincing.

"We want a peaceful resolution, but you are endangering a lot of people by not cooperating."

"Who's not cooperating? I said I'll be down when I'm done."

Agent Darbe reminded Lyle. "This isn't your rules, Mr. Thibodeaux."

"I beg to differ. If you haven't already looked, behind the dumpster is a box of cooking equipment. Come up and you will see just how explosive what I cooked is." Lyle figured they weren't well versed enough to know if that was fact or fiction, and to discover the truth would take at least the amount of time he asked for. Lyle put the phone down and moved to the window. He peeked through the curtain and could see the crowd being moved back. They weren't taking any chances. Lyle stepped back to the phone and listened.

"Okay Mr. Thibodeaux. What are your demands?"

"Demands?" He laughed. "You think I have demands? Or maybe I'm stalling?"

Agent Darbe negotiated, "What do you want?"

"I already said, I need to wait until I am done."

"What are you doing?"

"Do you seriously want to know?"

"If that will help us resolve this, yeah, I'd like to know."

"I'm watching TV."

Like a good negotiator, Agent Darbe tried to befriend Lyle. "Is it a good show?"

"I don't know; I haven't gotten to the part I want to see."

Agent Darbe asked. "Is it a movie or a TV show?"

"Neither." There was a pause, and Lyle laughed. "No, it's not porn either."

"I didn't say it was."

"I'm sure you were thinking it."

"So, then what is it?"

"Weather report, news, updates."

"Are you waiting for anything in particular?"

Lyle had finished the conversation. "Yeah, the sports. Bye." He hung up as Agent Darbe asked something. He sat on the floor behind the bed so he wasn't a target for a sniper's shot.

A news update ticker taped across the screen. 'Suspected serial killer pinned in at Longview motel.' They interrupted the weather-related program with a view of the outside of his lodging. "I hadn't expected this, but it could be entertaining." He reached up and grabbed his pillow. He rolled onto his stomach and rested his chin on soft downy. He used the remote to increase the volume.

"After a tip from a motel clerk, the FBI confirmed that the man who checked into this motel is the sought after brother and alleged mastermind of the brutal murders of several residents of Dirtwater."

Lyle couldn't believe they hadn't the energy to put together a decent investigation. No one had taken the time to do any forensics.

"What some are considering a miracle, the last and final victim was found alive on his farm."

The news cut to an interview of the farmer. "I'm lucky to be alive." He could see they filmed from the gravesite. "I was drugged and put in a cattle box four feet down. Thanks to one of my dogs, I was literally dug out."

Lyle couldn't believe he didn't kill those dogs. Then he heard something surprising. The farmer said something off camera but audible, "Be careful with her, and see she gets a proper burial. That woman died twenty years ago." How could he know that? How did he know his sister suffered all her life after the abuse of their father? He watched as they removed a body bag.

"Inside the bag is the body of Lauren Thibodeaux, the other half of the duo killers, killed by Mr. Gates in a home invasion. Lyle Thibodeaux buried his sister's body and a live Mr. Gates in this hole." The camera showed a deep excavated hole. "Where it is speculated Mr. Thibodeaux sought revenge for his sister's death."

"Well, they got that right." Lyle wasn't satisfied with the outcome. Revenge wasn't served, but he did misjudge the farmer; clearly, he'd spoken to his sister, maybe before she tried to kill him, and he understood her torment. There was nothing Lyle could do; he committed himself to another plan.

Lyle opened the vial and brought it to his lips. In a tilt, he drank the fluid. He sat up and walked to the bathroom. He washed the vial and took the second vial on the sink and poured the contents into the empty vial. He capped it and put it in his pocket. His heart had a sharp pain running through it. He carried the empty vial in his hand and staggered to the door. He opened the door and fell out onto the balcony. He had enough energy to roll to his back and catch the herds of gun-carrying soldiers-of-law ascend upon him.

In his spinning thoughts, an uneven echoing rhythm of voices called out, "He's ingested something."

Someone grabbed his chin. "What is this?"

Lyle smiled. "My apology." His mind slipped to darkness.

Chapter 63

Danny hurried to the bathroom as his first duty, the greatest pee of his life. He mumbled. "About time." He had convinced himself that if he had been permanently stuck in that box, he was never going to soil it; however, another half hour in that hole and he would have lost all control. Danny stripped off his hosed down clothes; dirt, mud, and water slapped against the tile of the bathroom. It felt good to stand and stretch. He turned on the shower and turned it tepid. The heat of the box left him wanting something a little cooler. He stepped in and closed the curtain around him. He let the water run over his face, drowning out the memory of the last two days. When he closed his eyes, he found himself reaching out in sudden jerks, afraid he'd feel a lid. The box had done a job on him.

He didn't hear the door open, and Karen' voice caught him off guard. "I have to admit, for someone I've only known a few days, and shared a drug induced midnight coffee with, I've sort of grown attached to you. If I'm being honest, when I woke up today, my first thought was that I wouldn't find you alive, and I panicked." She walked closer to the curtain, opaque images between them. "That doesn't sound too forward, does it?"

Danny straightened and rose above the shower head. He looked over the curtain and down at her. "I don't suppose so. I kind of feel the same way." Danny liked Karen, she was bold, she was shy, and she was wrapped up in duty. "Can you hand me a towel?" He continued eyeing her.

She grinned, "Get it yourself." She crossed her arms and Danny worried until she reached up and lightly tapped his chin. "Of course I'll get it." She stepped across the floor and pulled a towel out of the cabinet. "These are man size towels." She let it unfurl and it went from her head to her toes.

"I'm a big boy."

She smiled as he exited with the towel wrapped around him. "I remember." She looked up. "Bend down."

Danny bent, suspecting she wanted to whisper something.

Karen put her arm around his neck and kissed him on the lips. "I missed you."

He grinned. "I missed you too." Danny winked. "Did you leave John out there?"

"He's fine; he's taking care of your dog."

"Have you heard about the other two?" He walked to the sink and pulled his toothbrush out of the cabinet.

"John said they were recovering nicely."

Danny felt like a kid at Christmas. He grinned and left Karen standing there while he hurried to his room and changed. He shouted loud enough for her to hear, "I'm sort of hungry."

She stepped into the hallway and into view. "Yeah, I sort of thought you might be. Would a steak do?"

Danny held up two fingers.

"Two steaks?"

"Please."

She shook her head. "I've seen your steaks; they are like half the cow." She turned and walked away.

He ducked into the hallway and shouted, "Thank you!"

She raised a waving hand as she walked into the kitchen. "No problem."

Danny came out to the smell of beef. When he made it to the kitchen, John sat waiting as well. "Is she feeding you too?"

John smiled. "Courtesy of the Gate's farm."

Danny asked, "Shouldn't there be an entourage of police and news reporters here by now?"

Karen admitted, "We haven't called it in yet."

Danny looked bewildered. "Huh?"

Karen said, "If we call this in, and the news gets a hold of it, and it goes out. We might have another visitor again. So, if you are supposed to be dead, let's just wait until morning to let the world know you are alive, okay?" She put her hand on his.

He nodded. "Detail again?"

She winked. "Yep."

John shook his head. "I thought you weren't that fond of cops?"

Danny frowned. "I've put up with you for all 37 years of my life, so I must like some of them." While Karen finished up the eggs for the steaks, Danny nudged John. "What'd you find in the pit?" He stared at a friend and not at a sheriff.

John shrugged. "A lot of trash. I'll probably have to go back to clean it up." He pointed at Danny and whispered, "By the way, remind me to never try and steal one of your cows."

Danny straightened up and looked surprised. "You were busy; you dove into Harper as well?"

John winked. "I told ya', I was gonna' find ya' one way or another."

Danny reminded him, "You didn't find me—" John joined him, "the dog did."

Danny turned his head and said to Karen, "So they haven't found Lyle?"

Karen spun around. "So, you know his name now?"

"I told you, it's in the diary. I know all about the Thibodeauxes. I spent most of my time catching up with the succubus in the box with me." He turned serious. "She wasn't given a fair shake in this world, none of the kids were."

"Well don't turn all Stockholm syndrome on me, he did try and kill you."

Danny had his own code and trying to kill him broke it. "Yeah, he did, and I don't much care for that."

John interrupted, "Yeah, I don't think that was too smart a move on his part."

Everyone sat for a 2 a.m. meal. Danny ate his two steaks and when he was done, he turned to Karen. "Are you going to eat all of yours?"

She slid the plate to him. "No, I think a quarter of the slab you cut those in is enough for me, go for it."

John stuck his fork out when Danny eyed his. "I can eat all mine, thank you."

When they finished, Karen started washing dishes. Sheriff Scott headed to the front room and Danny came up behind her and insisted, "You don't have to do that."

She said, "You're right, so why don't you pull out a towel and help me."

He followed her order and together they picked up the kitchen to a woman's touch. "Thank you, Karen."

She smiled and pushed him in the back. "Let's make sure the Sheriff isn't in trouble." They stepped into the living room and John had fallen asleep with Tess curled up next to him on the couch. Karen pulled the blanket off the back of the couch and draped it over him. "Good night, Sheriff."

Danny asked. "Are you going to be okay in the guest room?"

She nodded. "Yeah, I'll be fine."

He continued on when she made it to her door, walking down the hall to his room. When he turned, she stood by her door looking with a gaze of gratitude, the same gratitude he felt for her. "Oh, I almost forgot." He returned and put his finger under her chin and lifted her head up. "Thank you for saving my life." He bent down and kissed her on the lips. He turned and she remained stiff as a mannequin. He winked as he opened his door. "You know, I might need you to return the favor when you needed someone to get you over your nightmare. I suspect the box might be in my dreams. I could use a live body next to me."

She stared, closed the guest room door and followed him into his room. "Yeah? Yeah, you are probably right." She took his hand. "Besides, a good detail would keep an eye on you all night."

They retreated to his room.

The following morning, Danny slept in; with so little sleep he ripped right through his five-a.m. internal clock. He would have slept longer except authorities began to descend upon the place within the hour after Karen called it in. By eight, Karen dragged Danny out of bed and put him in front of cameras so the media could ask questions ranging from, 'What was it like being in a hole,' to 'Did you think you were going to die?' Danny shrugged it off but the crowd reconvened at the gravesite when they realized the serial killer was in the hole. Examiners, diggers, reporters, and police buzzed around the opening like bees to a hive.

They had to navigate through the mud, but when they made it to the box, they were careful to locate all three parts of her. Danny promised them, "She's all in the box," as they searched for her right hand.

About the time they recovered all of Lauren, a reporter blurted, "What's running through your head, Mr. Gates?"

Danny was stoic. "I'm lucky to be alive."

"What happened?" The reporter looked at a crater of mud.

"I was drugged and put in a cattle box four feet down." He reached down and scratched Tess' ear. She hadn't left his side since he woke. "Thanks to one of my dogs, I was literally dug out."

Danny watched as they tossed the body bag up onto the ground above the hole. He pushed the camera away and tersely said to the men working the body bag. "Be careful with her and see that she gets a proper burial. That woman died twenty years ago." He felt a sense of loss for the little girl inside her, the one buried in a psychotic rage fueled by her father.

Danny started walking with the men carrying the body bag. He waved off the cameras and microphones. "You can talk to me later."

Karen walked beside him. "You okay?"

He turned and whispered, "I just think for all the damage she's done, the real issue isn't going to be raised."

Karen tilted her head. "Which is?"

"She was created, not born this way."

"Regardless of that, you can't go around killing innocent people."

Danny agreed. "No, no you can't but you can at least be given a eulogy that offers you peace in death."

Karen started to say something but held it in.

They walked in silence as they brought the body up to the farm and to a waiting makeshift examiner's room.

Danny watched as the battery of reporters followed Karen, looking for the continuation of the story. She shooed them away and said there was nothing more to tell until the other person involved was caught, and she would not let the body of Lauren Thibodeaux be photographed. She sternly ordered them to leave. One by one, everyone departed, even sheriff John Scott, who still had duties with his town, a town that lost three citizens. It was just Karen and Danny.

She winked. "Let's go get your dogs.

Danny smiled. Good idea.

Chapter 64

And the waters shall rest. Lyle spent his entire life in the project of his sister. She'd tested his resolve to family, kept him a slave to her moments, but he never wavered on his commitment, he never wavered in his love, and the waters shall rest. His final act defiance, defiance to society who declared him a menace when all he was, was a keeper. He would not let them deem him the villain, at least not to his face. He would take with him the secrets of a genius, and the waters shall rest. For nearly thirty-two years, Lyle Lawrence Thibodeaux, who had a shadow as large as any in the Thibodeaux family, lived beneath the shadow of Lauren Beatrix Thibodeaux. His neither amounted to resolve nor regret, but one of loyalty and the Thibodeaux way, one of unquestioned allegiance, and the waters shall rest.

They lifted his body from the second floor cement walkway of a dingy gray motel, four men hoisting him by limb and transporting him to a waiting ambulance, down a flight of cement steps, around the horde of onlookers, his head fallen backwards, his blonde hair draped loosely ground ward, and the waters shall rest. A blustery wind and fierce rain hammered his body, a limp lifeless vessel that had housed his thoughts and carried his hopes, whatever hopes those could have been for a man doomed to a

Thibodeaux code. A medic grabbed his wrist, then his neck. He put a stethoscope to his chest and shook his head. They put his body in a bag and placed it on a gurney. And the waters shall rest.

Like the procession of a funeral, they traveled a solitary path with no hurry to arrive. Lyle had become a toe tag in a morgue on the outskirts of a small town in Southwestern Washington. They deposited him in a chamber and closed the door, the echoing click of stainless steel as the remnants of a very bad week came to pass. No fanfare, no answers, no peace for a community who suffered the wrath of a psychotic breakdown, and the waters shall rest.

Somewhere else, four brothers touched down in a Seattle airport, four Thibodeaux men there to gather their brother and take him home to rest in the place where it all began. They started the journey with hope against hope, but news travels fast in the age of technology, they knew this wasn't a living reunion, but one of filling requests, and the waters shall rest.

In a home in Corvallis, a young woman held her hand over her mouth, tears streaming down her face as they replayed the body of Lyle Lawrence Thibodeaux carried down those cement steps, a gleeful sentiment of capture by those who knew nothing more. In the heart of that woman, ached sadness that she held blame, that this resolution was in part his answer to saving her the embarrassment of press; and the waters shall rest.

The day of rain, the day of rain, the day the rains wouldn't stop. The rivers would swell, as though the sky cleansed the earth below of carnage too gruesome and blood stained to remain. The wind would howl that day, the rains would march on, and four brothers made their way to take their family home. It was the Thibodeaux way, and the waters shall rest.

In the mountains of the Ozarks, a group of sisters huddle in tribute to a fallen sister and fallen brother. Theirs was the Thibodeaux way, whatever conflagrations the sister and brother had started, whatever unspeakable damage they unleashed, they were Thibodeauxes and the only victims of concern. In the mountain of the Ozarks it rained as well, but the rain which fell were tears of a family in grief, and the waters shall rest. April 2nd was a day like no other, the end of the journey for so many involved, a day where citizens unlocked their doors, and the police went off high alert. It was a day where everyone's anxiety eased, where the nerves of a shattered community began to mend, and the waters shall rest.

April 2nd was a day that all the troubles of a young man who couldn't catch his breath ended. As the life he'd always known collapsed in a rage fueled attack on people he didn't know finally ended; life left him as the reminder of who the Thibodeauxes were. He too would wind down the frantic pace of nerves, sorry for his part, aware that time can close in and expect a toll to be paid. He paid it, and the waters shall rest. And the waters shall rest.

Chapter 65

Danny and Karen pulled up to the veterinarian office of Parrish and Lazarz. Rain pelted the roof of the Silverado, dancing off the hood with a haze of vapor lifting high into the air. Danny exited with more than the normal gait others often saw. He had a lift in his step as he waved Karen to hurry up. They brought Tess with them and hurried indoors. When they heard the barking of the spaniels in a room beyond the entryway, Tess released a woeful cry, an animal's tearful happy reunion. The trio of dogs began a series of barking communication and Tess begged for allowance past the door.

The doctor's receptionist, Ms. McLaughlin, laughed. "Oh, you want your siblings, young lady?"

Tess danced at the door as Ms. McLaughlin stepped around the counter and pulled the handle. Danny and Karen followed Tess in, and the dog met her siblings behind screen cages. She howled and barked to be reunited. Danny's heart lifted seeing Trudy, she looked good, Wilbur too.

Doctor Parrish came out from his office. "I figured that was you with all the commotion. He looked down at Tess. "I see you found Tess."

Karen corrected him. "Tess found Dan." She nodded. "I mean, she literally found him."

The doctor peered at Karen over his glasses. "So this is the dog that dug him out?" He bent down and looked her over. "She seems pretty healthy, and I'd say you have three dogs, Dan."

Dan felt relief seeing the two Brittany spaniels. "Are these two okay?"

"Good as new." He bent down and released the cage so the two spaniels could touch their sister, a mob of fur wrestling with joy.

Danny kept his focus on the dogs. "You got food here they'd like? I have dried food, but they seem to want mine."

Doctor Parrish smiled. "Pat wasn't too good about their diet. She liked to let them eat leftovers." He escorted them back to the front where he pulled a case of canned food from a shelf. "They will eat this."

Danny pulled a pen and checkbook out. Ms. McLaughlin handed him a bill, but Doctor Parrish pulled it back. "On us."

Danny waved him off. "I'll pay. You run a good service and I want to make sure they get attention when they need it."

The Doctor shrugged and handed him the bill. Danny said to Ms. McLaughlin, "Toss two more cases of food onto this bill."

Danny thanked the doctor for saving his pets; he choked and coughed it off as a scratch in his throat. "You did a great job with them, Doc." Danny hoisted the cases as easy as a bag of chips. They stepped out into the blustery weather and Danny opened the cab.

"Will they all fit in that small back seat?" Karen watched as wet paws leaped in, one by one.

"Back seat guys." They scrambled over the back with Trudy and Wilbur taking seats and Tess lying on the floor.

Driving back to Dirtwater, they passed the Henricksen ranch, Danny noticed Trudy never took her eyes off the farm. "It's okay girl. I know, I know." He reached his arm over the seat and rubbed her head; she leaned forward and licked his neck.

Karen informed Danny. "They caught Lyle."

"When?"

Karen picked up her phone and typed a question. She waited and a few moments passed. "This morning."

"Where?"

She viewed her phone. "Longview."

Danny looked in his rearview mirror. "Did he give himself up or did he go down with a fight?"

She sighed, "Neither."

Danny squinted, puzzled.

"He killed himself."

Danny shook his head. "Unbelievable. He had to toy with me but he was able to kill himself. That's doesn't make much sense. If it was that easy, why didn't he just shoot me?"

Karen had an incredulous look. "Are you serious? Are you suggesting he made a mistake in not shooting you?"

Danny laughed at the irony. "Yeah, I guess I am." He continued, "How did he kill himself."

Karen read the phone with interest. "Poison."

Danny locked eyes with her. They shared a moment of realization. "We'll get the dogs home and take your vehicle."

"This is my collar!" Karen pounded the dash. "Hurry."

They blew through Dirtwater proper, Sheriff Scott sitting on patrol along the intersection of Main and First never moved. When they hit the driveway, Danny let the dogs crap in his yard and then ushered them in the house. He scrambled to the kitchen, tore open the bag of dry food and left it on the floor. "You kids will have to eat dry until we get back. Don't tear the place up." He turned to Trudy. "Watch your family."

Karen put the light on her roof, and they screamed out of there flashing a red emergency. In Dirtwater, Karen pulled up alongside the sheriff and Danny lowered his window. "If I don't get back before five, go check on my dogs."

John shrugged. "Okay." He didn't get another word out before Karen put her foot on the gas and used Main Street as a drag strip, tire tread leaving marks behind them. She handled the issued vehicle with all the power it possessed. They were getting to Longview as fast as possible. When they hit I-5, the next twenty miles were traveled over a hundred miles per hours, hard rain and all.

By two, they'd made it to the building of the examiner, with the morgue in the basement. Karen and Danny pushed through the doors, and Karen flashed her badge. "The morgue?"

A security officer said, "Take the elevator to the basement." As the two ran to the elevator, the officer hollered, "To the right."

When they made it to the morgue they entered and approached the desk clerk. "Can I help you?"

Karen was anxious. "You have a body that came in this morning. The body of Lyle Thibodeaux?"

The clerk smiled. "We had the body of Lyle Thibodeaux. It was identified and released to next of kin."

Karen spit back. "That body was involved in the death of seven people, two of which were law enforcement. How could you just let the body go?"

"They had this." He handed Karen a document. She read it and shook her head. She handed it to Danny.

Danny reviewed the judge's release, signed by the good judge, Michael Thibodeaux, from the great state of Missouri. "Wow."

Karen said, "Bullshit." She raised her voice, "How did they take the body out?"

"Carried it."

"No, you idiot, what did they transport it in?" She leaned over the desk.

"They had a small U-Haul."

She turned to Danny. "They are going to drive him back." They headed for the elevator. Karen whispered, "Not if I can help it."

Chapter 66

Lyle opened his eyes and heard, "Welcome, Brother."

He smiled. "You found me." He sat up and a dim light from the trailer of the truck gave a hazy glow to the space. "Where are we?"

"Just outside of Portland, heading east."

"Any problems getting me?"

His brother Michael shrugged. "Nope, I signed off on having you released and filed the papers with the state of Washington. "Went smooth. Nice plan."

Lyle sat up. "Get me out of this. I need some fresh air." Lyle knew Michael would understand his cryptic remarks about coming home.

Michael made a call, and the U-Haul slowed the rumble and came to a stop. The rear door slid open, and Lyle stepped out into a rain storm. "God this feels good." He turned around and his other brothers greeted him with hugs.

Walter eyed his brother. "What are you going to do about the farmer?"

Lyle shrugged, "Nothing for now, maybe not ever."

Walter protested, "He killed Lauren, he killed your twin."

Lyle shook his head. "No he didn't. She died a long time ago. He didn't start that fight and for right now I have no beef with him."

Walter shot back. "I disagree."

Lyle stepped forward, face to face with his younger brother. "Then maybe you should do something about it. I'm done. Maybe later, but for now, it's over." So was the conversation. "Let's go home."

He asked Michael. "Who's sitting in the back, because I'm not?"

Daniel grinned. "A little claustrophobic?"

Lyle nodded. "Yeah."

Everyone changed seats, Daniel and Zachary took the trailer while Lyle, Walter, and Michael sat up front. Their plan was to travel east along the 84, into Idaho, eventually meeting up with the 80 into Omaha and then south. They stopped in Hood River for a bite to eat, five downy white boys, entered a small café to the curiosity of all the other patrons. It wasn't just that they all were snow white blondes, but they shared the same height, the same build, the same facial characteristics of their father, a Thibodeaux.

Lyle politely whispered, "Do you have a table hidden away?"

The waitress gnawed on a piece of gum and moved her head like the second hand of a clock at each Thibodeaux. "Brothers?"

Lyle stood in the middle of the file, two to his left and two to his right. "Good observation."

"Follow me." She counted out five menus and led them to a sparsely seated rear. She laid the menus on table with no neighbors. "Private enough?"

Lyle smiled. "Perfect. Thank you."

She fiddled with a booth light until it clicked on. "I'll be back in a few with your waters."

The boys were in a corner booth, Lyle slid in so he could have the center, allowance to observe every person in the café.

Michael chided him. "Don't be paranoid. We legally have you."

Lyle reminded him, "You legally have a dead body."

Michael offered, "I also have a death certificate, so quit worrying."

Lyle wasn't going to quit worrying until he made it home on the mountain in the Ozarks. Until then, he would be prepared for anything. "I hope you're right, Brother."

When the waitress came back, she flipped a pad open and clicked her pen on. "What can I get you?" She didn't look like Cindy, she wasn't young like Cindy, but her delivery reminded him of her. He longed for Cindy but knew he could never reveal he was alive. He smiled. "What do you recommend?"

She raised her nose. "Seriously?"

Lyle laughed. "Yeah."

She leaned into the table and whispered, "Anything but the chicken fried steak."

Lyle asked, "Okay, then what's the special?"

She grinned. "Chicken fried steak."

Lyle smiled. "Meat loaf."

In a series of answers that sounded like a broken record, the boys said consecutively, "Meat loaf, meat loaf, meat loaf, meat loaf."

As the waitress poured their water, she said, "No wonder you boys look alike. You all eat the same food."

Lyle wished that was the reason, he wished it wasn't something so much more sinister. "That too."

In the privacy of seclusion, Lyle told his brothers why he found peace with the farmer, how the farmer told the authorities to treat the body well. Lyle admitted he'd love to bring her home, but he'd over played his hand and he committed plenty of felonies. If they caught him, he wouldn't see the freedom for many years, more years than life was worth.

They ate their meal and bid the town of Hood River goodbye, hopped back on the 84 and continued their journey. They traveled along the Columbia, a natural border to their left and a rising range to their right. The highway, a singular ribbon, connected little towns where pockets dug into the range, permitted enough level ground for dwellings to exist, even though they stair-cased upward like amphitheaters. The rains stopped as they dropped out of the maritime climate of the Western side of the state and leveled off into the eastern side. The ground turned barren, with desert air.

When they hit The Dalles, Oregon, a roadblock had traffic backed up a half mile, everyone crawled to a stop.

Lyle wondered why there would be a roadblock and why police allowed cars through one by one. He had a bad feeling. "We need to put me under and back into the bag."

Michael didn't disagree.

Walter pulled a bag up from his feet. "Pick your poison." He laughed.

"Lyle scanned the bag. He pulled two out. "This one," he handed to Walter, "Is the same thing you used to bring me out the first time."

Lyle held the other vial and grabbed a syringe. They were stopped in traffic and Lyle hopped out. He circled to the rear of the U-Haul and slid open the back enough to crawl in. His two youngest brothers helped him up. "I need to go under for a few minutes. We might have an inspection of my demise." Lyle injected himself and lay down into the bag.

"Don't forget the toe tag." Lyle's head spun. "You'll have to do it."

His brother's voice went in and out, a lost echo in a dark place. "Will do."

Lyle lost control of his motor functions but paid attention, the sound of the zipper was the last thing he remembered.

Chapter 67

Danny wasn't one to let things go when someone tried to kill him. He'd proven he wasn't one who accepted someone stepping on his property and challenging him, even a bear, without justice being served, but the truth was; he wasn't too keen on taking it to someone who had left the premises. He accepted calling it a draw with Lyle. "How do you plan on finding him?" He buckled up next to her.

Danny discovered the real detective in Karen. "They are going to drive home. They might still assume the coast isn't completely clear, so they won't drive too long on I-5. From here, they either drive north and cross the cascades on the 12, or they drive south and cross the gorge either on the Washington side or the Oregon side. I'm betting in that rig, they take the best road, the 84."

Danny shrugged. "They have a two-hour head start."

She smiled. "I have friends." She picked up her phone a placed a call. "Is this Sutcliffe?" She continued, "Adam, I need a favor." Danny listened to her. "I need a roadblock, looking for a small U-Haul with possibly five very blonde men in it." She listened and responded, "The 12 on the east side before it splits, the 14 at Lyle, and the 84 at The Dalles. Can you make that happen now?" She winked to Danny and told the person on the other end, "Thanks." She pushed out an easy breath. "Okay."

Danny asked, "And where to do we go?"

I'm gambling on the 84. That's as good as a fifty-fifty. If they are on the 14, we will be parallel." She put the red light on top of her car and they cruised out at a high rate of speed. They crossed the Columbia and passed Lang State Park when her phone rang. She answered, still hitting a comfortable ninety in the rain. "Yes." She concentrated on the road. "Where?" She smiled. "Thanks, we'll be there in 30 minutes." She disconnected and whooped. "Got em'." She slowed to seventy miles and grinned.

They pulled in behind the U-Haul, four of the Thibodeauxes with angered expressions on their faces stood surrounded by half dozen officers with guns drawn. Karen jumped out and Danny followed. An officer met her and asked if they were the party being sought. Karen turned to Danny. "Is it?"

The four men, carbon copies of the two Thibodeauxes he'd crossed. "I'd say so."

One of the men stepped toward Karen with his hands out and up. "I'm a Missouri State judge, and I have the legal right to this body."

She grinned. "You're a pretty damn young judge."

He offered, "Small County, and I'm a pretty good lawman."

Karen stood her ground. Well, so am I, and I would be derelict in my duties if I didn't follow through with forensics on other crimes. Crimes your brother may or may not have committed. If he's innocent, we can clear him."

"Innocent, Ms—"

"Zimmerman, Detective to you."

"Does it matter if he's innocent? He's dead."

"Yeah, it does matter, because there may have been others involved."

"What tests do you wish to run?"

"New fingerprinting and swabs. We had issues with the others."

The brother nodded. "That can be done right here, or at least here in..." He turned to the nearest officer pointing a weapon. "What town is this?"

"The Dalles."

He shrugged incredulous. "Really? They put a THE in the name?" He raised an eyebrow. "All that can be done here in The Dalles."

Karen said, "Fair enough, but this man here, she tilted her head to Danny, "He's going to place the body bag in my car."

"Are you serious, Detective Zimmerman."

"Serious as a heart attack."

"I have a good mind to call your superior."

She stared. "I have a good mind to let you." She ordered the man nearest the back door of the U-Haul, "Open it."

The brother doing all the talking nodded and the brother by the door turned the handle and slid the door up.

"Not that I am accusing you of being anything like your brother, but back the fuck up." She gestured to the officers to help enforce her request. They circled the four men and persuaded them to stand back.

Danny approached the bag; wary his adversary might spring up and hit him again with poison. He tapped the bag and felt a foot. He slid the corner of the bag to the edge of the trailer and handled it with ease.

One of the brothers, the one who looked the youngest, whispered loud enough for Danny to hear, "How was your stay with my sister?"

Danny snapped his head toward the brother. "You must be Zachery." He turned to another brother, "I'd guess you're Daniel." He stared the other two down. He pointed to the leader, "Based on you doing all the talking, you must be Michael. Your wife is Angela, right?" He looked at the last of them. "That leaves just Walter, and your wife is Helen." He had Lyle under his arm like a football. He towered over the brothers. "My stay was enlightening." Danny turned and marched back to the car, shoving the body bag hard into the back seat. He stood and placed his hand down onto the roof of the car. "He's dead, right? Don't look so shocked."

Karen motioned to one of the local sheriffs. "Can you take me to the morgue?"

"Absolutely."

Karen backed away, viewing the brothers. "Oh, one other test. I will need to do a toxicology test. You don't mind, do you?"

The brother Danny identified as Michael said, "You shall not draw blood from him; that is clearly stated in the order."

"So, sue me." She walked back to her car, and they drove off following the sheriff, and followed by the U-Haul."

Karen said, "You ever take blood before?"

Danny said, "On cows all the time."

"Good, it shouldn't be too much different."

Danny looked bemused. "And why will I be taking blood."

"Because he's going to make some calls and I'm going to be told to stand down. That A-hole isn't getting away. If you get that blood and it tests for anything that could fake death, I will hunt him down."

Danny no longer felt the same way. "Fair enough, but you are aware we have the killer, and it wasn't him."

She huffed at Danny. "You are aware that you should be dead right now, and he did it?"

"True, but I'm not dead."

They pulled into the local coroner's office and Danny yanked the body bag out and hoisted it over his shoulder. He observed. "For a body that's supposed to be dead for ten hours, this one's got a lot of give." It bent over Danny like a piece of carpet.

In the basement, they unzipped the bag and Karen said, "This body's not been dead for ten hours. He's not dead now."

The examiner put a stethoscope to his chest. "He has no heartbeat." He took his temperature. "But I agree he's too warm to have been dead ten hours."

The brothers came in at the last of the conversation. "We had the trailer heat turned up; two of our brothers were in back with him."

Karen insisted, "Shut up and get out of here."

Michael objected. "Sorry, but as a judge, and the one who signed off on this release, I will stay."

Karen came around the table and insisted, "Well guess what? We are leaving, and we are leaving with your dead brother. You can come pick him up in a week."

Michael held his ground. "You shall release our brother after you test him, is that clear?"

She pulled out her handgun and placed the barrel against Lyle's head. "So help me God, if you interfere with me, I will put a hole in your dead brother's head. You can have me removed from my job for desecration of a corpse. You want that?"

The youngest brother stepped between the two and broke it up. "Detective Zimmerman, whatever you decide, we will abide. He grabbed her hand and shook it. "You are the law here." He stepped over to Danny, "and you big guy, I thank you too." He reached out to shake Danny's hand and Danny stared him off.

"No thanks."

"Please, a gesture of apology."

"I don't want your apology and don't touch me."

The youngest Thibodeaux attempted to reach out and pat Danny's shoulder, but Danny backed up. "You make contact with me and I will punch you so hard, you will join your brother in that bag."

The brother squinted. "Have it your way then, farmer." He turned to his brothers and wanted to go, ushering them with his hands.

Karen said to the examiner, "Sorry, but we'll just take it to go."

Danny zipped the bag and picked it up. Karen kept her gun drawn as they left using the stairs. When they made it to the street, the U-Haul had departed but Danny suspected they weren't leaving without their brother.

Karen said, "Let's get this body back to Olympia. I think Sleeping Beauty here needs a good cell for his beauty rest. She put the car in gear, and they hurried west.

They'd gone maybe thirty miles when Karen admitted she didn't feel very well. "I'm sick to my stomach." Another ten miles and she asked Danny to drive. "I think I've been poisoned." She cursed. "Damnit, I shouldn't have let them touch me."

Danny had seen this before. She'd been hit with something like this the night he was buried. He pulled her red light out and popped it on the roof of the car. He started it up and pushed the gas down. By the time they hit Portland, her face had a glistening sheen of moisture and her eyes were listless.

He called John. "John!"

"The dogs are fine; I'm at the house right now."

"I need you to dispatch a hospital in Portland for me."

"Huh?"

"Karen's been poisoned again. But this one might be deadly."

"Okay, okay, where are you?"

Danny gave his location and John radioed in and asked for an ambulance to meet him. "They'll take her. Make sure you tell them to do blood samples immediately."

Danny took the directions, and the ambulance waited where John said they would. He stood over them as they took blood. The paramedic placed the blood in several solutions, and one came up colored.

The paramedic said, "Wow! Botulinum."

"Is that serious?"

"Would have been if you'd waited." He pulled a vial down out of a kit and slammed a dose into her arm. "How long ago?"

"She started complaining about an hour ago."

He nodded, "She'll make it, barely," he continued, "Uh, Mr—"

"Gates."

"Mr. Gates, we are going to transport your wife to Providence. She'll be in intensive care."

Danny didn't correct them. He liked the sound of Mrs. Gates. He followed the ambulance to the emergency room and kept the red light flashing the entire way. When he exited, a police officer noticed the car. "Excuse me, do you need my help?"

Danny stepped forward, and the police officer listened. "Watch this car. If anyone tries to touch it, shoot them."

"Good enough." The officer circled the car like a vulture. Danny followed Karen up three floors where the frantic pace of emergency flow turned to the gentle beeps of monitors. They rolled her into a room and shut the door behind them, leaving Danny in the hallway.

He waited until a doctor exited and caught his attention. "The woman, is she going to be okay?"

He smiled. "Yep, but how did she get Botulinum in her? That's a poison meant to kill."

"She was poisoned by a perp."

The doctor offered, "You can get some coffee down the hall, but she won't be awake until sometime tomorrow."

Danny nodded. "Okay."

Now it was personal again.

He went back to Karen's car and thanked the officer for watching. Danny said his partner was in intensive care and if the officer could check on her. He gave him her name and said, "The Olympia sheriff's department will arrive soon."

He then called John and told him to let Olympia know Karen had been hurt and where she was. Danny had business to do. "John, what have they done with the body of the attorney?"

"They buried her in Dirtwater cemetery. Dropped her right in, just like you asked."

"Thanks."

Danny knew what the brothers wanted. It was time to end this.

Chapter 68

Lyle took a deep breath, the heat of the bag cleared by a thoughtful gesture of being unzipped. It was dark and he strained to catch his bearings. Where was he? He thought about where he should be, shouldn't he be traveling? It was quiet, no rumbling. He felt solid beneath him, the feeling of earth, as though not on the trailer floor. "Zachery?" The words felt tight, as though enclosed inside a jar. "Zachery?" It was peculiar, diminished, alone. "Zachery, anyone?" No one answered.

Something had a rancid odor, foul—decaying. Lyle lifted an arm, stiff, tired, raised it up and found wood above his face. "What?" Something bumped his head, something hard, metal; cylindrical. Lyle touched the object in the dark—it was a flashlight. Realization and fear, found in a moment of nascent thought. "No, please don't let this be..." He closed his eyes and turned on the flashlight, a burning glow beyond his eyelids, he counted to three. Wood above him, a box. He rolled his head to the left and his sister lie next to him, peace became her, clean, silent, deceased. "No, no, no." He pounded the lid, "I'm not dead!" Frantic overcame him, he didn't feel the small draft of air to keep him alive or see the two fresh batteries. He didn't observe the finely wrapped sandwiches or the pen and paper. Lyle was overcome with the sensation of cellar, of his lack of loyalty and commitment, of the finality of the Thibodeaux way. In the box was his sister, food for a lifetime, a short lifetime, batteries to spend his hours reading Lauren's diary and discovering the truth of the Thibodeaux way. A tear slid off his face into his temple. "No!"

He gently whispered to fate, "I'm sorry."

The End……………………………………..

BIOGRAPHY

randall 'Jay' andrews lives in Southern California with his wife and sons. He's worked as a writer for his adult life and has several titles prior to Six Days in Dirtwater. If you wish to find them, they can be found at www.jacolpublishing.com along with the rest of the JaCol authors.

9 781946 675279